ved clos .. Tell me. Or, better yet, show me.'

Susanna forced herself to breathe. 'I want to sleep with my husband like spoons in a drawer. That's my secret.'

He lowered his hand, but not before she saw a glimmer of longing in his eyes. Instantly his expression shifted into the smirk of the man who'd offered her money for a night in her bed. Compared to the price she'd named, a thousand dollars was cheap.

He focused his eyes on hers. 'If you want a man, I'd be glad to oblige. But it's a one-time event.'

Susanna had no intention of saying yes to this proposition, but neither could she let him win. 'I'll keep it in mind.'

'Anytime, Doc. Satisfaction guaranteed.'

MIDNIGHT MARRIAGE

BY
VICTORIA BYLIN

MILLS
BOON®

First published in Great Britain 2007
by Mills & Boon, an imprint of Harlequin (UK) Limited,
Large Print edition 2011
Eton House, 18-24 Paradise Road, Richmond, Surrey TW9 1SR

© Vicki Scheibel 2006

ISBN: 978 0 263 22397 2

Harlequin (UK) policy is to use papers that are natural, renewable and recyclable products and made from wood grown in sustainable forests. The logging and manufacturing process conform to the legal environmental regulations of the country of origin.

Printed and bound in Great Britain
by CPI Antony Rowe, Chippenham, Wiltshire

Victoria Bylin has a collection of refrigerator magnets that mark the changes in her life. The oldest ones are from California. A native of Los Angeles, she graduated from UC Berkeley with a degree in history and went to work in the advertising industry. She soon met a wonderful man who charmed her into taking a ride on his motorcycle. That ride led to a trip down the wedding aisle, two sons, various pets, and a move that landed Victoria and her family in northern Virginia.

Magnets from thirty states commemorate that journey, and her new life on the East Coast. The most recent additions are from the Smithsonian National Museum of American History and a Chinese restaurant that delivers—a sure sign that Victoria is busy writing. Feel free to drop her an e-mail at VictoriaBylin@aol.com or visit her website at www.victoriabylin.com

To Dave and Joe,
the best sons a mom could have

Chapter One

Midas, New Mexico
October 1898

Rafe LaCroix looked down at the woman sleeping alone in Doc Randall's bed and muttered a curse. He wasn't surprised that the old goat had kicked the bucket. The last time Rafe had passed through Midas, a growing town in northern New Mexico, Randall had been knocking on death's door. He'd even talked about taking on a partner—some hotshot doctor from back East.

At the mention of "back East," Rafe had stopped listening. If he never crossed the Mississippi again, he'd die a happy man. As far as he was concerned, that muddy divide cut a line between the happy times in his life and the bitterness he tasted every damned day. It also marked the spot where he'd become a man about five years too soon.

Shaking the vicious memory from his mind, Rafe looked down at the lady doctor and pondered his options. Would she be willing to go with him if he politely woke her up? He doubted it. He'd spent half his life thinking up lies, but even he couldn't make himself believe he had a wife giving birth or a sick child—not when he thought about his bloodstained duster and the careless stubble on his chin.

He looked like hell and smelled even worse. No woman in her right mind would leave the safety of her bed with the likes of him. She'd have to be crazy or stupid, and he doubted that a woman with a house full of medical books was stupid. Crazy was another matter. Rafe couldn't take the chance that she'd say no to him—not with Nick delirious and calling out for his mama. Leaving his friend alone had just about killed Rafe, but he didn't know squat about festering wounds, nor did he have the stomach to take off the leg.

Damn his bad luck. A lady doctor complicated the situation—especially this one. He'd always been partial to brunettes, particularly leggy ones with high breasts and upturned lips, and she had those attributes and more. Her upstairs bedroom held the warmth of a woodstove and she had tossed off the covers, giving Rafe a moonlit view of bare skin where her shift had slid down her arm. Her breasts rose and fell with each breath, and her mouth was twitching as if she were living a dream. She also had pretty feet and strong calves. She'd be good in the saddle in more ways than one.

Rafe liked to look at women, that was for sure. But he figured sex was more like a horse race than a visit to a Boston art gallery. A man got excited when the gun went off, settled in for the ride and then finished strong. As for the race itself, he liked to win. Looking at the lady doctor, he wondered if she had similar inclinations. Damn him for a fool… he didn't have time for this nonsense. But that would change as soon as he and Nick reached Mexico. In another week he'd be swigging tequila in a cantina and visiting the ladies who'd gladly invite him upstairs, both for his money and his good looks. But first he had to take care of Nick.

Manhandling a woman went against Rafe's gut in the worst way, but the thought of burying Nick bothered him even more. He pulled back the canvas flap of his duster and put his hand on the butt of his gun. With her bed tight against the wall, trapping her was a piece of cake. He made his voice barrel-deep. "Lady, wake up."

He watched as she blinked away her dreams and took in the sight of him—his gun belt, his Colt .45 and the bulge in the front of his trousers. In a single motion, she gasped, clutched the blanket to her breasts and pulled her knees to her chest as she scooted against the headboard.

"Get out!" she cried.

Rafe roughened his voice. "Not without you. I'm guessing Doc Randall's six feet under and you took over for him. Am I right?"

"Yes, but that doesn't give you the right to barge in here."

Rafe felt her gaze all over his cheeks and chin. He'd pushed his hat low to keep from being recognized, but he couldn't hide completely. A beam of moonlight had cast his shadow on her bed, revealing his height and lanky build. It also lit up the blue coverlet she'd pulled across her breasts and revealed her intelligent brown eyes.

Rafe lowered his chin to deepen the shadow across his face. "Get moving."

"Tell me why."

"You don't need to know. Just get dressed."

"And if I refuse?" Her tone made him think of river ice—cold and hard but quick to melt in the warmth of spring.

"Then I'll change your mind for you." Raising his head slightly, he turned his eyes into shiny stones to let her know he meant business. Sidestepping, he opened her wardrobe and threw a dress across the foot of the bed. "Put that on."

The woman looked at it with stark longing. She wanted to cover herself, but the dress was out of her reach and she didn't want to rock forward to retrieve it. Nor did she want to give in to him.

"It's your choice," he said, smirking. "You can do what I say, or I'll tie you up and carry you out of here. It's a bit chilly, though. That cotton isn't going to keep you warm. It's not going to hide those breasts of yours, either."

As her eyes narrowed with loathing, Rafe rocked back on one heel to emphasize the gun strapped to his side. They both knew he wouldn't use it—she had something he needed—but he wanted her to see the worn holster and the blood on his coat. He had her cornered, but he knew that women could be sly and brave, more so than men who relied on brute strength. He might have enjoyed watching the lady wrestle with the choice he'd given her, but he didn't have time. He indicated the dress with his chin. "Get going."

She gave him a hard stare. "I'll go with you, but not alone."

Rafe reached inside his duster, pulled out a length of cord and snapped it tight. "You'll do as I say. Is that clear?"

Her eyes flashed with rebellion. "I'll do what's right and so will you. Put that rope away."

Rafe enjoyed trading sparks with a woman as much as any man, but this wasn't the time. He lifted a set of leg irons out of an inside pocket and dangled them in front of her nose. "I'd rather not use these on you, but I won't hesitate. You can walk out of here or be carried like a trussed-up deer. It's your choice."

Just as he'd hoped, the lady saw the wisdom of rocking forward on her knees and snatching up the dress. With the red calico clutched to her chest, she swung her legs over the side of the bed and glared at him. "Turn around."

Rafe gave her a wicked smile. "Not a chance."

"You're the one in a hurry. Not me."

"I'm also the one with the rope." Rafe respected her for holding her ground, but they were wasting time so he hardened his gaze. "Save the shyness for someone else. I've seen too many naked women to be impressed by a flat-chested spinster. Now move it."

She wasn't all that flat and she was too young to be a spinster, but Rafe needed to douse the fire licking at his belly. Judging by the heat in her eyes, she'd be a passionate lover, the kind of woman who'd fight to take more ground. The flames in his gut burned even hotter when she arched her brows like the cynical woman she wasn't.

"Since you're already an expert on breasts, you won't mind turning your back," she said.

"I'm not a fool." He nodded at her nightstand. "If I give you the chance, you'll thump me with that medical book."

When she didn't budge, Rafe stared at her fingers, pale and knotted in the dress. He couldn't waste all night, so he grabbed for her wrist. At the same moment, she slid her bottom off the bed and scrambled to her feet. She solved her modesty problem by turning her back on him.

He watched as she raised the dress over her head and let it fall past her shoulders, covering the white nightgown in a curtain of red calico. The dress caught on her hips, emphasizing her bottom as she shook the fabric free. Hunching forward, she worked the front buttons, glancing over her shoulder to give him the evil eye. Each time she turned, her braided hair swished like a mare's tail.

Rafe liked the looks of her. She was taller than he'd thought and more slender. Definitely coltish. She'd probably been a tomboy growing up—the kind of woman who'd know how to use her long legs in all the right ways. And if she didn't know, he'd be glad to teach her.

Ah, hell. He had no business thinking about such things—not with Nick scared and shivering in a damp cave. "Hurry up," he growled.

Ignoring him, she lifted a pair of her cotton drawers off a chair, stepped into them and somehow tied the strings without giving him more than peek at her calves.

Rafe was about to make a smart remark when she dropped to a crouch and reached under her bed. "I need my shoes."

As quick as fire, he snatched her wrist. "What else is under your bed?"

Their gazes locked, hers boiling like strong coffee and his resembling blue ice. Just as he expected, the heat of her turned his icy stare into steam.

When she tried to pull back her hand, he squeezed harder. Staring into her angry eyes, he reached under the bed and curled his fingers around the double barrel of a shotgun. The lady was full of surprises, but so was he. With lightning speed, he released her hand, raised the weapon to his shoulder and aimed it at the family photograph above her bed. "Nice Remington."

"Be careful," she said. "It's loaded."

He considered firing it into the wall to scare her, but he didn't want to risk waking a neighbor. Instead he cracked open the barrel, removed the two cartridges and saw they were full of rock salt. The pissant ammunition told him a lot about the lady doctor—she'd protect herself, but she didn't have the heart to kill. After dropping the cartridges in his pocket, Rafe pushed to his feet, letting the weapon dangle from his hand. He'd keep it as a souvenir or maybe give it to Nick for his birthday.

"Go on," he said. "Get your shoes."

He watched as she pulled out a pair of mannish boots. Sturdy and practical, they were perfect for tonight's journey. She lifted them by the tops and faced him. "I need stockings."

"Which drawer?"

"I'll get them." She stepped toward the highboy.

"No, you won't." Rafe planted his feet in front of her and squared his shoulders. She probably had a two-shot Derringer hidden between her camisoles. She needed to remember who was in charge. "I'm not in the mood for another surprise...unless it involves black lace and garters."

"Then you're going to be disappointed."

Rafe jerked open the top drawer and rummaged through her underthings—all cotton and plain. He tossed a handful on the floor. "You're right. I'm bored already."

Her eyes blazed with fury at the violation. He couldn't blame her. He'd gotten annoyed when Nick had gone through his saddlebag looking for a can opener, and the contents had been far less personal than her unmentionables.

She gave him a look of pure disgust. "The stockings are in the middle drawer."

He pulled on the knob, reached inside and tossed a ball of cotton on the bed. "Hurry up."

She sat on the mattress, untangled the stockings and pulled the first one over her bare toes. "Why don't you tell me why you're here? I'm going to find out soon enough."

"My partner got shot in the leg. It's festering."

"When did it happen?" she said, tugging on the second stocking.

"Five days ago."

Disgust filled her eyes as she wiggled her foot into her boot and yanked on the laces. "You're an idiot for waiting so long. He'll be lucky if he doesn't lose his leg."

The small room turned as fiery as a furnace. Rafe had known the minute Nick got shot that he needed a doctor, but he couldn't risk being found—not with Mexico a few weeks away. Instead he'd dosed Nick with whiskey and probed for the lead with his fingers, only to discover that the bullet had broken into fragments. He'd thought he'd gotten all of them, but he couldn't be sure. By the time he'd finished, Nick had passed out and Rafe hadn't been able to stomach a sip of water, let alone a swig of the whiskey he needed as much as his friend.

He blocked out the memory by staring at the lady doctor's fingers as she looped the laces on her second boot. The moonlight turned her knuckles bone-white, but there wasn't anything fragile about the way she made a bow and jerked it tight.

Standing straight, she said, "I need my medical bag. It's in the clinic."

"Then we'll fetch it." He wasn't about to let her get behind him on the outside stairs. Putting his palm on the butt of his gun, he gave a mocking bow and a sweep of his arm. "After you, miss."

The narrowness of the room forced her to step close to him. He smelled vinegar in her hair and figured she'd washed it earlier that night and rinsed the tangles just like his mother used to do before his father came to visit. Thoughts of the fair-haired man turned Rafe's stomach, but the tang of vinegar made him soft inside. Wise or not, he preferred it to perfume.

As the lady lifted her canvas coat off a hook, he smelled grass and mud, horse sweat and peppermint. The mix struck him as peculiar until he imagined her giving candy to a frightened child. He thought about searching her pockets for another weapon, but she had already opened the bedroom door and stepped into the alcove that opened to the stairs. Worried that she'd bolt, he grasped her upper arm. "If you cooperate, you'll be home by nightfall. That would be best for everyone."

He dropped his attention to her lips to scare her, but she stood still, forcing him to look into her eyes. "You should have knocked on my door and asked for help," she said. "You could have spared us both this nonsense."

"I doubt that," Rafe replied. Only a foolish woman would have left with him in the middle of the night, and this woman had both courage and a sharp mind.

Still gripping the shotgun, he let go of her arm and reached back to shut the bedroom door. Moonlight illuminated the frilly quilt heaped on the mattress and lit up the dust balls that had slid out from under her bed with the weapon. The lady doctor was full of surprises. He'd have to keep a close eye on her. Not that he minded…looking at a woman as bold as the doc was pure pleasure.

As soon as the door clicked shut, Rafe nudged her down the stairs. The risers creaked with each step, filling him with the worry that a neighbor would peek out a window and shout for help. Earlier he'd cursed the cold because of Nick, but now he welcomed the chill. The windows in the nearby houses were closed tight against the October night.

When they reached the bottom of the steps, the lady reached into her coat pocket, extracted a key and opened a door that led to a back room. In the darkness he saw the dim shadow of a ponderous desk and shelves full of books.

"I'll need some light to check my bag," she said.

The room was windowless, so Rafe nodded. "Light the lamp."

A match hissed and flared. When the wick caught, a yellow glow spilled into the cramped space. Judging by the cracked spines, the books had belonged to Doc Randall—all of them except a shelf holding novels, poetry and a copy of *Huckleberry Finn.* She carried the lamp into a second room where he saw an exam table, a counter full of bottles and a tall cabinet. Her leather bag was sitting on the counter near a doorway that led to a room that opened to the street.

Just below the bag, Rafe saw a drawer that could have held anything. Thinking about the shotgun, he paced to her side and snatched up the bag. "Let's go."

"I'm not ready." She set the lamp on the counter with a thud.

"What else do you need? Point and I'll get it."

She looked him square in the eye. "I need the amputation kit."

Rafe nearly puked. Nick deserved to ride horses, bed a woman without shame and to stand two-legged in a river, fishing for his supper without a care. If his young friend lost his leg, he'd never do any of those things. Guilt sluiced over Rafe like water in a miner's pan, only there was no gold in the bottom— just dirt.

He choked back a mouthful of bile. "Where is it?"

She pointed to a wooden box on the top shelf. "Everything's in that case."

He wasn't about to climb on a stepladder so that she could kick it out from under him, but neither did he want her to climb it. If he wasn't careful, she'd drop the case on his head. He also had to block both doors to keep her from running. He solved the door problem by slamming his boot against the exam table, causing it to skitter across the room. A drawer flew open and sent instruments and glass vials clattering to the floor. A foul odor filled the air as the table fell and blocked the door.

"You idiot!" The doctor ran to the broken bottles. "Those things cost money."

Rafe blocked the office door with his body, but instead of trying to escape, she dropped to her knees and scrambled to pick up the instruments.

Her frantic movements made him think of a squirrel gathering nuts—or an orphan hoarding crumbs. The picture reminded him of Nick, the promise he'd made and the hell that had come because Rafe had failed to keep his word.

Glowering, he said, "Just get the damn bone saw."

Susanna pushed to her feet and put the instruments she had collected next to her bag. Until now, she had been fairly certain the intruder had no intention of harming her, but that hope had vanished when he kicked over the exam table. No matter what he intended, he was unpredictable and capable of violence.

With his tipped-down hat, filthy coat and dishwater hair tied in a ponytail, he embodied the things Susanna hated most—violence, suffering and an emptiness of the soul. He wasn't drunk, but she smelled whiskey in his pores. He also reeked of dried blood—a bad-meat smell that made her more determined to get to the Colt Navy pistol hidden inside her medical bag.

The weapon had been a gift from her father and she knew how to use it. With the Benton gang using the trails between Cimarron and Midas as a route to Mexico, she'd been on guard for the past month. Her kidnapper was probably one of them. As for the man who'd been shot, he could be any one of the Benton cohorts—the one-eyed man who had set Bill Langley's barn on fire or Zeke Benton, the brother who had raped Melissa Greene. At least the patriarch of the group, Frank Benton, had been caught and hanged for his crimes. There had been hope the gang would disperse, but instead it had grown heads like the hydra in Greek mythology. For each head that was chopped off, the monster grew three more.

If the outlaw had shown her a shred of respect, Susanna would have risked going with him—it was her duty to treat the injured, no questions asked. Afterward, she would have gone to the sheriff, something this man had to realize. But knowing what she did about the outlaw gang, she feared for her life. The Colt was loaded with .45 caliber bullets. If she shot her attacker in the leg and dosed him with chloroform, she could run for the sheriff. If that strategy failed, she'd shoot him dead, and the world would be a better place for his passing.

To protect herself, she had to open her bag without raising his suspicion, and that meant convincing him she was scared witless. Clasping her hands to her cheeks, she let her eyes fill with tears. "D-don't hurt me," she whimpered. "I'll do what you say."

"That's more like it."

Idiot. Susanna made her bottom lip tremble. "I—I—need that box."

The outlaw gave a satisfied nod. "Then climb up on the ladder and get what you need."

With his gaze slicing into her back, she pretended to shake as she climbed the steps. The amputation kit was small but heavy. She'd lifted it before—not often, thank God—but now she pretended to sway as if it weighed a hundred pounds. If the intruder came to her aid, she'd hurl it at him.

But instead of footsteps, she heard a snort. "Don't ham it up, miss. If it were that heavy, you wouldn't keep it up there."

So he wasn't an idiot after all. Susanna set the case on the counter with a thud. "I have to put a few things in my bag."

"Just do it."

She opened the lid to the box and then turned to her bag where the Colt was buttoned into its own pocket. She could see the gun poking through the canvas and wanted to open the pouch, but he'd be expecting her to turn back to the amputation kit. Needing to keep up the charade of stocking her bag, she lifted a tray of suturing needles, set it in the bag and then twisted the button. The wooden disk caught in a tangle of thread.

"What's taking so long?"

"Nothing," she answered, tugging on the knot.

His boots hammered a warning as he strode across the room. Desperate to hide the gun, she wedged a bundle of bandages against the pocket. Just as he reached her back, she whirled around and tipped her face upward, putting them eye to eye. Neither of them moved except for the rise and fall of their chests. She could feel the heat of him spilling from the open collar of his shirt. It mixed with the odors of dust and blood, whiskey and the autumn air. His jaw twitched as he reached past her body, grazing her ribs as he put his hand in her medical bag.

With his eyes locked on hers, he pawed the sides where her instruments were strapped on thin boards. His arm flexed against her biceps as he squeezed the wad of cotton hiding the gun. If he pulled it out, he'd find the Colt. She had to stop him and she knew exactly how to do it. Without a flicker of doubt, she slammed her knee into his groin.

"Shit!"

The man jackknifed with pain and dropped the shotgun. Susanna raced to her office, screaming for help and praying someone would hear. Three more steps and she could slam the door and run for the street. Two steps…one step…but then he snaked his hand around her waist and spun her about. She felt his breath on her cheek. She also saw pain in his pale blue eyes as he jerked her closer, putting them hip to hip as he trapped her against the wall.

"You're going to regret that," he said in a reedy voice. With a twist of his arm, he whipped the rope out of his pocket, turned her and lashed her hands behind her back.

"No!" she cried as the cord cut into her skin.

"I warned you, lady." Looking disgusted, he pulled a red bandanna out of the same pocket and gagged her with it.

Terror pulsed through her veins as he dragged her back to the counter. After dumping the contents of the amputation kit into her bag, he lifted the shot-gun off the floor and laid it between the handles so he could carry both with one hand. After swinging her bag off the counter, he blew out the lamp and dragged her into the alley.

Chapter Two

About the only decent thing Rafe had done in the past hour was toss a blanket over the woman tied up in the back seat of her own surrey. It was cold and threatening to rain, but he'd done it more for himself than her. The infernal kicking against his back had worn his patience to a nub, and he hated the sound of her stifled cries for help.

God, he felt lower than dirt. But what choice did he have? Between secrets of his own and his time with the Bentons, he couldn't risk bringing Nick to town—not with handbills bearing his likeness wallpapering every train depot between St. Louis and Leadville in Colorado. He'd managed to stay a step ahead of the man he bitterly called his guardian angel, but if a traveler recognized him and put in for the reward, Rafe would never make it to Mexico. He'd be chopping rock in a Missouri prison or having his neck stretched on a gallows.

Whap!

The lady doctor had kicked his seat again, reminding him that she'd done a fine job of turning his balls into pancakes. He still felt nauseous, and each kick to the seat made him feel like more of a heel.

Whap!

As the seat jerked, an uncomfortable thought pierced Rafe's mind. It was close to dawn and they'd been on the road awhile. Maybe the woman needed to pee. Shifting his legs on the floorboard, he took stock of the circumstances. They were miles away from town and had about an hour to go before they reached Nick. Live oak and piñons fenced in the road, and the moon had dropped below the tree line. The murky shadows made running impossible. Rafe's horse, a roan some fool had named Punkin, was tied to the back of the carriage. She'd steal the gelding if she could, but Punkin was ornery and liked to bite.

Whap! Whap! Whap!

It seemed safe to stop, so Rafe reined in the doctor's old gray, hopped out of the surrey and lifted the blanket off her head. She sat up and dragged her chin against her shoulder in an effort to loosen the gag.

Rafe took pity on her and slid it off her mouth. "Do you need to visit the bushes?"

"Lord, yes!"

With a curt nod, he grabbed her ankle so she couldn't kick, untied the cord binding her feet and worked the laces on her boot. "This is so you don't get ideas about running."

As soon as he tossed the shoe onto the front seat, she shoved her other foot into his palm—a sure sign that she really had to go. He was doing his best to hurry when the shoelaces ended up in a knot. When she gave a soft moan, he glanced up at her face. She'd pinched her lips together in misery.

"Sorry," he said with a grunt.

She didn't acknowledge the apology—not that she should have—but he liked the way her voice mixed her highbrow education with tones of the West. He'd known a lot of bright women, but none of them had kept him on his toes like the doctor did. As soon as Rafe loosened the knot, he slid the boot off her foot. She scooted out of the carriage and turned her back on him, wiggling her fingers to draw his attention downward. "I need my hands."

With her braid swishing against his wrist, Rafe gripped her forearm while he untied the rope. As soon as he let go, she sprinted into the trees. "Make it quick," he called after her.

He counted to ten and then twenty. When he

got to a hundred, he started to wonder if Florence Nightingale had given him the slip.

Susanna relieved herself with calm efficiency and then hunted for a rock she could put in her pocket for self-defense. She could tolerate his smart mouth, but if he got fresh with his hands, she'd fight back. She had just a few minutes before he came looking for her—maybe less.

He'd been wise to keep her shoes. She had four brothers and had grown up with a fishing pole in her hand. She'd also gone camping with her father every year on the anniversary of their reunion until she had left for college. She knew the mountains even better than the bearded prospectors who hung around Midas in the winter. Not only could she find her way home, she'd be able to tell the sheriff exactly where she'd been.

As she bent down to hunt for a rock, Susanna prayed that something good would come from this horrid night. Maybe she'd be the link in the chain that would lead to the capture of the Benton gang. Dear God, she hoped so. But in the meantime, she needed to keep her wits about her. After curling her fingers around a chunk of granite, she pushed to her feet. She wished her parents were home. She had more confidence in her father than the sheriff, but John, Abbie and her three youngest brothers had traveled to Boston to visit Robbie, their half brother, at college.

"Hurry up, Florence, or I'm coming after you."

The outlaw's gruff voice grated on a raw nerve. She *hated* being called Florence—not because she felt superior to nurses, but because the men who hurled it as an insult were mocking a woman who'd been a pioneer and a true heroine. It also took Susanna back to her early days in medical school, when professors and students alike had dished out abuse in every class.

"My name's not Florence," she called back, insisting on respect. "You can call me Doctor."

"Fine, Dr. Nightingale. Just hurry up."

"I will…Mr. James."

A beat of silence told her she'd confused him. "Who's Mr. James?"

Susanna counted his annoyance as a victory. Maybe she could trick him into revealing his name. "So you're not Jesse James, the Missouri bank robber?"

A low chuckle whispered through the trees and brought to her mind a picture of the outlaw's lips curling into a smile. "Jesse's been dead for years," he said. "Rest assured, I'm no ghost."

"I can see that," she answered. "What should I call you then?"

"You'll hear my name soon enough. You can call me Rafe."

"I'd rather call you Mr. James—unless you have another last name." She was probing, but she also wanted the distance that came with formalities.

"Rafe's all you need."

"In that case, you can call me Dr. Nightingale."

Susanna had a reason for not revealing her identity. He didn't need to know she was John Leaf's daughter. Her father had traded his guns for a preacher's coat, but he'd once been an infamous shootist.

Wanting to avoid being tied up again, Susanna decided not to aggravate the outlaw and headed back to the road. She wanted to gather more information about him, but she was pleased with what she'd just gleaned. Having grown up in Washington, D.C., where she had lived until she traveled West at the age of fourteen, she had an ear for accents. She heard the South in this man's voice, but it had been muted by time and travel. She'd have to remember that detail when she went to the sheriff.

As she emerged from the pines, she saw the surrey with its large wheels and brocade seats. It had been a fancy ride in its day, and she liked having room for extra passengers. The outlaw must have sensed rain like she did, because he had put up the folding top. A soft clicking called her attention to the front of the surrey where he was holding her horse by the halter and stroking its nose. Poor Lightning had outlived the spirit of his name. He should have been retired when Doc Randall passed on, but Susanna couldn't afford another horse—not without a loan from the bank or sacrificing her pride and accepting charity from her parents.

As the man scratched Lightning's ears, she lingered in the shadows, filing away details of his appearance for the authorities. He was just over six feet tall, broad shouldered and undernourished. He was also flexing his neck, a habit that suggested fatigue or chronic tension.

The minute he saw her, he dropped the halter and walked toward her with the length of rope clenched in his hand. They met at the side of the carriage.

"There's no need for that," she said, matching his stare. "I'm not going anywhere without my boots."

"All right," he said. "But you'll have to ride next to me. I want to keep an eye on you."

With a curt nod, Susanna walked to the passenger side, climbed in and positioned herself as far from him as possible. As he took his place next to her, the carriage springs dipped and squeaked with age. With a flick of his wrist, he urged Lightning into a fast walk. The old horse managed to look spirited until the trail curved up a hill that grew steeper with every step. Lightning moved slower and slower until he'd come close to a dead stop.

"Damn nag," muttered the outlaw. "You should buy yourself a decent horse."

"I would if I could," she countered. "You may find this hard to believe, but some of us work for a living."

She was about to look away when he gave her a hard stare. "Why would I find that hard to believe?"

Because you're a liar and a thief. You take what you want and leave others to suffer. She was itching to lecture him about hard work and ethics, but his pale blue irises were flashing with bitterness and his lips had thinned to a sneer. She'd touched a nerve that ran straight to his heart. He knew something about suffering.

Circles of bluish exhaustion had spread from the bridge of his nose to the hollows beneath his eyes. Most of the cowboys she treated were men whose features had been carved by bar fights, hours in the sun and damaged dreams. Looking more closely at Jesse James, she saw that his nose had never been broken, his cheekbones bordered on aristocratic and his mouth made her think of the Boticelli angels she'd seen in the National Art Gallery. "Where are you from?" she asked.

The creases around his mouth deepened into a frown. Staring straight ahead, he replied, "It doesn't matter, but my pride does. I don't usually kidnap women. I was expecting Doc Randall when I broke into your house."

So he had been in Midas before. "When did you see Doc last?"

He shook his head, telling her that he wasn't going to answer. Instead he sat straighter in the seat. "After you take care of Nick's leg, I'll let you go. You can ride back on this old nag, but I'm borrowing your rig."

Susanna clenched her jaw until her molars throbbed. She had less than twenty dollars in the bank and she needed the carriage to make calls. Her parents would have helped her, but she had her pride. They'd already paid for her education and had three more children to raise. The bank wouldn't loan her money, either. She'd tried to borrow to build a new clinic with a special room for children and indoor plumbing, but Harlan Welsh had refused to help her.

I'm sorry, Dr. Leaf, but what's to stop you from changing your mind about this fancy building? You might decide to get married and have babies, and then where would the bank be?

She had politely negotiated with the banker, but it hadn't done any good. In the end, she'd been choking on her frustration. She was twice as educated as he was and ten times more committed to making Midas a good place to live. Her heart ached with compassion for people in need—especially orphans, because she had once felt like one. Married or not, that would never change.

Shivering against the chilly night, Susanna thought about the moth-eaten cloak hanging in her wardrobe and the need she'd have for it when winter arrived. As much as she wanted the navy-blue coat on display at the Midas Emporium—a full-length garment with brass buttons and a hood—it seemed like an indulgence compared to buying new obstetrical instruments, the latest medicines and a binaural stethoscope with rubber tubes. She *had* to keep the surrey. She would have begged for it, but she knew the outlaw wouldn't be impressed by weakness.

Instead she arched an eyebrow at him. "When do you plan to return it?"

He shrugged. "Beats me."

"Then you're stealing it."

"Call it whatever you want," he replied in a drawl. "I'm taking it for Nick."

No matter how much his friend needed the surrey, Susanna needed it more. Or more precisely, she needed to be able to replace it. "I'll make you an offer," she said. "If you steal it, I'll have to notify the sheriff. But if you buy it from me, we'll simply be transacting business."

His lips tightened into a half smile. "How much do you want?"

"A hundred dollars."

"For this piece of junk?"

"It's not junk," she answered calmly. "The rigging is almost new."

After giving her a sly glance, the outlaw stretched his arm across the back of the seat so that his fingers dangled an inch from her shoulder. "Your rig's not worth anything close to a hundred dollars…but I can think of something that is."

As one of four women in a class of a hundred at Johns Hopkins, Susanna had heard enough rude remarks to last a lifetime. She'd been teased, groped and harassed until she'd learned to hold her own. Ignoring the innuendo, she kept her voice level. "You can have the surrey for fifty dollars."

"I'll tell you what," he said, brushing her coat with his fingertips. "I'll give you two-hundred dollars for your surrey and a roll in the hay."

Susanna shoved his wrist away from her shoulder. "Forty dollars, and you keep your hands to yourself."

The outlaw clicked his tongue. "You drive a hard

bargain, Dr. Nightingale. I'll go up to three-hundred dollars, but only because you're nice looking—and probably a virgin."

Heat raced to her cheeks—not because he'd called her a virgin, but because he made her feel like one. He was right. She was innocent when it came to the intimacies of marriage. But she wasn't the least bit naive when it came to men. At Johns Hopkins, she'd eventually become one of the boys. After the barkeep had gotten over his surprise, she'd swigged beer in a pub, listened to lewd jokes and learned that men wanted sex while women yearned for love. To her way of thinking, women were the brighter of the two genders.

Arching her eyebrows, she gave Jesse James an appraising look. "Speaking clinically, there's a cure for what ails you."

The fool seemed pleased with the game. "Are you offering?"

"Absolutely," she replied. "But you should know I've only done it once—on a cadaver." Her anatomy professor had meant to humiliate her in front of the entire class, but the men had become remarkably quiet when she'd cut off the cadaver's testicles and proceeded to dissect them. She'd hated every minute of it, but the teasing had stopped for a month.

She had hoped her story would have the same

effect on the outlaw, but his eyes were twinkling. "Something tells me we're talking apples and oranges here."

"I'm talking about castration," she replied. "That's the surgical removal of—"

Jesse James burst out laughing. "No thanks, Florence. But I'll tell you what. I'll up my offer to five-hundred dollars, but that's only because I need a bath and shave."

"You need more than that," she said evenly. "You need to learn a little respect."

"Every woman has her price." He tipped his chin sideways and peered into her eyes. "What's yours?"

Romance...love...shared dreams...

She wanted the kind of love her parents had—a marriage full of surprises, tender touches and words that didn't have to be spoken to be heard. But she also wanted respect for her profession and her opinions, a husband who'd be proud of her accomplishments. In college, she had wondered if such a man existed. After graduating and returning to Midas, she had decided that her dreams were unrealistic and had shortened the list of qualities she wanted in a husband. She'd set her cap for Timothy Duke, a widower with three adorable daughters. In spite of his feelings about her career, he was hardworking and honorable.

Yes, Susanna had her price…but it had nothing to do with money. "That may be true," she replied. "But mine isn't what you think."

The outlaw looked at her from the corner of his eye. "So what is it?"

"You wouldn't understand."

Staring straight ahead, she unwillingly flashed on the dream she'd been having when the outlaw woke her up. It was always the same—she was alone in a lush valley, gathering a bouquet and feeling sad because no man had ever given her flowers. She would hold the bouquet to her nose, breathe in the scent and thank God for the gifts he'd given her—the ability to heal, a wonderful family and a heart full of love. But then she'd wake up alone in the dark and wonder why God had also given her bodily yearnings that never went away.

As the outlaw steered the carriage to the edge of the forest, Susanna felt that ache now, low in her belly and high in her chest. The first rays of sun were falling through the trees like shafts of gold. She heard the ripple of a stream running along the trail, the twitter of chipmunks and the distant squawk of a scrub jay. The music of the day gave her peace and made her lonely at the same time—just like her dream. She wanted so much…to laugh until her sides hurt and be held when she cried…to love a good man and give birth to babies of her own.

The beauty of the morning made her throat swell. She wanted to share it, but not with the outlaw at her side. She'd rather be the lone visitor in God's art gallery than have the moment spoiled by his disrespect.

She was relishing the sun on her cheeks when the outlaw took a deep breath, held it and exhaled with a rush. "We might get a touch of rain," he said. "I like the way it smells."

He had sounded wistful. "Me, too," she replied, eyes straight ahead.

As the trail left the shade of the forest, the outlaw steered the carriage into a valley Susanna recognized. The north side of the canyon was known for its caves and rocky peaks, and a narrow passage connected it to a trail that led to Cimarron. It had come to be known as Outlaw Alley, a fact that reminded her to fish for information.

"Tell me about your partner," she asked. "How did he get hurt?"

Jesse James shook his head. "I'd rather talk about you. What made you want to be a doctor?"

"I grew up in the District of Columbia," Susanna replied. "It's a beautiful city, but parts of it are so poor it's shameful. Before my mother came to

Midas, she was married to a terrible man. After he died, she opened her house to women who needed help. I saw what a little kindness could do."

A smile curled the outlaw's lips. "I admire your ideals, Dr. Nightingale, but a pint of whiskey does the same thing you do. It takes away the pain. In fact, it does it better, at least for a grown man."

"There's a place for whiskey," she said softly. "It dulls the mind and cleans wounds. But it also causes nausea and headaches."

The outlaw chuckled softly. "You just proved my point. Thanks to that kick you gave me, my head's pounding and my guts are in a twist."

"You had it coming," she said. "I won't apologize."

"I'm not asking you to."

He clicked his tongue at Lightning who picked up his pace as the trail disappeared in a sea of grass. Still tied to the surrey, Rafe's horse clopped behind them. As they made their way to an apron of rock below the canyon wall, the wheel-high blades dipped and swayed back into place. A third horse whinnied a warning, reminding Susanna of the gunshot man in the cave. As soon as the outlaw reined in Lightning, he hopped down from the surrey, lifted her bag off the floorboard and stuffed her shoes inside his coat pocket.

"I need my boots," she said.

"Not a chance. The cave's not more than thirty yards from here."

Susanna looked down at her toes, said goodbye to her stockings and climbed from the seat. The cotton offered some protection to the soles of her feet, but she felt every twig and pebble as she climbed around man-size boulders and bushes stunted by a lack of water and too much wind. Judging by the stairlike steps that had formed between the rocks, countless men—and maybe a few women—had hidden from the law in the cave she spotted at the base of the wall.

"Rafe? Is that you?"

Susanna froze in midstep. The voice coming from the opening was high-pitched and thin with pain as she expected, but it couldn't possibly belong to a grown man. It lacked the depth and the timbre, and most telling of all, the tiny cry had been full of tears.

A child...her patient was a child...a gunshot boy who was about to lose his leg.

Chapter Three

Susanna hoisted her skirts and sprinted up the trail as the outlaw called to the boy. "Yeah, it's me, kid. I brought a doctor. She'll fix you right up."

"My leg's a lot worse," said the tiny voice.

Susanna's heart pounded with dread. She heard the emotions she sensed in all her patients—exhaustion from the pain, relief that help had arrived and a shuddering fear of what would happen next. Judging by the boy's voice, she estimated his age as ten or twelve, shy of puberty but old enough to understand the facts.

A child...someone had shot a child....

It was an abomination against the human heart. She wanted to hang the person who was responsible—and the outlaw following her up the hill because he'd waited so long to get help. Terrified of what she'd see, Susanna stepped into a tomblike room made of granite and peered into the shadows.

Her gaze landed first on a fire that had died hours ago, leaving nothing but ash and charred wood in a circle of rocks. Next she spotted a saddlebag. The buckle had been left undone, revealing a wad of crumpled greenbacks. She also saw a Sharps carbine propped against the wall, angled so that the light from the mouth of the cave showed a swirl of roses engraved on the gun's receiver.

As she stepped deeper into the interior, she spotted a pallet of blankets against the back wall. Someone had folded them into a bed of sorts, leaving one loose for warmth against the cold night. Beneath the wool she saw bare toes, a thin leg in a blood-soaked bandage and finally the terrified eyes of a boy with red hair and freckles.

He pulled himself to a sitting position, leaned back on his elbows and looked at her with awe. "Are you really a doctor?"

Susanna knelt at his side. "Not only am I a doctor, I'm also a very good one. I went to a fancy school back East."

"So you can fix my leg?"

The hope in his voice broke her heart. She never lied to her patients, but she was sorely tempted to start now. Instead she said, "I'm going to try my best."

After giving her a solemn nod, the boy settled back

against the pallet. Susanna laid her palm against his forehead to gauge his fever, though she knew from his glassy eyes that he was burning up.

"Your hand's cold," he said. "It feels nice."

"What's your name?" she asked.

"It's Nicholas. Or Nick," he said, trying to sound grown-up.

"Hello, Nick. My patients call me Dr. Sue. How old are you?"

"I'm almost eleven."

"Then you're old enough to understand things. Can you tell me what happened?"

When the boy craned his neck toward the mouth of the cave, Susanna turned and saw the man standing in silhouette, gripping her medical bag and looking haunted. She understood that Nick was asking permission to reveal a secret. She also saw that he cared for the man. They didn't look at all alike, but it was possible they were related—cousins perhaps.

The outlaw stepped next to her and set the bag at her feet. "I cleaned the wound as best as I could, but the bullet broke into pieces. I don't know if I got it all."

While working in poor sections of Baltimore, Susanna had learned to keep her judgments to herself. Ignorant or not, people did the best they could with what they knew. The outlaw might not understand the need to wash his hands and use carbolic, but she could see no excuse whatsoever for waiting so long to get this boy to a doctor. Later she'd speak her mind, but right now she had to examine the leg.

Turning back to Nicholas, she said, "I have to take off the bandage. It'll probably hurt. Would you like a peppermint to suck on?"

"Sure." He looked almost pleased.

Susanna lifted two peppermints from her pocket, unwrapped the first one for Nick, opened the second for herself and popped it into her mouth. She was about to open her bag when she saw the boy waiting for her to offer a piece of candy to his friend. For Nick's sake, she took another peppermint out of her pocket and held it up to the outlaw. "Here you go," she said, looking over her shoulder.

His eyes met hers in understanding. The candy wasn't a peace offering. She intended to take him to task for Nick's condition, but she didn't want to upset the boy. He took the candy, thanked her with a grunt and unwrapped it.

Susanna turned back to Nick. "Now let's see your leg."

"It hurts all over," said the boy. "I feel sick, too. Like I'm going to puke."

"I'm hoping the peppermint will help, but it's all

right if you get sick. It's just your body trying to fix your leg instead of digesting what's in your stomach."

Susanna opened her bag and took out a pair of scissors. As gently as she could, she cut the length of cotton from the boy's leg. A row of buttonholes told her the bloody bandage had once been a shirt. Judging by the size, it had belonged to the man. It was also a fine linen with embroidered cuffs, the kind of Fancy Dan shirt that cost more money than she saw in a month.

Susanna peeled back the bandage and studied the wound. The bullet had struck the boy below the knee. If it had shattered like the outlaw said, it had hit bone and probably caused a fracture. Nick was young and the bone would mend. Six weeks on crutches and he'd be playing tag, but the bone was the least of his problems. The entry wound was ringed by hard tissue and full of pus, but what sickened her were the veiny streaks of red. He had signs of blood poisoning.

If Nicholas had been fifty years old, she would have told him that amputation was the surest way to save his life. Then she would have dosed him with chloroform and done her job. She'd been trained to do what science required, but taking a child's leg would be the most awful thing she'd ever had to do.

Rage burned in her empty stomach. Five days ago she could have removed the bullet with sterile instruments and treated the wound with antiseptic. She could have dosed the boy with echinacea tea and made poultices to draw out the infection. She could have given him laudanum for the pain. The final outcome was in God's hands—not hers—but she would have gone to war with the devil himself to spare the boy the misery she saw in his future.

Was it too late to wage that battle? Waiting to take off the leg was risky. If gangrene set in, he'd be in grave danger. But the solution was permanent and crippling. Glancing at Nick, she wondered about his parents and his tie to the man standing behind her. In the end, the decision to amputate the leg would be theirs, but she'd have a better chance of winning this war if she took him back to Midas.

The boy looked at her with wide eyes. "You won't cut off my leg, will you?"

Susanna refused to lie. "I'm going to try very hard to save it, but your life's more important."

"No!"

She touched his forehead. "Listen to me, Nick. I have some medicine in my bag and even more back in my clinic. I want to take you to Midas."

The boy looked at the outlaw. "Rafe?"

"The doctor's right, kid."

"Will you come with me?"

When the man didn't answer, Nick pushed up on his elbow. "You promised—"

"I know what I said, but that was before you got hurt." The outlaw dropped to a crouch and brushed back the boy's sweaty hair. "I'm worried about you."

Susanna didn't know which jarred her more—the tenderness in the man's touch or the knowledge in his eyes that an even harder decision might have to be made. Even more telling, she saw a guilt so strong that he couldn't blink it away.

Nicholas frowned. "I'm slowing you down, ain't I?"

"*Aren't I.* And no, you're not holding me up." The man pushed to his feet. "Partners don't walk out on each other. I say we let the doctor look at your leg and then decide what's best."

"But the Bentons—"

"Can go to hell in a handbasket." The outlaw dipped his chin and lowered his voice. "This isn't the time to talk about them."

As Nicholas sealed his lips, Susanna sifted through the information she'd gleaned. If the man and boy had been riding with the Bentons, why were they hiding now? She had assumed her captor was an outlaw, but she'd never heard of a hardened killer traveling with a child. She also realized he'd taken a chance by coming to Midas, and he'd done it because he cared about the boy.

Perhaps he had once run with the gang but had had a falling-out with them. He couldn't possibly be on the right side of the law. He had to be hiding something; otherwise he would have brought Nicholas to her days ago. Nor would he have kidnapped her in the middle of the night. Susanna wanted answers, but first she needed to drain the pus around the entry wound to make him more comfortable.

As she opened her bag, she took out a wad of bandages and saw the pocket holding her Colt Navy. She doubted she would need it, but she lifted her scissors and snipped the pocket open just in case she had misjudged the circumstances. Then she lifted out a small brown bottle.

"I'm going to give you a dose of laudanum," she said to Nick. "Then I'll wash my hands and make sure Rafe got all the bullet fragments." She didn't like saying the man's name, but she didn't have a choice.

"Will it hurt a lot?" Nick asked.

"Only for a few minutes, and then you'll forget about it."

When he nodded bravely, she wished to God she could spare him the suffering she was about to inflict. Silently she said a prayer—asking God for wisdom for herself and mercy for the boy. She also prayed for the man who would have to live with himself for the choice he'd made five days ago.

As she poured the laudanum into a spoon, she wondered again about the relationship between the man and boy. "Are you two related?"

Nick shook his head. "Not by blood, but we're partners. Rafe's teaching me things."

Susanna could imagine—how to lie, steal and kidnap women.

"Did you know he speaks French?" Nick said.

"Is that so?" she answered. Whatever French the outlaw spoke, he'd probably learned in a brothel. Susanna set down the bottle and lifted the spoon to Nick's lips. "Drink this."

The boy swallowed the drug without making a face. When a child didn't complain about the taste, she knew an illness was serious. As she corked the bottle, Nick went back to tales about Rafe. "He's teaching me to read, too. Have you ever heard of *The Odyssey?*"

"Nick, that's enough," said the man. "Try to sleep."

As she pushed to her feet, Susanna looked around the cave for a pot to use for water. She saw one in the corner and picked it up. "I heard a stream at the bottom of the rocks. I'll need fresh water. We also have to build a fire so I can boil my instruments."

"I'll fetch it," said the man.

"Rafe?" The boy's voice was just above a whisper.

"What is it, kid?"

"Thanks for helping me. You won't leave, will you?"

Ah, hell, thought Rafe. What could he say?

A month ago he had left his horse tied in front of an establishment where kids didn't belong. He'd come out after midnight and found Nick stealing food from his saddlebag. Seeing that the kid was half-starved, Rafe did for the boy what Lemuel Scott had once done for him. He bought the kid a meal. They'd gone back into the saloon where he'd ordered chili and corn bread for them both, beer for himself and milk for the boy.

While eating supper, Rafe had learned that Nick's mother had died a month earlier and that he didn't know his father. More of the story had come out during the long ride from Green River, a town in southern Colorado, to the mountains west of Midas. Rafe surmised that Nick's mother had been a sweet Irish girl who'd been molested in a rich man's house. When she discovered she was with child, she'd fled west where she'd made a living doing laundry and possibly things she hadn't shared with her son.

Times were hard in Green River. None of the

townsfolk had wanted an extra mouth to feed. Neither did any of the local farmers. Nick was old enough to be a burden but not strong enough to do a man's work. Rafe had been about the same age when his mother, Mimi LaCroix, died in her bed with a pool of blood spreading between her legs. He knew what friendship meant to a frightened boy, and so he'd told Nick they could partner up for a while.

That promise had turned into something more. Nick had become the little brother Rafe had never had. Over the past month, the decision to give up bounty hunting and settle in Mexico had changed from a desperate escape to a plan for a new life. With the money in his saddlebag, he could start a gunsmithing business south of the border. Thanks to Lem, Rafe knew all about firearms. He also had a talent for engraving—nothing fancy, just roses and the like—but he enjoyed it. He figured he'd gotten his eye for beauty from his mother.

Being with Nick had brought back some of Rafe's finest memories. He'd been eighteen and almost a man when he'd met Lemuel Scott, but he'd been greener than Nick when it came to surviving in dusty cow towns. Lem had taught Rafe everything he knew: how to trail a wanted man across miles of empty prairie, how to shoot to maim and the best ways to capture an outlaw when he was worth more alive than dead—like Frank Benton. The murdering bastard had been tried and hanged, and Rafe's saddlebag was bulging with the bounty.

As he glanced down at Nick's leg, Rafe felt his chest muscles tighten into a wall. The Bentons hadn't been pleased to have their pa locked up, and they had vowed to make Rafe pay, both for turning in their old man and for double-crossing them. Earlier, they'd accepted him as a friend, a brother even, and he'd betrayed their trust by tricking the old man into wandering alone into the night. After knocking Frank Benton stone-cold, Rafe had hog-tied him and turned him in to the authorities.

That had happened back in Colorado, but five days ago, Rafe had run into the gang near Cimarron and had traded shots. To his shame, Nick had taken a bullet meant for him. The kid was too damn brave for his own good. And too damn young to lose his leg.

As much as Rafe wanted to keep his promise to take Nick to Mexico, he couldn't risk being caught by the Bentons. Nor did he want his guardian angel to drag him back to St. Louis for a trial of his own.

Rafe's nickname for the man who'd been following him was pure sarcasm. He didn't know who his father had hired to track him down after that night in St. Louis, but the man was no angel. If he was anything like Rafe's old man, he had a heart of stone. He also had an uncanny ability to stay in the shadows. While riding with Lem, Rafe had often asked his friend to check out a town for the damnable posters. When he found one, Lem would ask questions at a local saloon. The story was always the same. The posters were delivered by a local railroad agent. If anyone made a claim for the reward, a nameless man showed up, listened and left.

It struck the average man as odd, but Rafe understood the tactic. His father's detective didn't want to draw attention to himself. He was laying a trap, one which Rafe had been able to avoid with Lem's help and by traveling farther west. Lem had been dead a year now, and Rafe found it harder to keep a low profile.

Every time he set foot in a town, he risked being recognized. Going to Midas was out of the question, but so was leaving Nick. He'd have to find another place for the doctor to treat the boy's leg. He dropped back to a crouch and squeezed Nick's shoulder. "We're in this together. Now get some rest."

The lady doctor pushed to her feet. "The laudanum needs a few minutes to work. May I have a word with you?"

After a curt nod, Rafe walked to the front of the cave, where a layer of clouds had dimmed the morning sun. He would have welcomed a heavy rain. Storms were nature's way of erasing a man's tracks and giving him a clean start. At the same time, the drop in temperature made him afraid for Nick. The boy looked even weaker than he had a day ago, and Rafe worried that he'd catch a chill.

He reached the mouth of the cave ahead of the lady doctor but motioned for her to go first. As she moved into the daylight, she tipped her face up to the clouds. A drop of rain struck her cheek as Rafe stepped to her side. He had an urge to wipe it away, though he didn't know why.

Maybe it was the vinegar smell of her hair or the knowledge that she was aching for Nick. Wordless, they stood together as clouds boiled over the ridge. Raindrops spattered Rafe's face and hers too, forcing them to walk back into the cave where they'd have to whisper to keep from frightening Nick.

Rafe dipped his head to her ear and said, "Level with me. How bad is it?"

She shook her head in despair. "If he were an adult, I'd take off the leg. But he's just a boy..."

When she bit hard on her lips, Rafe knew how she felt. He wanted to beat himself bloody for not getting help immediately. "How soon do we have to decide?"

In her eyes he saw both dread and a steely anger.

"Before I recommend anything, I want to take him to Midas. Judging by the look of the wound, he still has bullet fragments in his leg. I need to operate, and I'd prefer to do it in the clinic. I also have herbs that I can brew into a tea that's fairly effective against blood poisoning. The rest of the treatment is just common sense. Keeping him warm is critical to fight the shock, and I can't do that in this cave."

Rafe saw her point. The rain was coming in waves, gentle but cold enough to chill a man's bones. "I'll build a fire."

"That's not enough," she insisted. "Let me take him to town."

"I can't do that."

"Not even to save his life?" Her voice shook with annoyance. "I can see you two are close. Why don't you leave him with me and come back later? Maybe in a month or two."

If Rafe stayed in one place too long, his guardian angel was sure to find him. And if he hid out in the mountains, the Bentons would track him down. Was leaving Nick in Midas the right thing to do? Maybe so. The doctor would give the boy a home or see to it that he was adopted by a good family. Rafe wouldn't be abandoning Nick. He'd be seeing to the boy's needs. But he knew in his gut that Nick wouldn't see it that way. The kid would feel like a piece of trash being set aside. Rafe had felt the same way when his father had sent him off to school and the bitterness lived in him to this day. He couldn't do that to Nick. He shook his head. "That's not possible."

When her eyes caught his, he had no trouble seeing her with a scalpel in anatomy class. The woman was tough, but only when being firm was kindness in disguise. Rafe had the feeling she was about to pull his guts out, and he was going to let her because he had it coming.

"I don't know why you're on the run, mister. And I don't care," she said evenly. "But I *do* care about Nick. How could you involve him with the Bentons? He should be in school and shooting marbles, not facing an amputation."

Shame boiled in the pit of Rafe's stomach. He'd give his right nut to save the boy's leg. Hell, he'd give his left one, too. He'd risked his life and his freedom to bring the doctor when he did, but he didn't have to explain himself to a know-it-all woman. He'd wasted enough time already.

He curled his lips into a snarl. "You don't know squat about what's happened, so mind your own business."

She stared right back. "I know that a boy needs a clean bed and decent meals."

"Damn it, lady."

"And I know that a child should *never* face an amputation."

"Christ on crutches," he muttered.

Ignoring his profanity, she got right in his face. "I know something else, too. This could have been avoided. You should have brought him to me when it happened. I could have—oh God." Tears welled in her eyes, but she wiped then away before they spilled down her cheeks.

Rafe glared up at the clouds. He wanted to hock up a mouthful of spit, but the taste of peppermint stopped him. "There has to be another answer," he said. "Do what you can right now. I need to think for a bit."

"You've already wasted *five* days. What's there to decide?" She glanced back at Nick, who had fallen into a fitful slumber, then she jammed the cooking pot into his hands. "I need water. I'll build up the fire while you fetch it."

He was about to tell her to get it herself when he remembered he still had her shoes. Her feet had to be half-frozen, and the floor of the cave was covered with bat dung. He almost handed her the boots, but he worried that she'd carry Nick to the surrey and ride off—not that her horse could move faster than his. He just didn't want to go to the trouble of chasing her.

"I want my shoes," she demanded.

He looked down at the hem of the dress showing beneath her duster. It took him back to her bedroom where he'd seen her toes. It also reminded him of the shotgun under her bed and the struggle in the clinic.

"Not a chance, lady. I don't trust you for a minute."

Rafe pulled his hat low against the rain, tucked the pot under his arm and headed down the trail to the stream. Wrapped in worries about Nick and mad at the lady doctor for telling the truth, he wasn't paying attention when Zeke Benton emerged from behind a boulder and pointed his pistol straight at Rafe's head.

Chapter Four

"Hold it right there, LaCroix."

Susanna had just stepped to the back of the cave when a new voice reached her ears. Deep and gravelly, it belonged to a determined man. Had a U.S. Marshal caught up to the outlaw? Her heart pounded with hope, but she couldn't forget Nick's mention of the Benton gang. For all she knew, the voice belonged to the Benton brother who had slashed a bank teller's throat in Cimarron, going so deep that he'd nearly severed the man's head. Or perhaps he was the brother named Zeke. At the thought of what he'd done to Melissa, Susanna's stomach churned.

Whether the stranger was a marshal or one of the Bentons, she intended to be prepared. Dropping to a crouch, she opened her medical bag and curled her fingers around the butt of her Colt Navy. After pushing to her feet, she lurked at the mouth of the cave where she had a view of Rafe standing with his hands in the air. After the way he'd manhandled her at the clinic, she almost smirked. But that small satisfaction turned to a chill when she glimpsed the man aiming a revolver at Rafe's face.

The description of Zeke Benton on the Wanted posters said he was six feet tall and weighed over two-hundred pounds. The mug shot above it had shown a man with acne-scarred cheeks, black hair and crooked teeth. The stranger holding Rafe at bay matched the photograph perfectly.

Please God...anyone but the Bentons...

But even as the words formed in her mind, she saw the truth in Rafe LaCroix's eyes. "What do you want, Zeke?"

"I want to see buzzards eating the flesh off your bones. Our pa's dead and you should be too."

"He deserved to hang and you know it."

"You tricked us, you son of a bitch. You had Pa eating out of your hand, and then you turned him in for the goddamned bounty."

"Only because he was worth more alive than dead."

"Maybe so," Zeke drawled. "I bet you feel the same way about that boy, don't you?"

Killing went against every bit of Susanna's training, but she'd shoot Zeke Benton dead before she'd let him harm Nick. She raised the Colt and took aim, praying the whole time that he'd change his mind about harming anyone and ride away. At the same moment, she saw Rafe shrug off the threat. "The boy doesn't mean shit to me."

Liar. Susanna knew that he'd take a bullet to protect Nick. She could also see the tension in his neck and jaw. He was itching to tear Zeke Benton into pieces.

Benton gave a sneer of his own. "Maybe not, but what about the lady doctor? She's a pretty thing, ain't she?"

His voice dripped like honey—sickening sweet and as dangerous as a nest of bees. Rafe was trying to appear nonchalant, but she could see a tick in his jaw just below his ear. She knew his Colt was inside his duster. Benton had to know it, too, but he was enjoying a perverse litany of what he intended to do to her.

For once, Susanna was glad to be underestimated as a woman. It hadn't occurred to Benton that she'd be armed and ready to defend herself. After an especially foul reference to her anatomy, she cocked the hammer of the Colt.

"So what's your preference, LaCroix?" Benton said. "I can't decide which I'd enjoy more—shooting you first and taking my time with the lady, or tying you up so you can watch while I get between her legs."

Susanna focused on Zeke while keeping Rafe in her peripheral vision. Rafe had curled his lips into a smirk as if he were about to make a smart remark. At the same time, he went for his gun.

Before Benton could fire, Susanna shot him in the head. The bullet went exactly where she intended—into his temple where it took his life with more mercy than the Bentons had shown the bank clerk with the slashed jugular vein.

Later she'd be sick, but she had seen what Zeke Benton had done to Melissa. He'd torn her insides to shreds and left her fearing babies and how they were made. If the early signs were accurate, he'd also left her carrying his child. If Rafe LaCroix had put Frank Benton in jail, Susanna figured his life was worth saving—and that Zeke Benton's life had needed to end.

Rafe was scrambling to the cave, keeping low behind the rain-slicked rocks. "Get back!" he shouted. "The bastard's not alone."

Susanna took cover inside the cave and studied the terrain. The scattered boulders could have concealed a dozen men and Rafe had to cross an open patch of dirt. Keeping the Colt ready, she scanned the terrain for gunmen but saw nothing. The rain had eased, leaving a freshness in the air that didn't match the violence of the morning.

She heard Nick whimper. "What's happening?"

"It's okay. You're safe now."

"But I can help. I can shoot—"

"No! It's best if you stay put."

"But Rafe—"

"He'll be here in a minute."

At least that's what she hoped as he sprinted across the half-moon of dirt in front of the cave. He was just ten steps away when a gunman popped up from a boulder, fired and dropped out of sight. The bullet hit the granite above her head and sent daggers of stone flying through the air. A shard scratched the skin above her left eye and stopped her from getting off another shot.

Rafe charged into the cave, snatched up the carbine and took aim, but the shootist stayed low. With the sulfur smell thick in the air, he glanced in her direction. "Did they teach you that in medical college?"

Susanna smiled at the admiration in his voice. "No, it's a family talent."

When another gunman showed himself, Rafe took a shot and missed. Susanna had a better angle and fired a split second later. The bullet struck the man in the chest and sent him sprawling behind the rock.

Only his boots showed, dusty and twitching as he drew his last breath. If he was the man who'd slit the bank teller's throat, justice had been done. And if he'd been one of the onlookers, he still had it coming.

Susanna felt Rafe's gaze on her face. He had to be wondering where she had hidden her gun. Considering she had just saved his life, she decided it was time to bargain. "I want my shoes back."

"You can have them," he said. "Heck, I'll buy you new ones."

A bullet ricocheted off the lip of the cave.

"Watch the rocks to your left," she said. "Someone's running for cover.

Rafe took aim and fired, but they both knew the shot was impossible. The man was running like a rabbit and a hundred yards away. Seconds after he disappeared into the trees, a trio of riders galloped across the far end of the valley and disappeared through the cut that led to a southern trail.

Rafe lowered the Winchester. "That was Lester Benton. He'll be back with ten men. We have to get moving."

Susanna glanced at Nick, who was sitting up in a drugged stupor. With every minute that passed, the infection was spreading deeper into his body. "We have to go to town," she said. "There's no choice."

"No!" The sad cry came from Nick. "I want to stay with Rafe."

If her patient had been an adult, Susanna could have laid out the facts. Instead she became aware of the holes in her stockings and Zeke Benton's corpse. Something painful had welded Nick to Rafe LaCroix and the trouble wasn't over. Nonetheless, she had earned the right to speak her mind. "My boots, please."

"Put them on quick," Rafe said, tossing them at her feet. "We're leaving, but we're not headed to town."

Earlier he'd been ready to buy the lady doctor new boots and something pretty to say thanks for saving his life. Rafe had been a dead man when he'd gone for his gun. At best he and Zeke would have traded bullets, but Rafe hadn't even pulled the trigger when Benton's eyes had rolled back in his head. The magnitude of the doctor's decision hadn't escaped him. Even though he'd treated her badly, she'd spared his life when she could have shot him dead or dinged him in the leg.

All that kindness gave Rafe a headache. He didn't like owing favors to anyone, especially to a woman who could outshoot him. She was also doing a fine job of distracting him from the threat imposed by the Bentons. After stowing the gun in her medical bag, she had dropped to her bottom and bent her knee to put on her boots. Rafe had glimpsed her calf and a bit more.

She must have felt him staring, because she lowered her knee and glared at him. "Not only are you selfish, Mr. LaCroix, you have the manners of a stray dog."

She had a point. She had also picked up on his last name while he didn't know hers. Dr. Sue was fine for Nick, but Rafe refused to use the nickname. It made him feel like a little boy. Determined to remind her that he was a man—and an able one—he decided to turn on the charm.

"You're right," he said, extending his hand. "I've forgotten my manners. My name's Rafe LaCroix. I'm the bounty hunter who turned in Frank Benton. His sons aren't too happy with me, especially since I rode with them for a few months to get the drop on their pa. I owe you for saving my life."

His fingers looked like bare sticks until she grasped them. Using his strength for leverage, she pushed to her feet, faced him and shook his hand like a man. "I'm Dr. Susanna Leaf. I may have saved you from Zeke, but you were protecting Nick and me. I appreciate that."

When she tightened her grip, Rafe squeezed a bit harder. Their eyes locked with an unspoken challenge. If she wanted to arm wrestle, he'd oblige. But not according to her rules. Instead of breaking the handshake with a manly jerk, he eased his hold and brushed his fingers against her palm. The gesture was both suggestive and polite, a trick he used to gauge a woman's sophistication. Dr. Leaf's eyes narrowed, a sign that she understood what he had done and hadn't liked it.

As he lowered his hand to his side, he felt a niggle of worry. He'd heard the Leaf name before. Whenever Lem cozied up with a pint of whiskey, he'd told stories about his days with the Too Tall gang. The tales had gotten wilder over the years, particularly the ones about an outlaw-turned-preacher who still carried a gun. The last thing Rafe needed was an irate father hunting for his little girl.

Dreading her reply, he asked, "Are you any relation to John Leaf?"

"He's my father."

Rafe held in a curse. He'd planned to let her go right away, but the Bentons and Nick's condition made that impossible. "You're not going to make it home today like I planned. Do I need to worry about a search party?"

She shrugged. "Maybe. I usually leave a note on the blackboard outside my office. It'll depend on who comes by and what they see."

Rafe's memory flashed to the mess in the exam room. If a passerby saw the overturned table through the window, the whole town would be looking for her. Nonetheless, going to Midas was riskier than running. Rafe shook his head. "We're not going back."

"Why not?"

"That's my business."

The pity in her eyes stripped him to bare skin. But even worse was the shake of her head. "You should have told me the truth. I would have left a note like always and never told a soul that we'd met."

Like hell, Rafe thought. No one believed him, not ever. "You'd have thought I was lying. I couldn't take that chance."

"You took an even bigger risk when you drew on Zeke Benton."

"That was different." Rafe wasn't afraid of dying. He and the Almighty had parted ways in a New Orleans graveyard. He no longer cared about heaven, hell or anything in between, but he did trust in his own bad luck. It followed him like a rabid dog, snarling at anyone who stood too close. Right now, that short list included Nick and the lady doctor. "We have to get moving."

But Dr. Leaf didn't budge. "I know why you did it."

"No, you don't."

"You were protecting Nick and me. It was good of you."

The respect in her voice made him ache for the oblivion he found with whiskey and whores. Or worse, for the peace of waking up sober in a clean bed. Until Nick came along, Rafe hadn't given a thought to settling down. Nor did he ever look at a woman with more than sex on his mind. But the lady doctor...ah, hell. He needed to get to Mexico where *all* the ladies had brown eyes and long legs. And not a single one had a medical degree.

But first he needed to take care of Nick. "There was a fork in the road a few miles back. Where does it go?"

"To a ranch, but we can't go there."

"Why not?"

"Because the man who owns it has three daughters. I don't want the Bentons anywhere near that place."

Neither did Rafe, but he couldn't think of another solution. "You said yourself that Nick needs a clean bed. I expect you can use the kitchen for a surgery."

"Yes, but—"

"We don't have a choice." An ugly thought crossed Rafe's mind. His guardian angel had connections all over the West. If the rancher had an interest in the railroad, it was possible he'd recognize Rafe. "What's this fellow's name?"

"Timothy Duke."

"How big is his place?"

Her eyes narrowed with disgust. "If you're planning on breaking into the family safe, don't waste your time. He's not a wealthy man."

Once before, Rafe had cracked a safe. It had been in his father's study where a life-size portrait of the man's wife had watched his every move. He'd left that night with a load of cash, a price on his head and no regrets.

"I don't care about his money," he said. "Lester Benton is going to be looking for a hideout, some place that's worth robbing but not too much of a challenge. How impressive is the house?"

Her eyes clouded. "It's bigger than most."

"Then it's settled. Nick needs shelter and the family needs to be warned. Does this man have a wife? I don't want a bunch of gossip."

The lady doctor shook her head. "Bethany died in childbirth. It's been five years, but he still misses her."

Had that cozy tone come from the woman who'd shot Zeke Benton in the head? Rafe couldn't believe his ears. Unless he missed his guess, she had feelings for Timothy Duke. The information could prove useful, so he tucked it away like a new penny. "We'll leave as soon as I pack up."

She looked him straight in the eye. "I have a requirement of my own. I don't want Tim to know how we met. It would be best if he thought I came willingly, which I would have."

The request surprised him. "That suits me just fine, but I don't see why it matters."

"Because he worries."

Rafe teased her with a grin. "Don't trouble yourself, Dr. Leaf. My lips are sealed. I don't need a jealous beau chasing after me."

"He's not my beau."

She'd made her voice insistent, but Rafe could see that she liked the idea. He was tempted to tease her some more, but there wasn't time. "We'll tell him what he needs to know. Nick and I are a couple of drifters who ran into the Bentons. I asked you to see to the boy's wound and you agreed."

"That would have been the truth if you'd been honest," she reminded him.

Rafe looked pointedly at the medical bag. "Do you have any other surprises in there?"

"Only what you'd expect—catgut, bandages and a bottle of chloroform." She arched an eyebrow. "I'd dose you with it and take Nick to town, but he cares about you."

If Timothy Duke was the doctor's weak spot, then Nick was his. "Don't try it, Doc. You might be good with a gun, but I outweigh you by fifty pounds."

"You'd be unconscious before you could blink."

"I doubt it. When I wrestle with a woman, I win… and so does she." He had tried to intimidate her, but she looked more bored than impressed.

"We're both wasting time," she said. "You need to pack your things."

The lady doctor had a talent for being right. Annoyed, Rafe lifted the saddlebag and flung it over his shoulder. "Do what you can for Nick. I'll be ready in five minutes."

Susanna had finished bandaging Nick's leg when Rafe returned to the cave. She knew his last name now, but she couldn't think of him as either Mr. LaCroix or Mr. James. He was a man with worries and they'd become unwitting allies in the battle to save Nick's leg.

When she stepped back, he dropped to a crouch next to the boy who had been drifting in and out of consciousness.

"Are you ready for a ride in a fancy carriage?" For Nick's benefit, he'd made his voice hardy.

"I guess," the boy replied. "But I can't walk."

"You don't need to. Put your arms around my neck and hold tight."

Nick had what Susanna called bird-bones—fragile limbs that seemed better suited to flying than doing chores. At the same time, his eyes were filled with courage born of trust in the man who was a mix of brother, father and friend.

As Rafe pushed to his feet with Nick in his arms, he made a show of grunting. "Good grief, kid. You're heavier than a horse."

As Nick offered a weak smile, Susanna lifted her medical bag and followed them out of the cave. The morning glare made her squint, but not before she noticed Zeke Benton's body lying facedown on a patch of grass.

Rafe's boots chafed in the dirt as he walked past the corpse. "Don't even think about burying him."

In spite of the warning in his voice, Susanna hesitated. Laying the man to rest was a way of putting the "right" back in "right and wrong," but she also knew that the Bentons would be hunting for them.

Rafe called to her from over his shoulder. "He's not worth your prayers, Dr. Leaf. But if you're feeling the need, ask the Almighty to send rain. A gully washer would hide our tracks."

Susanna looked at the sky and saw a slate of tarnished silver. Rain would protect them from the

Bentons, but Nick was in danger of catching a chill. Behind the clouds she could imagine sunshine and blue sky. When she'd been a confused runaway, an old man named Silas had taught her to pray and she did so now—for their safety, Nick's well-being, even for Rafe LaCroix.

As surely as she had rips in her stockings, he had a hole in his soul that oozed bitterness like a wound formed pus. Susanna thought he and Nick had a lot in common. She could help the boy, but the man's needs were beyond the medicines in her bag. Walking behind him, she wondered why he didn't bother to cut his hair. It tagged him as a rebel—a man who'd spit in a person's eye and enjoy it.

But she also detected a lightness in his step as he avoided jostling Nick. The graceful stride emphasized the duster whipping around his calves and reminded her of his eyes as he'd looked at her legs. Heat rushed to her cheeks. For all of his rudeness, Rafe LaCroix was a handsome man with a sharp mind. How many bounty hunters carried a copy of *The Odyssey* in their saddlebags? Not many, she'd guess. The contradictions intrigued her almost as much as the I-dare-you look in his eyes.

Susanna enjoyed a challenge more than most women. Whether she was battling pneumonia or playing checkers, she liked to win. So it seemed did Rafe LaCroix.

She wanted to lag behind so she could observe him, but the surrey was in sight. He'd harnessed his packhorse to her rig and tied Lightning to a saddled pinto that must have belonged to Nick. On the back seat she saw an open bedroll. Rafe had placed Nick on the brocade and was tucking a blanket under the boy's chin.

Susanna set her bag on the floorboard and gripped the sides of the surrey. She was about to pull herself up to the passenger seat when Rafe clasped her shoulder.

"Hold on, Doc. I need a favor."

His tone was gentle and so was his touch, though she doubted he realized it. Turning, she saw a plea in his eyes. "What is it?"

"I'm trusting you to drive the surrey while I ride alone. I want your word that you won't try to run off with Nick."

His hand was still on her shoulder, holding her in place even though she had no desire to run. Considering the past hour, she thought the request was ridiculous. "Aren't we past that point?"

He tightened his grip. There was no malice in his touch, only a faint clinging that matched the anguish in his eyes. "I don't know," he said. "Are we?"

"Yes. At least where Nick is concerned. But you'll have to let go of me to find out."

He released her shoulder and rocked back on one hip while keeping his eyes tight on her face. "If the Bentons catch up with us, I'll hold them off. The packhorse is rested. Let him take the bit and he'll run. Can you handle that?"

"Of course." She had sounded confident, but her stomach churned at the thought of Rafe being alone in a gunfight.

He quirked a grin. "Don't look so worried, Doc. In spite of what you think, I'm pretty good at this sort of thing."

Susanna knew all about male bravado, but Rafe had proved himself by turning in Frank Benton. She also knew that he'd do anything to keep Nick safe. "I'll go straight to the Duke ranch. We'll wait for you there."

"I'd appreciate it."

She turned to the surrey and pulled herself up, belatedly feeling his hand on her elbow. The small courtesy seemed out of place in the empty meadow, yet it had come naturally to him. Looking down, she saw the deep lines shaping his mouth and wondered where he'd learned his manners and why he was determined to forget them.

As she slid across the seat, he strode to the roan,

pulled himself into the saddle and gripped the line securing the two extra horses. The gelding fidgeted with irritation, but Rafe took it in stride, murmuring until the animal gave a snort and stood still. After looping the line around the pommel, he turned the horse with the grace of a natural rider. Like herself, he sat straight with a bend in his knees, as if he'd gotten his training in a riding ring rather than on a ranch—not that she could see him in jodhpurs. His snakeskin boots lazed in the stirrups with too much defiance for that kind of elegance.

With a click of his tongue, he turned the gelding and stopped next to the surrey. They were eye to eye when he caught her staring at him. With a knowing glint, he tipped his hat. "After you, Dr. Leaf."

Susanna didn't know which disturbed her more—his insolent tone or the knowledge that he'd be ogling her as they rode. Since his scrutiny was unavoidable, she lifted the reins and urged the horse down the trail.

The rattle of the surrey blocked out the clop of the gelding's hooves, but it did nothing to ease the sense of Rafe's gaze on her back. She considered telling him to keep his eyes on the trail, but acknowledging her awareness would have been a defeat. Instead she sat still with her braid tickling her neck. As annoyed as she'd been by his teasing, she would have welcomed it now. A rude remark would have given her a reason to put him in his place. Instead his silence felt like a wall at her back, trapping and shielding her at the same time. Given his rude proposition, she didn't like that idea at all.

But she had also seen him be careful with Nick. In spite of his toughness, Rafe LaCroix had a streak of goodness, as if he knew how it felt to be lonely. Did he crave companionship like she sometimes did? Did he look up at the stars and wish for things he didn't have?

Star light, star bright...

She hadn't thought of the rhyme since her twin brothers had been out of diapers, but she had wished on countless stars over the years and still yearned for a few of those childhood dreams. A husband. Children. A house full of chatter.... Her thoughts drifted to Timothy Duke and she sighed. Showing up in his yard with a bounty hunter and a gunshot child wasn't going to help their budding courtship, which wasn't going well anyhow. Last week he had invited her to Sunday supper at his sister's house. Susanna had been charmed by the invitation, but his sister had been quick to criticize her.

Are you sure it's safe, Susanna? A woman shouldn't make calls alone.... It isn't respectable....

Maybe not, but Susanna didn't care a whit about

what people thought. She had a gift and she'd been born to use it. She'd never say it to Tim, but she might have saved Bethany and their newborn son. At the very least a Cesarean section would have given them a fighting chance.

Spurred by her convictions, Susanna sat straighter in the seat. Tim hadn't defended her against his sister, but she could overlook that lapse. Like most men, he didn't understand her vocation. On the other hand, he was hardworking and honorable.

She couldn't say the same for Rafe LaCroix. With his smart mouth and wandering eyes, he was all spark and no substance. Of the two men, she knew whom she preferred.

Chapter Five

In spite of a limp and a blind eye, Garrett Albright had spent the past five years tracking Rafe LaCroix. All along the Santa Fe Railroad, station managers had received posters offering a sizable reward for information concerning his whereabouts. The photograph was old—a graduation portrait taken before that night in St. Louis—but Rafe couldn't change his most distinctive feature. Anyone who saw his pale eyes remembered them.

Garrett did, and the memories weren't good.

Each time he received a wire telling him that a man resembling Rafe had been spotted, he traveled west in his private railcar, gathering information and making notes in a journal. That's how he'd learned of Rafe's friendship with Lemuel Scott and his recent pursuit of Frank Benton.

Until last month, the man Garrett called "the boss" had been satisfied with a knowledge of Rafe's travels, but the news of his connection to the Bentons had driven the old man to midnight vigils on the stone portico overlooking the Mississippi. Garrett knew how it felt to breathe in the night and smell the past. Some scores in life could be forgotten, but others gnawed at a man's heart and had to be settled.

Because of that understanding, he couldn't say no when the boss asked him to bring Rafe to St. Louis. Garrett had read his notes, determined that Rafe was in southern Colorado and left the next day. For three days he had done nothing but indulge in scenery and cigars, but the blast of the whistle signaled the train's approach to Green River and the end of his respite.

A valet knocked on the door. "Mr. Albright?"

"Come in, Roberts."

"We'll be arriving in Green River, Colorado in five minutes. The stationmaster is waiting with the clerk who spotted Mr. LaCroix."

Garrett snuffed out his cigar. "Thank you. I'll make my own way to his office."

After the valet departed, Garrett put on his coat and checked his billfold for the silver certificate he'd offered as a reward. Money was power in the boss's world, and Garrett had plenty of it at his disposal. The paper was worth a hundred dollars—a small fortune to a working man.

As the brakes squealed, the momentum of the train threw Garrett off balance. While bracing against the wall, he reached for his cane. It had been a gift from the boss and Garrett treasured it. The brass handle sported three rubies, but what pleased him most was the sword hidden by the cane's length. With his poor vision, he didn't trust himself with a gun.

After putting on his low-topped derby, he braced for the final lurch. Within seconds, Roberts knocked and opened the door, revealing a baggage handler with a small cart.

"The hotel is expecting you, Mr. Albright," the valet said. "I'll see that your baggage is delivered."

"Thank you."

In addition to hunting for Rafe, Garrett had a business obligation in Green River. The man he hoped to hire as the stationmaster for the new Midas depot would be arriving any day for an interview.

Gripping his cane, he ambled into the depot where he spotted Jason Monroe. The young stationmaster offered his hand but then lowered it when he realized Garrett couldn't return the grip without letting go of the cane.

Unconcerned with the awkwardness, Garrett extended his left hand in greeting. Of all the losses from his injury, not being able to properly shake a man's hand was the most humbling. Instead he deepened his voice. "It's nice to see you, Jason. Is the clerk waiting in your office?"

"Yes, sir. Follow me."

The two men walked down a hallway and into a room where a balding man with spectacles pushed to his feet. After introducing Garrett to Harlan Biggs, Jason excused himself. Garrett sat in a chair in front of the desk, motioned for Mr. Biggs to do the same and withdrew the photograph of Rafe from his coat pocket.

He handed it to Biggs. "Is this the man you saw?"

"Yes, sir. Except he's older and his hair's long."

"Did you get a look at his eyes?"

"Not up close. But I can tell you he's got a boy with him. The kid's ma died awhile ago."

Garrett took back the photograph. "Then he wasn't LaCroix."

"But I'm sure of it, sir. I saw them having breakfast at Madeline's place. She's from New Orleans and makes fancy things for her bakery."

A coincidence? Garrett doubted it. "Go on."

"They were making jokes about crepes. The boy called 'em crey-pees and the man started talking in French. That's why I remember him."

It was also how Garrett knew he'd picked up Rafe's

trail. He opened his billfold and handed the silver certificate to the clerk. "You've convinced me, Biggs."

"Thank you, sir. The missus and I—"

Garrett didn't have time for gratitude. "Did LaCroix mention where he was headed?"

"He said something about going to Mexico. I believe it, too. He rode with the Bentons for a while, at least that's the rumor."

At the mention of the outlaw gang, Garrett held back a frown. If Rafe had been tarred as one of them, he'd be in danger all the way to the border. Until now, Garrett had limited his search to Colorado, but that was no longer wise. It was time to travel south. Aware that his job had become more urgent, he pushed to his feet. "If you think of anything else, I'll be at the Imperial Hotel."

"Yes, sir."

As the clerk left the office, Garrett motioned for the stationmaster to step back inside. "What can I do for you, Mr. Albright?"

Garrett gave the man a large envelope. It held a second photograph of Rafe, a terse description of his appearance and information about the reward. "Take this to the local newspaper. Have him turn it into a poster and see that copies are delivered to every train station between here and Mexico."

"I'll take care of it today."

Garrett thought for a moment. "One more thing. Up the reward to a thousand dollars in gold and add these words, 'Must be found alive.'"

Young Jason's eyes flared wide. "He must be important to you."

"He is, but he's even more important to the boss."

As he followed the surrey into Timothy Duke's yard, Rafe looked around the small ranch. With curtains in the windows and a swing on the front porch, the log house had a homey feel to it. The outbuildings included a good-size barn, a chicken coop and a two-man bunkhouse. Knowing how the Bentons worked, Rafe held in a curse. The Duke place was a prime target for a midnight raid.

Next to the house he saw Timothy Duke chopping wood. The rancher had just raised the ax when he noticed his visitors. The blade came down with a crack and shredded the pine. Glaring at Rafe, he leaned the ax against the stump, took off his gloves and strode across the yard.

Rafe didn't care for the man's expression. They hadn't exchanged a word, but Duke had already sized him up as trail trash. Rafe had been judged before—back in St. Louis and in a Boston prep school where he'd learned to defend himself. When words didn't do the trick, he'd been glad to swing his fists.

As Dr. Leaf halted the surrey, he slid off Punkin and watched as she waved a greeting to Duke. Even in the duster, she looked pretty this morning. Her cheeks had a glow, and the braid brushing between her shoulder blades was loose enough to give a man ideas. If she liked Timothy Duke as much as Rafe guessed, the rancher was a fortunate man. Someday he'd be untangling that hair with his fingers, a picture that annoyed Rafe as much as Duke's scowl. What she saw in the rancher, he didn't know. The man walked like a constipated buffalo.

Rafe tied his horse and went to check Nick, who hadn't made a peep in the past hour. Glancing at the boy, he saw that he'd fallen asleep with the blanket over his head. "How's he doing?" he said to Dr. Leaf.

She leaned over the seat and rested her hand on Nick's forehead. "We need to get started."

Before Rafe could ask if he felt hotter, Duke reached the surrey. He glanced at the blanket in the back seat, then at Susanna. "What's going on?"

Refusing to be intimidated, Rafe stuck out his hand. "Good morning, Mr. Duke. My name's LaCroix. My friend and I had a run-in with the Bentons. He took a bullet in the leg and it's got to come out."

The rancher shook Rafe's hand but his grip was lackluster. "When did it happen?" he asked.

"Five days ago, but they're still in this area," Rafe explained.

Duke frowned. "Does the sheriff know?"

"Not yet," Susanna answered. "That's the second reason we're here—to warn you. Maybe Chester can go to town and spread the word."

Rafe figured Chester lived in the bunkhouse. He didn't want a lawman visiting the Duke ranch, but he couldn't argue without looking suspicious.

"He should be back this afternoon." Duke looked down at the blanket just as Nick swatted it away from his face. The rancher whipped his eyes back to Rafe. "He's just a kid."

"And he's hurt," Susanna interrupted. "I'd like to use your kitchen for a surgery."

"That's fine." Duke had answered Dr. Leaf, but his focus stayed on Rafe. "You say your name's LaCroix?"

"That's right."

Rafe didn't like being eyeballed, especially by a man with kingly airs. With his barrel chest, scrawny beard and cropped hair, Timothy Duke bore a striking resemblance to Henry VIII. Rafe had seen the famous picture in a history book and had loathed the man on sight. He felt that way about all kings.

If Nick hadn't been burning with fever, he would have told Duke where to stuff his crown. Instead he blanked his face.

The rancher hooked his thumbs in his belt and tried to look intelligent as he quizzed Rafe. "I'm wondering why you didn't take the boy to town and notify the sheriff yourself."

Dr. Leaf interrupted. "Nick can't ride. Mr. LaCroix fetched me last night and I suggested we come here. We're wasting time."

She had one foot out of the surrey when Duke cut in front of Rafe to offer his hand. "Go on inside. I want a word with Mr. LaCroix."

Susanna gave him a look of disgust. "Can't it wait?"

"No, but it won't take long. He can bring the boy in a minute."

If the rancher was going to ask questions, Rafe preferred to answer them in private. He handed Dr. Leaf her medical bag, waited until she was out of earshot and struck a casual pose. "What's on your mind?"

The rancher lowered his chin. "I don't know who you are, mister. But I don't like those guns lashed to your saddle or the blood on your coat."

Rafe's jaw tightened. "It's Nick's."

"Nonetheless, Dr. Leaf and the boy are welcome

to stay in the house, but you'll have to bed down in the barn."

Most men would have offered him a cot in the bunkhouse, but the rancher was making a point. Judging by the snorts coming from the outbuilding, Rafe would be sleeping with a family of pigs. He gave Duke his best impression of a Boston Brahmin. "Thank you, sir. I appreciate your *fine* hospitality."

Duke heard the sarcasm and glared. "Like I said, the boy and Miss Leaf are welcome in the house."

The way he'd said Miss Leaf made Rafe wonder how cozy they really were. He could understand not using her first name, but she liked being called *Doctor* and had earned the title. Rafe barely knew her, but he understood that respect mattered to her. He also knew that she'd killed a man this morning and would need a friend tonight. Would Duke understand? Rafe doubted it.

Irritated by everything, he lifted Nick from the surrey and followed Dr. Leaf's path to the back of the cabin. She had left the door ajar, so he nudged it with his knee and stepped inside. Judging by the steamy air and the vegetables on the counter, the oldest Duke girl had been fixing a stew when Dr. Leaf had recruited her to scrub the kitchen table.

The lady doctor had taken off her coat and was

jabbing pins in the braid she'd looped around her head. "Can you hold him until the table's ready?"

"Sure."

Satisfied that her hair wouldn't fall, she opened her medical bag and removed the bone saw, a knife and an assortment of devices Rafe didn't recognize. She was putting the instruments in the boiling water when Duke walked into the kitchen.

"I've asked Emily to help," she said. "Do you mind?"

"That's fine."

"I also need Mr. LaCroix. Would you see to his horses, please."

King Henry didn't look pleased, but he mumbled "sure" and left the room. Dr. Leaf took a last swipe at the table and faced Rafe. "You can set him down now."

For the next few minutes, she gave orders and he followed them. He took off his coat, rolled up his sleeves and washed his hands with carbolic like she did. As she arranged her instruments on a towel, he took his place at Nick's feet.

"Rafe?" The boy sounded terrified.

"I'm here, kid. So's Dr. Sue."

"Hello, Nick." She aligned her face with the boy's and looked into his eyes. "I'm going to put a piece of cotton on your nose so you'll go to sleep. I want you to breathe deep, okay?"

After he nodded, she laid the cloth across his cheeks. Confident he was out, she snipped off the bandage, positioned the leg and looked at Rafe. "Your job is to hold him steady. Position your hands like this."

After she demonstrated the grip, Rafe put his hands in place. Satisfied, she selected a scalpel and began to cut. Blood and pus erupted from the incision and filled Rafe's nose with a foul odor.

He'd smelled infection once before. His mother had died in a room as hot and damp as this one. Only instead of a kitchen, she had been in her bed in their New Orleans apartment. A hurricane had been raging through the city, rattling windows and threatening to tear off the roof. At the time, he hadn't understood why she'd sent him out in the storm to fetch a midwife. Now he realized she'd been with child, and something had gone terribly wrong. She'd bled out that day, and he'd vowed to never forget the man who'd been to blame.

His father...the king of St. Louis...a wealthy man with a real wife and a legitimate son.

Nick gave a soft moan, bringing Rafe back to the sight of Dr. Leaf probing the wound with a metal rod. She glanced at Nick's face and then spoke to Emily.

"More chloroform, please."

The girl upturned the bottle on the rag and applied it to Nick's nose. When he settled down, Dr. Leaf blotted the blood with a piece of cotton and went back to probing. Rafe's stomach twisted with worry. If she found the bullet fragment and the bone wasn't shattered, Nick had a chance. He couldn't bear to think about the other possibilities.

"Can you see anything?" he asked.

"No, but I work by sound," she explained. "The probe has a porcelain tip that makes a different tone when I tap lead instead of bone."

She could have been telling him how to bake bread—she was that calm. As she removed the probe from the wound and lifted the scalpel, Rafe fought the urge to look away. He'd caused this misery and felt compelled to share it, so he watched as she widened the incision. A sliver of white caught Rafe's eye. "Do you know yet if the bone's broken?"

"It's a simple fracture," she answered. "It'll mend."

"That's good, isn't it?"

"Yes, but the infection has to be stopped. If I can't find the cause, it would be best to—"

"Don't say it," he snapped. "Don't even *think* about cutting off his leg!"

Ignoring him, Dr. Leaf lifted the probe and went back to work.

Rafe felt like a fool. While she was trying to save

Nick's life, he was pitching a fit. "I'm sorry, Doc. I've got no business talking to you like that."

"I know it's hard," she said. "I'm doing my best."

He didn't doubt her for a minute. Perspiration had beaded on her forehead and her eyes were creased with worry. If anyone was more troubled than he was, it was the lady doctor. He couldn't imagine her using the bone saw, but he knew that she'd do it—just as she'd shot Zeke Benton. He owed this woman far more than a few dollars for her time.

At the soft intake of her breath, Rafe looked up from the wound. "What is it?"

She ignored him again. "Emily, hand me the forceps."

The girl passed the instrument to Dr. Leaf, who slid her fingers into the handles and proceeded to remove a piece of lead the size of a dried pea. She dropped it onto a tin plate with a plink.

Rafe stared at the metal with disbelief. How could something so small cause so much harm? But that's how poison worked. He looked up at the lady doctor. "Does this mean you can save the leg?"

"I'm going to try, but I won't lie, Mr. LaCroix. Nick would have a better chance at the clinic."

"What do you need?" Rafe asked. "I'll go get it."

"Echinacea for a tea and chickweed for a poultice."

Emily spoke up for the first time. "I have an herb garden. Would dandelion work?"

Dr. Leaf pinched the flaps of Nick's skin to close the wound. "That would be a good start. Chester can bring what we need tomorrow."

Rafe didn't want to take that chance. He also saw an opportunity to keep the sheriff away from the Duke ranch. "I'll go tonight."

"I'd rather you stayed." Her voice had been soft, but he saw a hard light in her eyes. "If Nick gets worse, I'll have to take off the leg."

Rafe felt sick as she lifted a needle and thread. He wanted to believe that Nick would recover, but the last time he'd hoped for anything had been in New Orleans and his mother had died. He'd been a cynic ever since.

Emily interrupted his thoughts. "He's so young. The herbs *have* to work."

"I hope so, too." Dr. Leaf pulled a stitch. "Where's the dandelion? Can you start that tea?"

"Sure."

Emily left to get fresh water, leaving Rafe holding Nick's ankle as Dr. Leaf finished closing the wound. The black thread looked out of place on Nick's skin, but her stitches were as delicate as embroidery. Rafe had seen plenty of fancy stitching—mostly on corsets—but he'd never seen work done with such care.

She took the final stitch and snipped the thread close to the skin. After setting down the scissors, she rested one hand on Nick's knee while Rafe continued to steady his ankle. She didn't speak or bow her head. She didn't do anything except close her eyes, yet somehow Rafe knew she was praying.

Just as the sight of her legs had shot an arrow of desire to his groin, the love in her expression traveled straight to his heart. He knew it was for Nick, but that didn't change the pressure building in his chest as he looked at her upturned lips. She had a talent and he had to admire it. She was also full of hope and he wanted to share it. He wasn't optimistic by nature. His attitude was bad and his luck was worse. But somehow he felt her goodwill seeping into him.

It was almost better than whiskey and a whore. Somehow he'd pay her back for what she'd done today. He didn't have much to offer—just money and his guns—but somehow he'd find a way to thank her.

Chapter Six

Susanna put down the towel she'd been using to dry her hands and glanced around the kitchen. Her instruments were clean and stowed in her bag, and the chairs had been put back around the table. Rafe had gone outside, and Emily was sitting with Nick, who had been given her bedroom. The girl would be sleeping with her sisters tonight, while Susanna napped on a pallet at Nick's bedside. For the second night in a row, she'd be short on sleep.

"May I have a word with you?"

She turned and saw Tim filling the door frame with his wide shoulders. Dressed in a flannel shirt and dungarees, he looked as solid as a mountain. "Of course," she said with a smile. "This must have been quite a surprise for you."

"Yes, it was." He walked across the kitchen, lifted a shawl off a hook and handed it to her. "Let's take a walk."

She would have preferred her own coat, but she was too worn-out for even a small disagreement. After draping the wool over her shoulders, she followed Tim out the door. Side by side, they walked down a path that meandered through a stand of pines and emerged at the edge of a stream.

Susanna's heart beat faster when she saw the pretty spot. Swollen with rain, the stream rushed over the rocks and under the willow branches hanging from the bank. With the sun low in the sky, ponderosas cast fingerlike shadows that turned the daylight into a dusky-blue that was her favorite color. Close enough to touch, scrub oaks lined the meadow, giving the spot an air of privacy. Had Tim picked it on purpose? She wanted to think so. After the past twenty-four hours, she would have welcomed a strong shoulder to cry on. At the very least, she needed a friend.

As they neared the water's edge, she smiled at him. "It's a pretty day."

"Not in my book."

Disappointment dropped in her belly like a stone. To hide her reaction, she crouched at the edge of the stream, dipped her hand in the water and wiped her face. She heard Tim's boots trampling the grass, then his shadow fell across her shoulders and stretched to the opposite bank.

"I know it's none of my business, Susanna. But I've *got* to speak up."

She dried her face with her sleeve and pushed to her feet. "You're angry that I brought Nick here."

"No, that's not it. I like kids. What I don't understand is how you could have left your house with that LaCroix character."

She could have defended herself with the truth, but what was the point? She would have left with Rafe if he'd asked. "I did what was right."

"You took a chance for someone who's not worth it."

Susanna saw three shades of red. Who was Tim to stand in judgment of Nick and Rafe? And what right did he have to question her judgment? She had a call on her life. It had been honed by science and education, but the profession of healing ran in her blood. Knowing that anger would hurt her cause, she kept her voice level. "That's not how I practice medicine."

"Maybe it should be," he insisted. "You take too many chances and today proves it. What if—"

Susanna clutched the ends of the shawl. "What if Emily had a fever and no one would come? What if Maggie had the croup and couldn't breathe?"

He didn't reply.

Fed up with his attitude, she let her voice rise. "If

I hadn't left Midas when I did, Nick might have lost his leg today."

Tim shook his head. "That doesn't change the facts. You could have been hurt...or worse."

Susanna feared the threat of assault as much as any woman, but she refused to let dread rule her life. Wanting to end the discussion, she made her voice firm. "I appreciate your concern, but I can protect myself."

I did it this morning...I killed a man....

The scent of gunpowder filled her nose. She blinked and saw Zeke Benton's corpse. Right or wrong, death was an ugly business. She needed to talk about the shooting, but Tim wouldn't understand. She'd have to wait until her parents returned from back East. Her father would sit her down on the porch, give her a shot of whiskey and tell her a story of his own. She'd listen and they'd talk—all night long if that's what she wanted.

Susanna felt tears pushing behind her eyes. After all she'd been through with the Bentons and Nick, she really needed that drink. Instead she swallowed back her upset. It caught in her throat and made her stomach hurt.

Tim had crossed his arms over his chest and was glowering at her. "Everyone knows you carry a gun. You don't have to remind me."

Why did it matter? If she'd been a man, her skill would have been admired. Even closer to tears, she touched the water with the toe of her boot. "I'd like to change the subject."

She'd spoken softly, but her voice still trembled. Tim must have heard it because he came up next to her. "I'm sorry, Susanna. I don't mean to be irritable. It's just that I'm worried sick about the Bentons. Chester's not back, and I've got the girls and you to think about."

Did being included with his daughters make her more than a friend? She didn't know, but his voice had softened, revealing the man who was pleasant at church and quick to help his neighbors. Reminding herself that he had good intentions, she tried to reassure him. "I'm worried, too. Let's hope they went south."

"I'd like to see LaCroix disappear with them," Tim said. "How long is he going to be hanging around?"

"It depends on if I have to amputate. Nick's not out of the woods."

"Good Lord."

"I know," she said. "It's awful. He'd heal quickly after the surgery, but I'm hoping it won't be necessary."

Tim stared up at the pines and then looked into her eyes. "I feel bad for the kid. For his sake, I'll put up with LaCroix but I don't like it. The man's a bad seed."

"How do you know?"

"It's written all over him—the guns, the blood on his coat. He even talks funny."

Susanna had heard the changes in Rafe's accent, too. The nuances intrigued her. So did his way with Nick. As the chloroform had worn off, Rafe had been the one to comfort the boy. When Nick had vomited, Rafe had cleaned up the floor and his fancy boots without a word of complaint. He'd even put Nick at ease by telling him he'd puked a few times himself for less noble reasons.

Susanna had glanced at Rafe and they had shared a smile. The memory filled her chest with a glow and a yearning she didn't understand. Putting aside the lump in her throat, she looked at Tim. "I don't know anything about Mr. LaCroix, but he cares about Nick. That counts for something."

Tim frowned at her. "If he cares about the kid, why isn't he in school?"

"I don't know," she answered. "Does it matter? Besides, Rafe's teaching him to read. Nick told me."

"What else has he told you?"

"Nothing."

While twisting the ends of the shawl, Susanna stared downstream where the water curved out of sight. Why was she defending Rafe? And why had she called him by his given name instead of Mr. LaCroix? She hadn't lied to Tim, but neither had she told him the truth. She felt dishonest, as if the bounty hunter had corrupted her.

Tim stepped to her side. "I don't mean to be so harsh."

"I don't, either," she answered. "It's been a hard day."

He gave her a crooked smile, the same one she'd seen in church when he invited her to his sister's house. She didn't feel a thing—not a flutter in her belly or a tightening in her chest—but she saw a good man. He was respected by his friends, thrifty when necessary and generous when it counted. They both loved children and Midas was their home. Sparks aside, she liked him.

And most of all, she was sick and tired of feeling alone. With nothing to lose, Susanna decided to take a chance. The Santa Fe Railroad had chosen Midas for its western headquarters and had built a new depot and a fancy hotel. The entire town had been invited to a grand opening that would include a ten-piece orchestra, shipped-in flowers and platters of food. She wanted to go and she wanted to dance. All she needed was a partner.

She couldn't ask Tim directly, but she could drop a hint. Keeping her voice casual, she said, "Emily tells me you're all going to the dance at the new hotel."

Tim shrugged. "I could do without the fuss, but my sister shamed me into it."

"You might have fun," Susanna insisted.

Ask me to go with you....

When Tim replied by scratching his neck, Susanna held in a sigh. She'd have to be as dumb as a post to say another word. Besides, what did it matter? She often went to social functions alone. Her profession made her unique among women and she enjoyed that freedom.

But just once, she yearned to go to a dance filled with anticipation. She wanted to wear her blue satin ball gown, sway to a waltz and melt into the moonlight as a man kissed her good-night. She also wanted to see elephants in Africa. Of the two events, the latter seemed more likely.

"It's getting dark," Tim said. "We should go inside."

Susanna hugged herself against the chill. "You go ahead. I need a minute."

"All right, but be careful. That drifter could be hanging around."

Susanna stifled a laugh. Tim didn't know half the story, and she had to keep it that way. "Rafe's harmless," she said. "Now go say good-night to your girls."

* * *

Harmless?

Rafe had a good mind to push his way through the bushes and show her just how harmless he was. No man wanted to be called harmless, but even as his jaw tensed, he knew he was being stupid. The lady doctor had kept the roughness of their first meeting to herself, and even more, she'd called him Rafe.

Overhearing their conversation had been unexpected. Earlier, he'd wandered to the stream in search of a place to clean up. He'd just finished shaving and had put on a clean shirt when he heard them approaching. A gentleman would have slipped away unnoticed, but Rafe had never benefited from being polite. He had needed to know what Dr. Leaf would say to Duke, so he'd stayed behind the hedge.

Now he couldn't leave without revealing his eavesdropping. He also wanted to down the whiskey in his pewter flask. Then there was the matter of why Dr. Leaf was lingering by the stream. Maybe she wanted to wash up. He could imagine her opening her dress and rinsing her throat. Maybe she'd wade into the water in nothing but her chemise… or maybe nothing at all. Harmless old Rafe wasn't above sneaking a peek.

He also knew how good it felt to get clean and had bathed in the stream himself. Without the whiskers and the dirt, he looked respectable, except for the hair that he wore long on purpose. It was a tool of his trade. With a few swipes of his knife, he could change from "that man with the ponytail" into a faceless drifter.

But he'd never change on the inside. He was itching for a look at the lady doctor and wanted Duke to leave.

"All right," the rancher said. "But be careful."

Silence.

"Susanna? Are you all right?"

Curiosity was eating Rafe alive, but he couldn't see through the branches. Was she nodding? Had Duke wised up and pulled her into his arms? Any fool could see that she'd been through hell today. Men forgot their misery by getting drunk. So did some of the women he knew, but kissing was even better.

Dr. Leaf took a deep breath. "I'm fine. Now go on home."

"Only if you're sure."

"I am."

The thud of the rancher's boots made Rafe mad enough to spit. How could he leave her alone? She had tried to hide it, but her voice had a quaver in it. As for that fancy dance, Duke had to be stone deaf to miss the hint she'd dropped.

Spying on Dr. Leaf no longer appealed to Rafe, but neither did it seem right to make his presence known. She'd be angry that he'd eavesdropped and embarrassed by what he'd heard. It seemed both smart and kind to stay put until she left.

But then he heard a whimper…a sniff…and finally a sob.

Rafe knew that her tears weren't born of weakness. Men got mad and broke things. Women cried and watered the soul. Seeds of hope would grow inside her and reach for the sun. Nonetheless, he wanted to throttle Timothy Duke. If the rancher had possessed a lick of charm, he would have pulled the lady into his arms and kissed the daylights out of her. He'd have chased away the darkness with a touch of fire, but instead the fool had left her to cry alone.

Rafe thought about pushing through the hedge himself, but he doubted she'd appreciate his company. Instead he wished her well from afar. He even closed his eyes for her, a silent hope for good things. But then she heaved a sigh.

"I am *such* a fool," she said to the trees.

Like hell, he thought. She was human and needed a friend. Or at least someone to yell at. Anger cured sadness almost as well as whiskey, and Rafe could offer both.

"Hey, Doc," he called. "Want a drink? You sound like you need one."

A startled gasp reached his ears.

"I don't know what you see in that fool," he added. "He looks like a buffalo."

Rafe had just pulled the flask from his pocket when the branches parted and Dr. Leaf emerged on his side of the hedge. Teary or not, the woman was hopping mad.

"How dare you eavesdrop on me!"

"It's a good thing I did. Someone needs to set you straight on men like Duke." It dawned on Rafe that he'd found a way to pay her back for helping Nick. He considered pushing to his feet but changed his mind. Height gave a man an advantage, but he'd already one-upped her.

He uncorked the flask and held it out to her. "Drink up."

She shook her head. "No, thank you."

"Are you sure?" Rafe took a swallow and made a show of enjoying it. It wasn't often that he got to be an expert, and he decided to play it to the hilt. After wiping his mouth, he said, "Forget about Duke. He's not right for you."

She glared at him. "You should have made your presence known."

"I'm glad I didn't. You'd still be mooning over an idiot."

"I'm not *mooning* over anyone."

She was telling the truth. Her tears had sprung from a deeper place—the part of her that worried about Nick and was sickened by men like Zeke Benton. Later he'd ask her about Zeke, but he wasn't done talking about the buffalo. "Maybe I should have a talk with old Tim. Dancing's not that bad once a man figures it out."

"Don't you dare—"

"It's kind of nice. You get to hold a woman close and feel how she moves. I like it."

Dr. Leaf looked ready to eat him alive. "I don't want to hear about you and dancing."

"Then why are you still here?"

Before he could annoy her more, she pivoted toward the stream, giving him a view of her shoulders sagging beneath the shawl. Earlier she'd pinned up her braid. Now that halo was drooping and begging to be undone. If she'd been like his usual women, he'd have whispered sweet things and led her upstairs. He'd have kissed her until she didn't care about anything but the moment. Instead he took another sip of whiskey and felt lonely for them both.

As the whiskey sloshed to his belly, she turned

around and gave him a rueful smile. "I made a fool of myself, didn't I?"

"No, Duke did." Rafe puffed out his chest and mimicked the rancher's baritone. *"I could do without the fuss."*

Dr. Leaf sealed her lips, but her eyes shimmered with laughter. The look told Rafe everything he needed to know about her feelings for Timothy Duke. She liked him, but she wasn't in love. Rafe knew from experience that people got cozy for all sorts of reasons, and he suspected he knew the cause of Dr. Leaf's need. She'd been through hell today and needed comfort.

There weren't many things Rafe could do for her, but offering a strong shoulder was one of them. He slid to the side of the rock. "Sit down, Doc. We need to talk."

She shook her head. "This is none of your business."

"It's not about Duke."

"Then what?"

"It's about Zeke Benton."

Her eyes filled with relief and her mouth softened into a faint smile. "I lied," she said. "I could really use that drink."

Rafe patted the spot next to him. "There's room for two."

She walked toward him with her arms crossed over her middle and the shawl fluttering behind her. After she sat down, he handed her the flask. "Drink up."

"Thank you."

As she gripped the pewter, their fingers brushed and she looked up. After smiling her thanks, she raised the whiskey to her lips and took three slow gulps. No sputtering for this woman—she'd tasted fire before. She lowered the flask, dabbed at her lips with her trigger finger and got ready to shoot Zeke Benton all over again. This time she'd be killing the memory instead of the man.

Rafe took a swallow of his own and then dangled the bottle between his knees. Out of habit, he traced the roses engraved on the side. He'd done the work himself, mostly by firelight while he and Lem traded stories. Rafe had a story, too. That's how he knew that dusk was a hard time of day.

He turned to Dr. Leaf and made his voice strong. "Don't feel bad, Doc. Zeke had it coming."

"I know. The Bentons did terrible things out at the Greene ranch. They stole the family blind, and Zeke raped the daughter."

"Jeez."

"Melissa's seventeen and so shy that I don't think

she'd ever been kissed. When her father brought her to see me, she could hardly talk."

Rafe squeezed the flask, wishing it was Zeke's throat. "You did the girl a favor."

"But I hated it."

"I know." He took another swallow, then wiped the bottle with his shirttail and held it out for her. "Want some more?"

She shook her head. "I have to be clearheaded for Nick."

"Just one?"

She laughed softly and took the flask. "You're a bad influence."

"Not tonight," he said. "You need a friend and I'm all you've got."

After she took a last sip, Rafe corked the bottle and slid it into his back pocket. He wasn't anywhere near forgetful, but he wanted to be her friend more than he wanted to get drunk. Trusting his gut, he lifted her hand from her lap and warmed her fingers with his. "When you think about this day, there's just one thing to remember. Zeke Benton deserved to die."

Her fingers curled against his palm. "I know it was self-defense, but—"

"There *are* no buts." Rafe lifted her hand as if

he were weighing gold. "You saved at least three lives—yours, mine and Nick's."

"Maybe so, but I'd rather cure sore throats."

Rafe almost wished he had one so she'd put her hand on his forehead to check for fever. She'd have found the heat and lots of it. Just looking at her made him eager, but touching her hand made him feel something deeper, a desire to make her smile and carry some of her burdens. Still holding her hand, he stared at the trees. "I bet you've cured a lot of sore throats."

"A few, but the best is delivering a baby. That's a joy."

A chill ripped through Rafe. "Not when it's too soon."

"That's true," she answered. "Sometimes things go badly. You sound like you've had experience."

He wasn't about to go down that road by remembering Mimi, so he thought about a night in a Leadville whorehouse. He'd been with a redhead named Jennie when the screaming started. For all his casual ways, Rafe was careful to keep from putting some poor woman in that position. "I heard it once," he said to Dr. Leaf. "The girl screamed herself hoarse."

Dr. Leaf nodded. "It's an ordeal, but it's also a happy time."

"Do you always see the bright side?"

"Mostly."

He gave a soft chuckle. "You're amazing, Doc. Most people run from trouble, but you run to it. I can't decide if you're stupid or crazy."

She flashed a smile. "I prefer crazy, but hopeful is more like it."

What she called hope, Rafe called naiveté. "Wishing for something won't make it true."

"No, but it's a start."

He suspected she was thinking about Duke. In Rafe's opinion, the two weren't suited at all. She had a fire in her belly and the rancher was a mule. Rafe could see the lack as plain as day, but Dr. Leaf was blind to it. Or maybe not.... Maybe she'd grown weary of sleeping alone and had decided to fill the emptiness as best she could.

Rafe did it all the time. He filled the hours with whiskey and women, by engraving roses on his guns and with books. The lady doctor filled her life with her work. He admired her for it, but what did she do on a lonely night when there weren't any sore throats to cure? Rafe knew what *he* did...what most men did.

He watched as she knotted her fingers in the shawl and pressed her fist between her breasts. The far-away look on her face made him worry, so he decided to set her straight about dreams. "You know that old rhyme, 'Star light, star bright'?" he asked.

"'Wish I may. Wish I might.'"

"Don't believe it."

He'd lightened his voice, but she looked so sad that he ached along with her. The moment called for a joke, a whisper, even a touch. He could feel her skirt touching his boot and her shawl tickling his elbow. He smelled vinegar, too. Just a trace from her hair, but it was enough to make him think about undoing her braid.

"I should check on Nick," she said.

As she pushed to her feet, her shawl brushed his cheek and reminded him that she'd been crying. Good manners pulled him to his feet, but something else made him trace the dried tears with his knuckles. Knowing what she needed, he made his voice low. "I meant what I said about Duke being a fool."

"That's kind of you."

"No. It's the truth."

Rafe took pleasure where he could find it, and right now he saw that possibility in Dr. Leaf's brown eyes. A better man would have waited for a flicker of invitation, but he wasn't anywhere close to being good. Instead he cupped her face in his hands and brought his mouth down to hers.

He tasted whiskey on her lips and made the kiss

tender, warming her with his hands and mouth. He reminded himself that she'd been crying and needed a friend, but her lips had become as hot as his. She planted her hands on his chest as if she were about to shove him away, but then she curled her fingers against his shirt. Her caress tickled and teased, as if she wanted more but knew it was foolish.

One touch of their tongues…if she pulled back, he'd let her go. Hungry for more, he teased her lips with his, telling her with a tender glide what he wanted to do. Instead of pushing him away, she slid her arms around his neck and angled her head to take advantage of the slant of his mouth. She'd been kissed before, he was sure of that. But it hadn't been with the questions she was asking herself now. How long? How much? How far?

Rafe was glad to supply the answers. As long as she wanted. As much as she needed. As far as she wanted to go. With their tongues tangling and lips wet with whiskey and each other, he wrapped her in his arms and pulled her hips against his.

The doctor would know what to expect from an aroused man, but did the woman? He got his answer when she caught her breath and froze. Definitely a virgin, he decided. But then she exhaled with a slow glide that tickled his face, and he wondered if she still wanted to be one. He understood that impulse for what it was. Killing Benton had made her hungry for a taste of something good. Death made men and women alike aware of the shortness of their days and the glory of life's pleasures.

Rafe felt it, too. The only cure was to make the fire burn hotter and he knew how to do it. With a firm touch, he trailed his hand over her ribs and up the soft side of her breast until his thumb grazed the sensitive tip.

She gasped and pulled back, giving him a view of the flames in her cheeks and her smoky-brown eyes. She wasn't cold anymore.

Neither was he and it scared him. The fire in his belly was more than a spark from two sticks rubbing together. Just for a moment, he'd wanted to steal her heart instead of a few minutes of pleasure. She made him feel whole, as if he were strong and wise and had something to share with her.

Damn him for a fool, what was he thinking? Kissing wasn't special. It was the shot that started a goddamned horse race. A man climbed on, rode hard and got off. Rafe liked women who knew the rules—whores who were grateful for the money and a man who bathed now and then. He had no interest in virgins and especially not the lady doctor.

So why was he staring into her eyes and feeling so damned confused? Being an experienced rider of women, he knew what he had to do. It was time to grab the reins. Deliberately leering, he perused her breasts, lingering on the visible effects of his kiss. "I see you liked that, quite a bit as a matter of fact."

Her mouth gaped with shock. She'd probably been expecting sweet talk, but Rafe wasn't done looking. Slow eyed and lazy, he slid his gaze to her hips, the tips of her shoes, then back to the pulse in her throat, and to her face where he saw astonishment, revulsion and, most terrifying of all, compassion.

He didn't want her kindness. It made him feel like Nick, a hungry kid who'd been caught stealing. But Rafe wasn't a boy filching cookies from a jar. He teased her with a slow grin. "You're a real prize, Dr. Leaf. In fact, I'll up my offer for your surrey."

"Don't—"

"A thousand dollars, but I want a whole night with you, naked in a real bed." Why the hell didn't she leave? Rafe tried a smirk. "It'll be your first time, won't it?"

He expected her to curse at him or slap his face. He had it coming and he wanted the punishment, because his intention to make her feel better had disappeared in a blaze of selfishness. But instead she still held his gaze, saying nothing as the shadows under her eyes deepened to the color of a bruise.

Rafe ground his teeth together. He would *not*

apologize. He had no regrets, no shame. Dr. Leaf should have left when she had a chance. She should have followed Duke to the cabin and wished on the stars until her dreams came true. For all of his pomposity, Duke was hardworking and decent. He was a family man, something Rafe would never be.

In need of more whiskey, he walked away with a small consolation. Unless she was crazy, she'd never call him harmless again.

Chapter Seven

A horse whinnied in the yard, awakening Susanna from the nap she'd been taking on the pallet by Nick's bed. Blinking, she saw that dawn had arrived. After last night's battle with the boy's fever, she welcomed the light. She could hear Nick breathing but found little comfort in the shallow rasps. Surrendering to a yawn, she sat up and touched his forehead. He was still burning up.

Yesterday she had believed that dandelion tea was the best treatment. Now she wished she had told Rafe to fetch the echinacea from her clinic. She had learned about the herbal at Johns Hopkins and some doctors considered it revolutionary. Besides, if Rafe had gone to town, she wouldn't have made a fool of herself yesterday. She could count on Tim to forget her hints about the dance, but Rafe LaCroix was sure to tease her about yesterday's kiss.

She still didn't know what to think. She'd been

glad for his whiskey and insight. He was intelligent and even wise. And that kiss… Desire shivered through her all over again. She'd let the spark between them burn out of control, at least until he'd made that crack about her first time. He'd been dead set on offending her and had almost succeeded, but he'd overestimated her shyness. Sex was part of life, and she wasn't at all embarrassed by it.

Even so, she'd been avoiding him. Twice last night he'd come in from the barn to see Nick, and each time she had stepped into the kitchen. After he'd left, she had gone back to Nick's room, where he'd left behind the smell of whiskey and questions she'd be foolish to ask. Why was he running? Where was he from? And why had a simple kiss made him so mean?

Susanna was checking Nick's pulse when she heard someone race into the cabin. Emily appeared in the doorway to Nick's room looking panicked. "It's Chester," she said. "He just rode in and he's hurt."

Susanna reached for her bag. "What happened?"

"I don't know. I was gathering eggs when I saw him fall off his horse."

"Go find your pa."

As Emily went to get Tim, Susanna hurried into the yard where she saw Chester's pinto standing at the water trough. A few feet way, she spotted the ranch hand lying on his back in the dirt, struggling to talk to Rafe who had dropped to one knee.

"What the hell!" Tim barreled past her with traces of shaving soap lining his beard. He reached Chester before she did and was unbuttoning his coat. "Dear God, man. What happened?"

"I dunno," Chester rasped. "Someone took a shot at me."

"Who?" Tim demanded.

"I didn't see 'em. Figured they were after the cattle."

Susanna looked at Rafe who shook his head. "It had to be the Bentons."

Tim looked over his shoulder. "Damn you, LaCroix! That bullet was meant for you!"

Rafe turned his head, but not before Susanna saw shame tighten his jaw.

Tim turned back to Chester. "Did they follow you?"

"Not a chance." Pride rang in the hired hand's feeble voice. "I went south and doubled back. I lost 'em, boss. For you and the girls."

Relief weakened Susanna's knees, but she didn't feel safe for more than a breath. The Bentons seemed to be headed away from the ranch, but they could always double back. Right now, Chester needed her help. Dropping to her knees, she asked, "Where are you shot?"

"In the back."

He was pale and gasping for breath—signs that the bullet had collapsed his lung. "When did it happen?"

"Last night."

He'd been in the saddle for hours. With every breath, more blood would have filled the lung cavity and put pressure on the heart. Pure courage—and love for the Duke family—had carried him home to warn them about the Bentons. Barring a miracle, he wouldn't survive. She touched his shoulder. "We need to get you inside."

"There's no need." A rasping cough brought up blood. "It's just like your pa said. I'm not afraid."

Susanna thought of her father's many sermons about heaven. The Reverend John Leaf had a way with words. As for herself, she had seen death arrive before. Some of her patients saw loved ones and cried out with joy. Others left this earth with closed eyes and the gentle slowing of their respiration. Chester was minutes away from that divide.

He looked at Tim. "You're a good man, boss. Take care of the girls."

"Don't talk," said the rancher. "Save your strength."

But Chester's eyelids had already drifted shut. Susanna gripped his hand and held it until he let out a breath and didn't take another. Bowing her head, she prayed that he'd feel the peace of knowing his

Lord, and that his family would be waiting for him with open arms—the wife he'd outlived by a decade, the parents he'd left in Tennessee, even the old dog he'd befriended when he'd arrived in Midas.

Silence hovered like incense until the sudden intake of Tim's breath broke the spell. "God damn it!" The rancher pushed to his feet and glared at Rafe. "This is all your fault!"

Susanna stood at the same time as Rafe, deliberately putting herself between the two men. She grasped the rancher's arm. "Tim, don't. This isn't the time."

He jerked away from her. "Then when the hell is? My family's in danger. So help me God, LaCroix, I'll—" Sidestepping her, Tim charged at Rafe and shoved him against the barn.

Instead of taking a swing, Rafe sneered. "You're going after the wrong man, Duke. We came here to warn you."

"That's right," Susanna added. "Nick needed help, but you needed to know they were in the area. Even if we hadn't shown up, Chester would have been hurt."

He stared hard at Rafe. "Why are they here in the first place?"

Susanna intervened. "Only the Bentons know the answer to that."

When Tim stayed silent, she turned her attention to Rafe. Tiny red veins made his blue irises even brighter, and deep creases shaped the corners of his mouth. Had he slept at all? Probably not, she decided. Judging by his appearance, he'd been up all night, standing guard over all of them. Susanna understood that fact even if Tim didn't. "We need to make some decisions," she said to the rancher.

Without taking his eyes off Rafe, Tim crossed his arms over his chest. "The boy can stay, but I want you gone."

Rafe shook his head. "I'm not leaving. Besides, if the Bentons show up, you'll need help."

"Not yours," Tim said.

Susanna stifled her irritation. "We don't have time for head-butting. Someone needs to tell the sheriff what happened."

"Forget it," Rafe said. "It's too dangerous."

"That's all the more reason to get the word out," she insisted.

Rafe shook his head. "It would be smarter to stay put. If they come back this way, we should be ready to defend ourselves." He shifted his gaze to Tim. "That includes Dr. Leaf. She's a crack shot."

"How do you know?" the rancher countered.

Susanna froze, but Rafe didn't blink. "She told me."

Tim frowned. "That goes against my grain. She can stay inside with the girls."

"Good grief!" Tim's chivalry irked Susanna, but so did Rafe's refusal to notify the authorities. "You're both being stubborn. I'll go for the sheriff myself."

"No!" Two male voices boomed in unison.

After giving her an irritated look, Rafe scowled at Tim. "It's a fool's errand, but I'm the one to go. Stay here with your girls."

"That's fine with me," Tim replied. "Don't bother coming back."

Rafe glared at him. "Don't hold your breath. I'll be back for Nick."

Susanna was about to ask Rafe to bring the medicine when he focused on her face. She saw the criticisms of Tim he'd made yesterday along with an "I told you so" expression.

Rafe made his voice formal. "If you don't mind, Dr. Leaf. I need a word with you in private."

"Of course. I'll be there in a minute."

As Rafe went to saddle his horse, Susanna laid her hand on Tim's arm. "I'm so sorry about Chester. He's worked for you for years."

His eyes filled with sadness as he put his palm on top of her fingers, lifted her hand off his arm and stepped back. He wasn't an affectionate man— she'd known that. But she still felt a sting when he brushed off her sympathy. She followed his gaze to the cabin where Emily was standing with her sisters. The youngest had her thumb in her mouth, and the middle girl was holding her sister's hand.

"I better tell the girls," Tim said.

"Would you like me to do it with you?" She had to speak to Rafe, but that would only take a moment.

"No. I'll handle it."

She watched as Tim walked across the yard and up the porch steps. She couldn't hear his words, but she saw the girls nodding solemnly.

Later she'd stand with the family while they buried Chester, but first she had business with Rafe. As she walked into the barn, she spotted him in a middle stall. He'd already put on his coat and hat and was saddling the roan. The only spot of brightness in the cavernous building came from a square window near the roof. It put a diamond of light on Rafe's back and made the ends of his long hair shine. The mix reminded her of the locket in her jewelry box. The outside had become tarnished. To see the gold and the person inside, she had to open it.

Yesterday she'd had a glimpse of the man hidden inside Rafe. She'd needed whiskey and he'd given it to her. She'd needed to talk and he'd listened. And that kiss... He'd been tender and passionate, pointing her down a road and asking her to follow—until

he'd turned back into a jackass. Judging by the look
of him now, that man was gone for good. Susanna
cleared her throat. "You wanted to speak to me?"

He glanced over his shoulder with the same scowl
he'd worn in the yard. "I have a favor to ask."

"What is it?"

"If I don't make it back, will you see that Nick
finds a home?"

"Of course."

"It won't be easy. He's at an awkward age."

"If it comes to that, I'll adopt him."

"You'll need a bigger place." He motioned toward
a corner of the barn. "My gear's stowed in the tack
room. You know what's in the saddlebag. Take it for
Nick."

"That won't be necessary, but I'll keep it in mind."

Her voice had sounded strong, but her stomach did
a flip. Jackass or not, Rafe would be in danger. A
lone rider had the advantage of speed if he ran into
the outlaw gang, but Rafe would be outnumbered.
She hadn't bothered with a shawl when she'd raced
out of the house and now she felt the cold in her
bones.

He'd turned his back on her, but she had to remind
him about the medicine for Nick. "You'll need to go
to the clinic. Nick's worse."

"Christ Almighty," he muttered. "That kid has worse luck than I do. How bad is it?"

Susanna dodged the question. "I need echinacea for a tea. It's in the cupboard by the door that leads to the waiting room. Everything's labeled, so you won't have trouble finding it."

Rafe pulled the cinch tight. "Anything else?"

She needed clean clothes, but she didn't want him to go into her bedroom. He'd invaded it once and that was enough. But she *did* need another favor. "There's a blackboard outside the front door of my office. I usually write a note when I'm gone. Would you leave a message saying where I am?"

Rafe hesitated and she knew why. If someone came looking for her, he'd be noticed. Susanna didn't care. Her patients had needs, too. "It's what I always do," she said. "Melissa Greene is supposed to come by today. If I'm not there, she'll start asking questions."

He pulled his hat low. "Sure. Whatever you say."

She'd never heard a man sound less sincere. "It's important, Rafe. Promise me you'll do it."

When he didn't answer, Susanna realized that his reasons for going to Midas were less than perfect. He'd fetch the herbs for Nick, but she doubted he'd do anything more. Her temper flared. "You're not going to see the sheriff, are you?"

He gave her a hard look. "No, I'm not. There's no need."

"That's ridiculous. The Bentons could be headed this way right now."

"They're not."

"How do you know?"

"They don't attack during the day." He led the roan out of the stall. "Frank likes to wait until a house is dark, then they break in, tie everyone up and take what they want. They'd have struck last night. I know these men. Judging by what Chester said, they're headed south."

His explanation rang true. At the same time, he'd made a selfish decision. "You should still report what happened."

"I'll leave that to you." He led the roan into the yard where he stopped several feet away from Chester's body. Someone, probably Tim, had covered the corpse with a blanket. In the distance, she heard the thud of a pickax, but her eyes stayed on Rafe, who was unlashing his carbine from its scabbard.

After lifting the weapon, he held it out to her. "Keep this for me."

Susanna accepted the gun with both hands and

turned it for a better look at the engraving. She'd never seen such fine work. Like the locket in her jewelry box, it was etched with roses. "This is beautiful. It must be special to you."

"It is." He looked into her eyes. "If I don't make it back, keep it for yourself. I owe it to you."

The gift touched her, but she also felt unsettled. He treasured the gun and had spent hours doing the etching. It felt too personal, so she said, "I'll keep it for Nick, but we're expecting you back for supper."

"Don't wait up. Anything could happen."

She wrinkled her nose. "Are you always this grim?"

"Yes, and I'm usually right."

He was looking into her eyes with a knowledge that took her back to the moment his lips had found hers. The heat of it warmed her now. So did the realization that he'd been right about her need to talk and be held, even her innocence. She had welcomed his understanding, but then he'd turned back into a saloon rat.

She frowned at him. "You owe me an apology."

"Not a chance, Doc." He'd made his voice low and deep. "I'm not at all sorry I kissed you. You needed it and I wanted it. But I *will* give you a compliment. You're an exceptional woman and a damn fine kisser. Don't ever doubt yourself."

"I don't."

But she'd just told a lie. She believed in herself as a doctor, but she wasn't so sure about the rest of her life. As a child she hadn't fit in and she still felt that way. When she chatted with other women, the conversation usually turned to their families. She had no one—except her parents and four younger brothers. As for male attention, she was caught between her gender and her career. By necessity, "Dr. Leaf" was a sexless creature who could pick shotgun pellets out of a man's buttocks without embarrassing him. But she was a woman, too. Alone at night, she had thoughts that would have burned down a barn. She wanted kisses in the dark, a man's hands on her breasts, the feel of him inside her.

Heat rushed to her cheeks. At Hopkins, her best friend had taken a lover and encouraged Susanna to do the same. She had been tempted by one of her professors, but she didn't have the heart for an affair. What good were sparks that would die out? She wanted a love that would last a lifetime. Susanna believed in that dream, but she'd grown discouraged over the past year. If she never married, she'd survive. She had her practice, her parents and her brothers. She loved Midas and believed in her work. If she overlooked the loneliness that crept into her bed, she had a perfect life.

Except she had liked kissing Rafe and wanted

to do it again. Heat spread from her belly to her back. It burned even hotter when Rafe brushed her cheek with his knuckles and brought her back to what he'd said about doubting herself—and being a good kisser. No one had ever said anything like that to her.

He gave her a tender smile. "I meant what I said, Susanna."

Her cheek burned as he lowered his hand. Shaking inside, she watched as he pulled himself into the saddle and rode down the trail leading to Midas. He looked at ease, but she wasn't fooled. The trip put him at risk and he was on guard.

She had never known a man with such shifting moods. She wanted an apology from the jackass, but she had been charmed by the man who had dosed her with whiskey. With his ponytail hanging down his back, he was a troublemaker to the core. But to Nick he was a father, brother and friend.

Susanna was saying a prayer for his safety when he looked over his shoulder. Their eyes locked across the space of the yard and he grinned. He'd caught her looking, but he'd been doing the same thing.

Rafe...a mix of a rogue and waif. The name suited him. He had the hard edges of a troubled man, but in his eyes she saw an unloved child. Had he been an orphan like Nick? Perhaps he'd been the youngest in a family with too many mouths to feed. Or maybe he'd grown up in a house full of violence as she had. She'd been fourteen when she discovered the truth of her blood and had run away from home. That search had reunited her parents and brought them all to Midas where she had met her father for the first time.

Looking at Rafe now, she recalled the lost girl she'd been on the train headed west. She wanted to tell him that she understood the need to run away from hurtful things, but before she could open her mouth, the waif vanished. Loose and lazy in the saddle, the rogue let his attention linger on her eyes and cheeks. Heat spread up her throat like a wild vine.

Refusing to be shy, Susanna stared back until he tipped his hat in salute.

I know what you're thinking, he seemed to say.

Maybe he did…but she understood him, too. She wasn't at all surprised when he kicked the roan into a gallop, as if he couldn't get away fast enough. He could ride all day and night. He could spend the rest of his life in the saddle, but Susanna knew a simple truth. Rafe LaCroix couldn't run from himself.

Chapter Eight

When he reached Midas, Rafe pushed his hat even lower and hunkered inside his duster. He looked like a half-dead saddle tramp, but his nerves were prickling with awareness. With wagons rattling and the shouts of children in a nearby schoolyard, the town had a lively feel to it. A stranger would be noticed but not questioned.

He had been here two years ago with Lem. His friend had taken sick, so they had paid a call on Doc Randall. The old man had told Lem his heart was skipping beats and that he needed to settle down. Lem had laughed it off and they'd gone back to trailing a fellow wanted for a double murder.

A few months later, Lem had died in his sleep. Rafe had buried him on a hill in the middle of nowhere, said goodbye and gone back to work. Bounty hunting wasn't the only life he knew, but it suited him. Thanks to Lem, he was good at it. The older man had taken a greenhorn kid and taught him how to track and shoot. As for being sneaky and clever, Rafe had honed those abilities in a snotty prep school in Boston. He'd liked learning but had hated everything else about that gray-stone world, especially being called a bastard.

He'd been called that name by his half brother, too. The memory of blood on the bricks in their father's study reminded Rafe that he was just a few steps away from prison or the gallows. Because of Nick, he'd been stopped for over a week, which meant his guardian angel could have plastered the town with those damned reward posters.

Rafe hated the thought of riding through Midas in broad daylight, but he needed to know if his past had caught up with him. Maybe his guardian angel had stopped the hunt at the Colorado border. Rafe hoped so. He wanted to give Nick time to recover and, foolish or not, he liked Dr. Leaf. He'd never met a woman who was both innocent and wise. She had a smart mouth, too. Rafe liked that in a female—not that it mattered. He'd be gone in a few weeks.

Figuring it was best to hide in plain sight, he turned up the main street where he saw the Midas Hotel, a bank and a café that was advertising pot roast and chocolate cake on a blackboard. Rafe's stomach rumbled, but he ignored the need and rode to the sheriff's office where he found a wall covered with Wanted posters. He saw Zeke Benton's ugly face and three more handbills showing men he recognized.

He looked twice to check for himself on the board. He'd turned in Frank Benton a month ago and that should have cleared his name, but a man couldn't be sure of such things. Justice, he'd learned, was fickle.

Relieved that he wasn't mentioned, Rafe turned Punkin down the street and rode to the train depot. If his guardian angel had been to Midas, he would have left a poster offering a reward for information. Months ago, Rafe had spotted one in Leadville and had laid low for weeks.

He found the station by following the scent of diesel. Oil clung to everything it touched. So did the smells of money, Cuban cigars and sumptuous meals. Bristling at the memory of his father's St. Louis palace, Rafe halted in front of a shabby train station and looked at a display board. It was covered with advertisements for land in Los Angeles and patent medicines, but he didn't see his own face staring back at him. His guardian angel hadn't come this far south. Judging by the run-down building, he probably wouldn't.

Except a little ways down the track, Rafe saw a crew of men painting a brand-new building. The two-story structure boasted a pitched roof, large windows and elaborate cornices under the eaves. Judging by the location, he guessed the building was a new depot. He decided to keep his distance and turned back to Dr. Leaf's clinic, where he left his horse in her stable.

Using the key she'd given him, he walked through the side door to the clinic and straight to the exam room. He'd forgotten about the mess he'd made when he kidnapped her. Broken glass lay on the floor and medicinal smells filled the air. The exam table was still on its side, a reminder that he'd tried to scare the daylights out of her and that she'd retaliated with a kick to his groin.

Rafe almost grinned at the memory. He'd had it coming and she'd delivered the blow like she kissed—with utter sincerity. He refused to think of kissing her as a mistake. He'd enjoyed it a bit too much, but that didn't mean he cared about her. Even so, he couldn't look away from the mess on the floor without feeling guilty. Because of him, she'd had a bad two days and her clinic was a shambles.

Rafe wasn't accustomed to cleaning up his own messes. He usually left and didn't look back, but he could still hear Dr. Leaf's outrage.

You idiot! Those things cost money!

He'd planned on paying her for seeing Nick,

enough to cover the damage and something extra for a warmer coat. But as he looked at the broken jars, money seemed like a token. It was the kind of thing his father would have done—ruin a poor woman's Sunday dress with a splash of mud from his brougham and toss her a sawbuck.

I'm sorry...

Not once had Rafe heard the old man utter those words; nor was he inclined to say them himself. Remorse had no place in his life. Except he could see Dr. Leaf on her knees with a dustpan and a broom. The lady was right. He owed her an apology, probably two considering his offer to buy her buggy, but hell would freeze before he'd make one. Rafe figured guilt was like a hangover. A man could endure the headache until it faded on its own, or he could stay a little drunk.

He usually picked the whiskey, but Dr. Leaf deserved better. After retrieving the broom from a tall cupboard, he began sweeping the glass into a pile. The whisk of the straw took him back to New Orleans where his mother had made him sweep their apartment every day. They had lived alone in a tiny set of rooms in the French Quarter, but the rent had been paid by the man who had met Mimi LaCroix in a high-class brothel and claimed her for his own—by deed if not by law.

Rafe had called the man Papa, but he'd been more like a king. He had taken them for carriage rides into the countryside, given Rafe toys and made his mother laugh. The infrequency of the visits only made them more special—until Rafe heard the word "bastard" for the first time. He'd bloodied the kid's nose, but it hadn't stopped the bullying. Nor had it helped that his father took to visiting more often. Late at night, Rafe would hear them making noises he now understood.

His stomach sickened at the thought. A pregnancy had killed his mother. Whether she'd miscarried on her own or had sought to end it, he didn't know. But one thing was certain. He blamed the man who had made Mimi LaCroix his mistress.

After he'd finished sweeping, Rafe tipped the dustpan of glass into a trash bin and turned to the cupboard where he found the apothecary jars. He put the one marked echinacea in his pocket and then browsed the shelves for a bottle of whiskey to replace the one he'd emptied last night. He found a brown bottle, held it to the light and saw it was half-empty. Knowing Dr. Leaf, she would have a spare somewhere else.

Rafe walked into the back room and went through her desk. In the bottom drawer he discovered a stack of letters tied with a ribbon. Most were postmarked from Baltimore, but some were from a man named Silas in Wyoming. That surprised Rafe. So did a copy of *Madame Bovary*. He had read it on the sly in prep school. Most of the boys had, and they'd all snickered about Emma Bovary and her wanton ways. Being a boy, Rafe hadn't understood the woman, but he did now. Lust and loneliness were a dangerous mix.

After closing the drawer, he opened a second one where—bless her heart—Dr. Leaf had a pint of Texas Gold. He took it and then perused the bookshelves for something for Nick. After passing up volumes by the Brontë sisters, he selected a collection of short stories by Mark Twain. He could have done without the memories of the Mississippi, but Nick would laugh at the jumping frog. He was about to leave when he spotted the candy jar on the doctor's desk. Thinking of the kids, he took it and headed out the side door.

Rafe had one more mess to clean up. Seeing no one in the alley, he climbed the stairs to Dr. Leaf's apartment and let himself in. Her undergarments were still in a tangle on the floor, so he knelt and pulled out drawers and a chemise. He gathered the remainder in his arms, jammed everything back into the highboy and opened the wardrobe holding her dresses. A navy skirt and striped shirtwaist looked like her office clothes, so he added them to the underthings.

He was about to close the wardrobe when a flash of blue caught his eye. Curious, he pushed aside her day dresses and took a long look at the sleekest ball gown he'd ever seen. The neckline dipped low, and the front was as smooth as skin. Beneath the heat of a man's hand, the silk would melt until it disappeared entirely. Had she worn it to an East Coast gala? Had she waltzed with every man in the room or had someone special broken her heart? He didn't know, but he was certain Timothy Duke didn't know what he was missing.

Rafe did, though. Most women made love like they kissed, and she had a knack for it. Her first time... he couldn't stop himself from thinking about what it would be like to be that man. He'd never been anyone's first—not a first son and not a first lover. But he knew what he'd do. If the opportunity knocked, he'd take Dr. Leaf on the ride of her life.

Rafe looked at her rumpled bed and saw her all over again. He'd start with slow kisses and build up her need. If she was skittish, he'd take even longer. But if she was ready to run, he'd touch and tease until she was crazy with wanting. Just thinking about her made him hard, but he also felt a pounding in his chest. First times mattered, and she'd remember him forever. But it would be best if she didn't remember him at all.

Determined to block his thoughts, he took an old satchel from under her bed, set it on the rumpled sheets and packed it with the clothes, the book and the candy. He considered adding the apothecary jar, but decided it would be safer in his coat. As he lifted the satchel, his eyes strayed to her pillow. He'd never lie here with Dr. Leaf, but what harm could there be in stretching out for five minutes? After last night's vigil, his eyes were as dry as paper. A catnap was just what he needed before the ride back to the Duke place.

Rafe stretched full length on the bed and tipped his hat over his eyes. Then he crossed his hands over his chest and his boots at the ankle. As his breathing deepened, the scent of her bedding filled his nose. When was the last time he'd smelled sun-dried cotton? He didn't know. Nor had he read himself to sleep since Boston where he'd discovered Robert Louis Stevenson.

Smiling at the memory, Rafe relaxed into the mattress. Maybe he could find a copy of *Kidnapped* for Nick in some emporium between here and Mexico. Or maybe he'd filch Dr. Leaf's copy of *Madame Bovary* and read to himself late at night on the trail, remembering her bed and the way she kissed.

* * *

Rap. Rap. Rap.

Rafe jarred awake. Someone was knocking on the apartment door. "Dr. Sue?"

The voice was young, female and close to tears. Rafe damned himself for a fool. He should have left the note on the board like Susanna had asked. Instead he'd fallen asleep like a baby.

The visitor knocked again with even more desperation. "Are you there? It's Melissa. Please...I *have* to talk to you."

Rafe clenched his jaw. He hadn't locked the door. If she turned the knob, he'd be forced to do something drastic. What the devil was wrong with him? Only a fool got caught lying in a woman's bed with her underthings in a satchel. The bed would creak if he moved, so he couldn't hide. He sure as hell didn't want to pull his gun and tie her up. All he could do was lie still as he listened for the knob.

She knocked again...and again.

Every tap sounded like a nail in his coffin. But then he heard a thump, as if she had leaned her head on the door in defeat. When a choked sob filtered through the crack, he dared to hope. And when he heard footsteps on the stairs, he took a deep breath.

He waited five minutes to be sure Melissa was gone, then he jumped to his feet, snatched up the satchel and hurried to the front of the clinic where he'd seen Dr. Leaf's blackboard. He lifted the chalk out of the tray and wrote "At the Duke ranch."

Thankful to escape, Rafe headed for the alley.

"Mister?"

Three more steps and he would have been around the corner and out of sight. Instead he turned, being careful to stay in the bright sun so that his hat hid his face, and looked at Melissa Greene. The best way to stay anonymous was to act innocent, so he nodded politely. "Can I help you, miss?"

"I need Dr. Leaf."

"She's at the Duke place. Chester got hurt." When she looked befuddled, he added a lie. "I'm the new hand."

"I see." Her shoulders sagged and she pressed her hand to her belly as if she were about to puke.

Rafe had been in enough whorehouses with expecting women to recognize the gesture. Thanks to Zeke Benton, she was a carrying a secret she wouldn't be able to keep for much longer. He wanted to give her some comfort, but what could he say? He settled for making his voice gentle. "Can I give her a message?"

"No!" The girl turned red with embarrassment. "I'm not sick or anything. I just need to talk to her."

Rafe clenched his jaw to keep from talking. Shame

had no place in this girl's life or her baby's life, but Zeke Benton had damned her to the judgment of fools. She deserved to know that he'd paid for his crime. But if Rafe told her about the man's death, she'd talk. Word would spread around town, and the sheriff would ask her questions about how she heard the news.

But at the sight of her puffy eyes, Rafe felt about an inch tall. Three days ago, he could have walked away and not looked back. He could have forgotten the girl and lied to Susanna. In his line of work, he fibbed all the time. It was second nature. But a small part of him didn't want to take that road with Susanna. She deserved better.

Deliberately slouching to disguise his height, he looked at Melissa. "I'm wondering if you would do Dr. Leaf a favor."

"What is it?"

"She sent me to town for some medicine, and I'm in a hurry to get back. Would you tell the sheriff that Chester's been shot? He ran into the Bentons in Outlaw Alley, the trail that runs west of here. He'll know where it is."

The girl nodded solemnly. "I'll go right now."

"You can also tell him that Zeke Benton's dead."

Worried that she'd ask questions, Rafe pivoted and strode toward the corner of the building.

"Mister, wait! What's your name?"

Keeping a leisurely pace, he raised his hand in farewell, giving her a good look at his ponytail so that she'd remember his hair and not his face. He didn't want to cut it off unless his guardian angel closed in, but at least he had the option.

With his hair brushing between his shoulders, Rafe turned the corner to the stable, climbed on the roan and headed back to the Duke ranch.

Chapter Nine

Where did hope end and foolishness begin?

Susanna had spent the day at Nick's bedside, asking herself that question. The infection was spreading, and every minute that passed without the echinacea brought Nick closer to an amputation. She didn't want to make that decision without Rafe. Even accounting for the bad weather, he should have been back hours ago.

Standing alone on the front porch, Susanna peered into the rain from beneath the shelter of the long eaves. Supper had been a dismal event with the girls missing Chester and talking in hushed tones. As soon as the dishes were done, they had gone to bed and Tim had excused himself to do paperwork, leaving her free to catch a breath of air.

The silence of dusk usually calmed her, but she felt herself straining to hear the splash of hoofbeats. As she huddled inside Emily's shawl, vicious pictures filled her mind…of Rafe lying dead on the trail, the Bentons invading the Duke home and, just as awful, of herself taking off Nick's leg. As thirsty as Nick was, he couldn't keep anything down—not even water. The fever had stayed high and he'd mistaken her for his mother, weeping when he realized where he was. Then he'd cried out for Rafe. She had tried to explain that his friend had gone for medicine, but the boy hadn't understood.

Susanna rubbed the muscles in her neck as she breathed a prayer for Nick. She said one for Rafe, too. Whether he'd admit it or not, he was a troubled man. Nick would have a scar, maybe a limp. If he lost the leg, he'd walk with crutches. Rafe's scars were on his heart and mind. They made him unpredictable, even dangerous.

"Susanna?"

Turning, she saw Tim standing in the doorway with two cups of coffee. As the door swung shut, he handed her the steaming blue enamel. "I thought you might be chilled out here," he said.

Touched that he'd thought of her, she took a generous swallow, savoring the heat as it filled her stomach. She lowered the cup and smiled at him. "Thank you."

For a man standing on his own porch, Tim seemed ill at ease. "What do you think happened to LaCroix?"

"I don't know."

"If it weren't for the kid, I'd be glad to see him gone."

Susanna bristled, but what could she say? *He shared his whiskey and saw into my heart...he listened like a friend...*

Until he'd turned back into a jackass.

Even so, she was worried about him and Nick needed the medicine. Rather than argue with Tim, she sipped her coffee. She had just taken a swallow when he stepped a little closer. "About that dance... would you like to go with the kids and me?"

No, she wanted to go with *him*. She wanted to wear her blue satin dress and think about kissing and romance and snuggling in the dark. But at the same time, she knew a baby step when she saw one. Hoping to feel a bit of excitement, she smiled at him. "I'd like it a lot. It's supposed to be very nice."

"Then it's settled." With a flick of his wrist, Tim dumped the dregs of his coffee over the railing as if he'd just made a business deal with a fellow rancher. Where was the romance?

Susanna didn't know whether to laugh or cry. It was a thoughtless gesture, but it was also his nature. Looking up at him, she wondered if he'd ever felt more awkward in his life and took pity on him. "We'll have a nice time," she said.

Tim nodded and then looked toward the barn. "I better get to the chores. Without Chester—" He clamped his mouth shut.

"I understand," she said. "Go ahead."

After setting the cup on the railing, Tim strode across the yard without glancing back. Susanna raised her own cup to her lips, but the liquid was lukewarm and disappointing. She drank it anyway, hoping for a jolt of energy, but instead she tasted the sugary dregs and felt foolish. Bethany had taken sugar in her coffee. Susanna drank hers black and strong. Mildly nauseated, she dumped the last few sips over the railing just as Tim had.

Had she been wrong to say yes to him about the dance? Until a few Sundays ago, they had been friends and it had seemed reasonable to hope for sparks. But that was before she'd kissed Rafe LaCroix, whom she was going to cheerfully murder when he showed up.

If he showed up...

Hugging herself against the chill, she started to hum one of the old spirituals she'd learned from Silas Jones, her father's best friend and the man who'd brought her to Midas when she'd run away from Washington. She'd been traveling as a boy named Sam and Silas had come to her rescue. He'd also opened her eyes to God's love in a way no one else had. She still wrote to Silas once a month and always got the same reply.

I'm proud to know you, Sam.... Do good and love hard...you can't go wrong with that.

Silas had been her first true friend. Tonight, even humming alone, she felt the old harmony in her heart. It soothed her worries, but an even deeper relief came when she heard the slosh of hooves coming down the trail.

Please, God...let it be Rafe....

The rider came into the yard at a trot, reined in his horse and jumped to the ground. As soon as she saw Rafe, she knew that he'd had a hard time. Streams of rain dripped from his hat, and steam rose in a cloud from the horse's withers. The roan had been ridden hard through the mountains where the storm had been most severe.

Susanna stepped into the drizzle. "What happened?"

He didn't look her in the eye. "Things took longer in town. Then I got spooked about five miles out. I thought I was being followed, so I cut through Needle Canyon."

Susanna winced. The narrow ravine would have funneled wind and rain into a torrent of water. Sometimes the trail disappeared completely in mud. She never rode through Needle Canyon and wanted to scold Rafe for taking that chance. But instead she shivered at the reason for his detour. "Did you see someone? Did the Bentons—"

He cut her off. "How's Nick?"

Later she'd finish her question, but first he needed to hear about the boy. "He's a fighter," she said. "I'll brew the tea right now."

The hardness in Rafe's eyes melted to raw pain. "He's worse, isn't he?"

Susanna never lied about her patients. "Yes, but there's hope. Take care of your horse and then come inside. Nick will be happy to see you."

Rafe led his horse to the barn, while Susanna went to the kitchen to brew tea and make a fresh poultice. She hadn't said it to Rafe, but if the boy's condition didn't improve soon, she'd have to take the leg off to save his life. She added a handful of herbs to the teakettle and set it to boil. Then she used Emily's mortar and pestle to mash another mix of leaves for a poultice. After spreading the paste on a cotton square, she folded it tight, dipped it in a pot of boiling water and squeezed away the excess before setting it aside.

When she could smell the tea, she filled a cup and carried everything into Nick's room on a tray. Just as she expected, the boy was tossing in his sleep. She set the tray on the end table, sat in a hard chair and placed the poultice on his leg. After covering it with a towel to keep in the heat, she lifted the cup.

"Nick?" she said softly.

As she slipped her arm around his shoulders, the boy's eyes fluttered open.

"Rafe's back with the medicine. I'm going help you sit up so you can drink it."

"Where is he?" asked the boy.

"Right here."

Rafe's deep voice had come from behind her. She heard something thud against the floor but couldn't look while she was holding the tea and trying to lift Nick's head. She wished she'd asked him to bring some of the paper straws she ordered from a catalog.

He must have seen the awkwardness, because he wedged himself between the chair and the night-stand and put his arm behind the boy's back. His reach pinned her hand between his muscular fore-arm and the boy's torso. As she extricated herself, his sleeve pulled back so that she felt a patch of cool male skin. He must have been half frozen by the ride and he had to be hungry. As soon as she took care of Nick, she'd warm his supper.

Using both hands, she raised the cup to the boy's lips for another swallow. She knew the tea tasted awful, but Nick didn't seem to care. She took it as a bad sign. Neither was she encouraged when he fell back to sleep without trying to talk to Rafe. Aware of the boy's weakness, Rafe had lowered him to the pillow and stepped away from the bed.

As Susanna set the cup on the nightstand, Rafe bent to pick up the object he'd set on the floor. "I brought a few things besides the medicine."

Her satchel. She had carried it close to three-thousand miles. It had held secrets, hope and the fears of a fourteen-year-old girl. The leather was worn, but the old case was her most cherished possession. It was also a reminder that she'd once been on the run and afraid of being found—just like Rafe LaCroix.

As she lifted the leather from his hand, Susanna wondered what she'd tell her friend about Rafe when she wrote her next letter. She had a knack for spinning tales and this one was a dime novel.

> **Dear Silas,**
> I was kidnapped by a bounty hunter who's teaching an orphan to read. He speaks French and reads Greek myths. He seems kind, but he's also unbearably disrespectful. I'd like to wash his mouth out with soap. I'd like…

Unable to complete the thought, Susanna held the satchel as Rafe pulled up a second chair. Dressed in dungarees and a chambray shirt, he looked like an ordinary ranch hand, but his face held an intelligence she didn't often encounter. She liked sparring with him, and she sensed a battle of wits was about to begin.

After shifting the bag in her lap, she worked the familiar buckle. "What did you bring?"

He teased her with a smile. "Your unmentionables. Considering I'd already ransacked your bureau, I didn't think you'd mind."

Her cheeks turn slightly pink. He could have asked her for permission, but she suspected he didn't often ask for anything. She decided to honor his good intentions. "I'm glad you did. People have to be practical."

Their gazes met from a distance she could have spanned with a touch. But even more personal was the glimmer of respect in his eye and the tilt of his mouth. "That's one of the things I like about you, Doc. You're not shy."

"What's the point?" she said. "The human body's hardly a mystery."

Rafe gave a soft laugh. "Is that a fact? It seems to me a woman's body is the most mysterious thing on earth. Think about it—"

"I'd rather not."

Trying to look peeved, she reached inside the

satchel and discovered her navy skirt and a shirt-waist, stockings and the candy jar she kept on her desk. She'd stocked it two days ago with a mix from the Midas Emporium. In addition to the peppermints she considered medicinal, it held a rainbow of butterscotch, licorice whips, gumdrops and the chewy Tootsie Rolls she'd asked Mrs. Wingate to order from New York City. When it came to chocolate, Susanna had no shame. It was also a safer topic than the mysteries of a woman's body.

She lifted the jar from the satchel and set it on the nightstand. "I see you found my vice."

Rafe arched his brows. "You call that a vice? A sweet tooth isn't even a bad habit. Whiskey, gambling, smoking opium—those are vices."

"You sound like an expert."

"I am."

Susanna felt a chill. "Even the opium?"

"I've tried it," he said, sounding wise.

When he leaned back in the chair and gave her a sidelong glance, Susanna realized that Rafe was trying to scare her. It wouldn't work. Wolves in the wild didn't warn their prey, and that's what he was doing with her.

She was about to close the satchel when he said, "There's a book in there, too. I borrowed it for Nick."

As she withdrew the copy of Mark Twain's stories,

she smiled. "He'll like it. It'll help pass the time once the fever breaks."

They both looked at Nick's face. His cheeks were blotched with fever, but the skin over his facial bones looked bloodless. Nor did she like the rise and fall of his chest. His respiration was rapid, and each breath rasped like a saw. Worst of all, though, were the red lines on his leg. The poultice covered them completely, but she knew his condition was worsening.

Rafe sucked in a lungful of air. "How soon?"

He was asking when they'd have to decide about an amputation. "I want to give the tea and poultice time to work," she answered. "But if he has convulsions, or if the red lines spread above his knee, it would be wise to take the leg."

Rafe muttered an oath. A better man would have offered up a prayer or bargained with God. *Take me instead...take my leg...take them both...*

But he didn't believe in making deals with Mother Nature, God, Father Time, Zeus or anyone else. Instead he leaned back in the chair and stared out the window, watching as raindrops trickled down the black glass and disappeared. He felt sick inside, mostly from guilt. He'd expected to be back hours ago, but that nap had lasted close to three hours.

To make up the time, he'd taken a short cut through Needle Canyon. He'd had no idea that the pass would be full of the storm. Twice he'd almost turned back to the main road, but both times he had visions of Nick and forged through the mud and rain.

Dr. Leaf leaned forward in her chair and adjusted the poultice on Nick's leg. She had pretty hands. They were smooth and strong, and he knew from yesterday's kiss that they'd be generous to a man's need.

"You're later than I expected," she said. "Did something happen?"

He'd enjoyed seeing her blush and decided to tease her some more. "Only in my dreams," he said, sounding husky.

She pinched her lips together, then relaxed them as curiosity got the better of her. "What does that mean?"

"I took a nap in your bed."

"I hope you changed the sheets."

"Don't worry, Doc. Without you, it wasn't that much fun."

The woman was trying to look bored, but her cheeks had flushed again. "I'd tell you to mind your manners, but you'd say something even more disreputable."

He smiled at her. "Probably."

"So instead I have a question for you." She looked straight into his eyes. "Why are you on the run?"

She'd turned the tables on him and he didn't like it. "It's none of your business."

"But it is," she countered. "If the Bentons—"

"You're not in harm's way."

"But what about you? Are you in danger?"

Hell, yes. Maybe it was the dim light that made him want to spill his guts to her. Or perhaps it was the talk of mysteries and sex. Either way, her interest in him had gone too far. "Just take care of the boy."

"That's what I'm trying to do." She lifted the poultice off Nick's leg and pushed to her feet. "I need to heat this up. There's a plate for you on the stove."

Rafe hadn't eaten since that morning, but he didn't want to follow her into the kitchen. "I'm not hungry."

"You're either a fool or a liar. Which is it?"

"Neither."

After giving him a look that said she knew the truth—that he was both—she walked out of the room. Alone with his rumbling stomach, Rafe listened to the patter of the rain. A sudden burst made him grateful for the roof over his head. It also made him feel stupid for passing up a meal just because the lady doctor wanted him to eat it.

Seeing that Nick was asleep, Rafe ambled to the

kitchen where Dr. Leaf had set a plate on the table, along with a bowl of cherry cobbler and a glass of milk.

She glanced over her shoulder and smiled. "I thought you'd change your mind."

"And why is that?"

"Men are predictable." She had looked him in the eye, but he could see it was taking an effort. "If they're not thinking about sex, they're thinking about food."

Rafe chuffed with irritation. He didn't like know-it-all women, but she had a point. He'd walked into the kitchen like a stray dog sniffing out scraps. Wanting to prove to her that he was a cut above a cur, he lingered in the doorway where he could see her standing at the stove. Steam was rising from a pot and glistening on her cheeks. When she wiped them with her sleeve, he recalled their conversation in the barn. "I left the note like you asked."

"Thank you." Relief rang in her voice and she smiled at him.

"I also swept up the mess from the other night." He hadn't planned on telling her, but it felt right.

"The instruments weren't damaged," she said, sounding matter-of-fact. "And I can replace the broken jars."

"I'll pay for everything. And for the extra time with Nick."

She gave him a sideways glance. "In cash? Or are we going to bargain some more?"

They were on his turf now. He flashed a smile. "Name your price."

"Twenty dollars will cover everything."

The amount was a fraction of what he intended to pay her. "You work cheap, Doc."

"I'll put it to good use. Not everyone pays me with money."

Rafe could imagine—chickens, cherry pies, maybe a ham now and then. As he watched her at the stove, he added up the cost of a new horse, a coat, work boots and pretty shoes. Then he doubled it. He wasn't motivated by guilt. Nor was he trying to buy his way into her bed. He just wanted to do something nice for her.

Feeling more comfortable, he sat at the table and took a bite of ham. While she prepared the poultice, he cleaned his plate. As enjoyable as it was, the food took second place to the pleasure of watching Dr. Leaf as she worked. She had her back to him, but he could still see the flex of her arms and the slight sway of her hips as she squeezed excess water from the poultice with a plate.

He was swigging down the milk, something he

hadn't done in years, when she turned to him. Her gaze dropped to the empty plate. "Don't forget dessert."

She left to tend to Nick, leaving Rafe alone with the cherry cobbler. The sweet treat wasn't his idea of dessert, but he ate every bite, rinsed his plate in the wash bucket and walked back to Nick's room.

Dr. Leaf had draped a damp towel over his scrawny chest, but Rafe could see the fever raging in the boy's cheeks.

"You should know that waiting is risky," she said gently.

"I realize that."

He'd sounded angry and he was—mostly with himself. He couldn't stand the thought of sitting helplessly in a chair, but neither could he leave. He had Dr. Leaf's whiskey bottle in his pocket, but the thought of a drink brought no comfort. Instead he crossed the room where he could look out the window. A swaying branch caught his eye. He was fairly confident the Bentons had traveled south, but he'd be wise to stay alert tonight.

When Nick moaned, Rafe turned and saw that the boy had opened his eyes.

"Rafe? Is it really you? I thought—"

"Hi, kid. How are you feeling?"

"Sick."

Dr. Leaf lifted the cup of tea to the boy's lips. "Drink this, then I'll give you a peppermint."

When Nick downed the nasty brew without complaint, Rafe felt a chill. The tea smelled like moldy grass, but Nick was too weak to notice the taste. After a couple of slurps, Dr. Leaf set the mug on the nightstand and reached for the candy jar. "Here's the peppermint," she said to the boy.

Rafe's mouth burned with the memory of the candy she'd given him in the cave. For a few seconds, he'd tasted the sugar and felt good. But he doubted it was going to help Nick. The boy was too weak to notice the sting of the mint. Rafe watched until he closed his eyes and drifted away.

He looked up at Susanna who was unwrapping a Tootsie Roll. Oblivious to him, she popped it in her mouth and started to chew. She caught him staring and said, "Want one?"

At least that's what she tried to say. With the candy in her mouth, she sounded tipsy and they both smiled.

Rafe knew what the smile meant. They were whistling in the dark, taking what comfort they could find. Wanting more of that closeness, he sat next to her and took the candy. Her fingers, still damp from the poultice, brushed his palm and sent a wave of longing through him. He could smell chocolate and mint, her warm skin, carbolic and the herbs. For some foolish reason, he wanted to hold her hand. Instead he popped the candy into his mouth and watched as Dr. Leaf checked the boy's fever with her palm.

Rafe had no trouble telling the truth. "He's worse, isn't he?"

"Yes, but the tea needs time to work." She sat back in the chair. "We have a long night ahead of us. Why don't you tell me what else happened in town?"

Rafe was glad to think about something other than Nick's leg. "I saw Melissa Greene."

He told her the story, including how he'd gotten trapped in her apartment. When he mentioned sending Melissa to the sheriff, Susanna smiled. "That's good. People need to be warned."

Maybe, but Rafe was more concerned about the reward posters. "I did it for you—not me."

She looked at Nick but spoke to Rafe. "I don't understand why you're on the run. Turning in Frank Benton would make you a hero."

He wasn't about to tell her he'd killed his half brother and robbed his father's safe. What did it matter? His brother was gone and he'd squandered every cent he'd stolen. But neither was he in the mood to spin a lie. He settled for part of the truth. "It has nothing to do with the Bentons."

As she adjusted the towel on Nick's chest, he leaned forward so that his shoulders were aligned with hers. For the first time in years, he wanted to spill his secrets. Not even Lem knew about that night in St. Louis, mostly because the old man hadn't asked. Not that Rafe cared. A man's past was his own business.

He decided to change the subject before Dr. Leaf asked another question. "I told Melissa that Zeke Benton was dead but not how he died."

"I hope it gives her some comfort."

"I think it did. But the way she touched her belly, I wonder if she's with child."

"I'm afraid so," Susanna murmured. They both knew what Melissa had ahead of her—shame, money troubles and the judgment of fools. Susanna's eyes filled with pity. "It's going to be hard for her."

"She could leave town. There's a place in New Orleans where girls can go. She could have the baby and then give it up."

Susanna gave him a sidelong glance. "It's her child, too. She didn't do anything wrong."

"That's true, but they'll both be judged."

"It sounds like you know about these things."

"I do."

When he refused to say more, she went back to wiping Nick's forehead. "It's not quite the same, but

I was fourteen when I found out that my mother was carrying me when she married my stepfather. He was a horrible man."

The loathing in her voice piqued Rafe's curiosity. He hadn't expected Dr. Leaf to understand bitterness. "How did you learn the truth?"

"He wanted to spite my mother, so he told me about my real father. I ran away from home and went looking for John Leaf."

"So you know how it feels to have someone yank the rug out from under you."

"I do," she answered. "And I know what it's like to be alone, just like Nick. You two are an odd pair."

To pass the time, Rafe told her about the first bowl of chili he'd bought for Nick in Colorado and finished with their run-in with the Bentons. "We'd have been in Mexico by now if it weren't for Zeke. He was gunning for me when Nick tried to warn me. The kid rode right into the line of fire."

The lamp flickered, reminding Rafe of the cave where they'd taken cover. Why on earth had he waited five days before getting help? The answer was easy—he was a selfish son of a bitch, more concerned with himself than the boy.

He shook his head. "I should have taken him to town."

"We all make mistakes." Her voice sounded like

silk catching on rough skin. "No matter what happens, he was lucky to find you."

"Lucky?" Rafe pushed to his feet and glared down at her. "If he loses his leg, he'll wish he'd never been born." The kindness in her eyes nearly dropped him to his knees. Without a bit of hesitation, she set the damp towel in the basin and took his hand in both of hers. When she tugged him down to the chair, he sat because he had nowhere else to go.

Clasping his hand in both of hers, she looked into his eyes. "When I first saw Nick, I thought you were just an outlaw on the run. But there's more to the story, isn't there?"

Rafe felt like a bug under a microscope. *Yes, God damn it!* But instead of shouting, he clenched his jaw. "Don't concern yourself."

She squeezed his fingers even harder. "You made a mistake. I've made them, too."

Rafe knew all about mistakes. His father had made a colossal one, and Rafe had paid the price. He'd made one of his own, and his brother had paid with his blood. If he forgave himself for Nick's misery, he'd have to forgive his father as well. But he'd sworn on his mother's grave to hold that bitterness to his dying day. Mistakes exacted a price, and someone had to pay.

Rafe jerked back his hand. "You're naive, Dr. Leaf."

"I'm hardly that."

For a young woman, she had sounded unbearably wise, even bitter, as if she had survived more heart-aches than he cared to imagine. Leaning forward, she put her hand on the poultice to check for warmth. "Do you ever pray, Rafe?"

"Hell, no."

"Why not?"

"Because the last time I tried it, the Almighty spit in my eye."

In spite of the chill in the room, Rafe felt the humid air all over again. He saw Mimi's coffin lying in a hole in the ground. It had been painted white and adorned with roses. The cemetery had been full of her friends—all women—except for Rafe's father. When the burial was over, the man had gripped Rafe's scrawny shoulder with clawlike fingers.

You'll be going to school in Boston...I'll do my best for you.

His best? Rafe hadn't been fooled for a minute. The man's wife and older son had his name and a fancy house in St. Louis. Mimi, on the other hand, had earned a pretty white casket.

Rafe had wanted to stay with his mother's best friend, a Creole woman named Shanna who had six kids of her own. They were like brothers and sisters to him. But his father had dragged him screaming into a private railroad car. He could still see the teak panels, each one carved with a scene from an ancient myth—Dædalus flying too close to the sun, Medusa with her snakes, and Zeus towering over them all.

Terrified, he had cried for help, but Mimi's God had turned a deaf ear. Rafe doubted he was listening now, but Susanna was looking into his eyes, waiting for an explanation he didn't want to give. She also looked exhausted and in need of a kind touch.

"You look beat," he said.

"I am." She stretched her neck and rubbed it with her own hands, kneading the muscles without fully relaxing.

Rafe had a knack for neck rubs. It came from having an artist's hands and a man's intuition. Right now, those instincts were telling him that Dr. Leaf needed his touch. Duke had left the barn before Rafe. Judging by the light under his bedroom door, he was reading in bed and unlikely to check on Nick or Susanna. After pushing to his feet, Rafe positioned himself behind her chair, put his hands on her shoulders and started to rub.

She stiffened but didn't stop him.

"Help me out, Doc," he murmured. "Relax a little."

She lowered her chin, but her muscles stayed stiff. Was she worried that Duke would walk in and see them? Or maybe she was afraid that she'd enjoy the neck massage a little too much? Holding in a smile, Rafe decided to give that worry a run for the money. Using his thumbs, he smoothed the muscles fanning away from her spine. He worked up to her shoulders, down her biceps and then up to her hair where he slid his fingers along the base of her skull.

A soft moan escaped from her throat. "You shouldn't be doing this."

"Want me to stop?" Rafe put a dare in his voice.

"Not yet."

Her shoulders rolled forward, giving him a view of the hairs that had strayed from her braid and the skin behind her ear. If they'd been in her bedroom, he'd have kissed that spot and made her shiver. Instead he worked his fingers deeper into her hair, watching as the lamplight turned the ends into filament.

With each stroke, she felt softer in his hands until she reminded him of a deer lying in the sun. When a deeper moan came from her throat, Rafe felt a rush of pride and wondered if anyone else had ever given her this small pleasure. He hoped not. A neck rub wasn't the biggest first in a woman's life, but it counted for something.

He could have kneaded her back for hours, but just when he wondered if she had dozed off, Nick went into convulsions.

Chapter Ten

Rafe pushed his way to the bed and grabbed Nick's legs to hold him still. Susanna had already leaped to her feet and grabbed a padded stick off the nightstand. After putting it in the boy's mouth, she held his shoulders against the mattress.

"We have to cool him down," she ordered. "Get another towel."

Rafe plunged a strip of cotton into the washbowl and spread it over Nick's chest. Then he gripped the boy's ankles to hold him still, feeling every jerk of his body. Rafe didn't know much about medicine, but he had some common sense. "Maybe we should dunk him in the stream."

"It would be too much of a shock."

"Then I'll open the window."

She shook her head no, focusing instead on Nick as his limbs stiffened and he arched his back. When his skin turned bluish, Rafe feared for the boy's life and faced the truth. The fight to save Nick's leg was about to end.

When the seizure eased, it left Nick pale and still. Susanna feathered her fingers through the boy's hair and then looked at Rafe. Her brown eyes had a tearful sheen, but all the softness had gone out of her stance. "I have to take off the leg."

Rafe knew she was right, but he couldn't stand the thought. He glared at her. "You said yourself the tea needs time to work."

"It does, but we're out of time."

She'd sounded like a banker turning down a loan. Filled with disgust, Rafe turned his head and stared at the wall with its family photographs and alphabet samplers. The lamp was burning bright and Nick had more color in his face. Rafe wasn't accustomed to hoping for things, but he wanted to try.

He stared pointedly at Dr. Leaf. "One more hour."

She shook her head. "I know it's hard—"

"So is being a cripple."

Her eyes, hard but glistening with tears, reminded him of rocks in the rain. "Without the surgery, he'll die. It has to be done."

"Damn it! How can you be so sure?"

When she didn't reply, he read the answer in her eyes. She knew the difference between medicine and wishful thinking. He also knew that she prayed to the God who had left him standing at his mother's grave and was about to turn a boy into a cripple. Or had Rafe done that with his selfish need to get to Mexico? Sick to his stomach, he pleaded with her. "Just a little longer, Doc. What can it hurt?"

Pity filled her eyes, as if she knew that he hadn't hoped for anything in a long time. "All right," she answered. "But only because I need to prepare the kitchen for surgery."

"How long?"

"Maybe ten minutes."

Rafe dragged his hand through his hair. "Christ on crutches," he muttered. But the profanity brought no satisfaction. Nick would be using crutches for the rest of his life.

Susanna's gaze locked on his. "I'm going to need help and it's too much for Emily. If you can't do it, I'll wake Tim."

Rafe shook his head no. He'd gotten Nick into this mess and he wouldn't abandon the boy now. "It's my place."

"Then it's settled."

But Rafe felt no peace at all. When Susanna left the room, he sat on Nick's bed and started to talk. He told the kid he was sorry and promised that he'd do a better job of looking out for him. "I'd trade places with you if I could. I'd give anything, Nick. Anything…"

When he ran out of words, he lifted the boy's hand in his own. If he'd believed in miracles, he would have begged for one. But he didn't believe in anything except his own bad luck. Old feelings of betrayal welled in Rafe's belly. His mother had been right. *Be wise, my Raphaël. Good intentions can go awry.*

Mimi had never explained that comment, but Rafe suspected she had been referring to his father. *We must forgive…*

Not in Rafe's book. Some hurts were too deep and an amputation had to be one of them. He couldn't imagine facing Nick in the morning. "I'm sorry" wouldn't come close to expressing his remorse; nor would it give Nick back his leg. Unable to bear the sight of the boy, now tranquil with sleep, he hung his head.

"Look!"

Nick's cry pulled Rafe out of the dark. Wide and bright, the boy's eyes were focused on the wall. Rafe craned his neck to see what had roused him and felt the same jolt as Nick.

An angel had entered the room. Filmy and gray, the shadow stretched from the floor to the ceiling, giving the woman's figure a slender strength. Instead of a halo, she had a braided crown. And in the place of wings, she had bent elbows and hands that were laced behind her back, forming two triangles with silver centers.

Nick was seeing a miracle, but Rafe understood the laws of light and shadow. He also recognized Susanna's shape and the way she had tied her braid before the first surgery. Backlit by the lamp in the kitchen, she was casting a shadow that was both human and unearthly. The three of them stayed still, tense and breathing together, until Nick let out a sigh.

Terrified that the boy had drawn his last breath, Rafe looked at his face where he saw beads of sweat rising like diamonds. As the boy's eyelids fluttered shut, his lips curved into a contented smile. In another minute, his entire body was drenched in perspiration.

The fever had broken, leaving Rafe to wonder if angels were real after all.

For the next three days, Rafe made himself useful around the ranch. Chopping wood and mucking out stalls gave him time to think about the angel on the wall and what had happened next.

Susanna had put away the bone saw and not mentioned it again. Instead she had brewed more tea and stayed up all night changing the poultice. By the time the sun rose, the wound had faded to pink and Nick was complaining about the taste of the tea.

They had all seen the shadow, but Nick had seen the woman in detail. Once, when Susanna was out of the room, he had informed Rafe that angels wore white dresses that glowed, but that they didn't have halos like he'd thought. He'd also insisted that they were ten times prettier than the pictures he'd seen in his ma's Bible, and this one had talked to him.

She had told him that the leg would hurt for a while and he wouldn't like the tea, but that he was going to get better. She had also told him that heaven was a special place and someday, when he was a very old man, he'd see it for himself.

Alone in the barn, Rafe tossed a forkful of hay with more force. He wanted to think he'd been reading too much of *The Odyssey* to the boy, but he had seen the angel for himself. Nick was right. Angels didn't have halos—they carried medical bags and tended to the wounded.

They also made boys—and grown men—fall in love with them. Not that Rafe was in that kind of danger. Nick was the one who couldn't stop talking about the lady doctor. *Rafe, don't you think she's pretty? Don't you think she's smart?*

Rafe thought those things and more. He recalled

rubbing her shoulders and the way she had hummed with pleasure. She had made him feel generous and even kind. But most haunting of all was the look in her eyes when she'd told him the leg had to come off. She could have judged him, but instead he'd seen the deepest kind of compassion.

I've made mistakes, too.

But not like his. Every minute that passed brought him a step closer to prison. As he tossed more hay to Lightning, Rafe weighed his options. He and Nick were stuck until the fracture healed. The sheriff had ridden out two days ago and had believed Rafe's story, but staying in Midas wasn't wise. Boarding-houses were full of losers like himself and he was likely to be recognized.

Even more troublesome was the longing in Nick's eyes. Twice he'd hinted to Rafe about settling in Midas. The Duke girls had been talking to him about school and he wanted to go. He'd also been gabbing about meeting Susanna's three young brothers—J.J., Silas and Law—or the holy terrors as she called them. She'd told Nick all about fishing in the stream behind the parsonage and collecting tadpoles in jars. She'd made it sound like so much fun that even Rafe wanted to roll up his trousers and go wading.

That night, Nick's eyes had filled with hope. *Do you think we could stay here?*

Sorry, kid. But we've got to head south.

Nick had nodded, but his eyes had dulled with heartbreak. Rafe understood the feeling too well. The boy had it bad for the lady doctor. He wanted a mother and a home, friends and a normal life.

As for his own feelings, Rafe could handle himself. Lust was lust. He knew where to go and what to do. When he got to Mexico, he'd find a woman. He'd forget Susanna's brown eyes and that silky braid. Someday he'd taste peppermint and not recall her name.

"Ah, hell," he muttered. Who was he fooling? He didn't *want* to forget her. In his dreams he'd already bedded her a dozen times. He'd imagined her telling him that she'd never forget him and that she cared for him. There was no denying the truth. He had a bigger crush on the lady doctor than Nick did, but he knew how to solve it. A night in her bed would cure what ailed him. Unfortunately, that event wasn't too likely.

Unless he got creative…. Rafe gave in to a smile. He didn't expect the lady doctor to hop into bed with him, but he sure as hell was going to enjoy the chase. Judging by that kiss, she'd enjoy it, too.

Lingering in Midas had a definite appeal, but he still needed an inconspicuous place to stay. As much as Rafe disliked the thought, he figured the Duke ranch was the safest place to hide. That meant eating a plate of humble pie and asking King Henry for a job. After hanging up the pitchfork, Rafe walked to the house. He wiped his boots and stepped into the kitchen where the middle daughter was serving breakfast with the help of her little sister. Duke was sitting at the head of the table like Zeus. "Bonnie, I need more coffee."

The girl lifted the pot off the stove and poured. Then she looked at Rafe, who was still in the doorway. "Would you like some, Mr. LaCroix?"

The girl had sounded like the maid in his father's house, the one who had looked terrified every time she served breakfast. Rafe tensed at the memory. "No, thanks. I just want a word with your pa."

Duke looked up with a scowl. "What is it?"

To Rafe's way of thinking, he hadn't done a thing to deserve Duke's scorn. He'd been sleeping in the barn and had paid for his keep and Nick's. He'd done chores and carved the ABCs into a set of blocks for the youngest girl who didn't get a lot of attention. Still, he needed a favor, so he made his voice friendly. "First off, thanks again for opening your home to Nick. He's a good kid."

"Susanna tells me he's healing."

"That's right. The infection's gone."

Duke nodded. "So you two will be on your way."

It was an order, not a statement. Rafe forced himself to be amiable. "That's what I want to talk about. The fracture still has to heal. You need a ranch hand and I need a place to stay. I'd like to work for you until Nick can ride."

Still standing, Rafe wished he'd pulled up a chair on his own. With Duke glaring up at him, he felt like a beggar.

"Girls, go outside," the rancher said.

As Bonnie and Maggie slipped through the door, Duke crossed his arms over his chest and leaned back in his chair. "I don't know who you are, LaCroix, or where you've been. But I want you out of here."

Annoyed, Rafe dropped lazily onto a chair and drummed his fingers on the table. "What did I do to piss you off so bad?"

"Breathing would have been enough."

"It's more than that."

"All right," Duke said. "Here are the facts. I've seen that money in your saddlebags and you're packing three rifles. That carbine is a work of art. Most men don't love their guns."

The carbine had been a gift from Lem and Rafe treasured it. He was a breath away from calling Duke an idiot, but he needed a place for Nick. Trying to sound nonchalant, he said, "I'm a bounty hunter. I turned in Frank Benton and that's why they're after me. It also explains the money you saw."

Duke dipped his knife in the butter crock. "Bounty hunters aren't much better than the scum they chase."

"Some, not all." Lem had been in the business for the money, but he'd had a sense of justice, too.

As if he had nothing better to do, Duke slathered the biscuit with butter. With each turn of the knife, Rafe's annoyance deepened. Determined to outlast him, he stared at the rancher's nose until he set down the knife.

Duke took a bite, chewed like a cow and swallowed. As the dough went down his throat, he glared at Rafe. "I won't hire you, LaCroix. For one thing, I don't like you. For another, there's no need. The boy's well enough for a trip to town."

"How do you know?"

"Susanna told me."

"When?"

"This morning."

Rafe didn't like the rancher's smug tone, nor had he missed the emphasis on *Susanna*. The man was claiming her as plainly as he branded one of his steers. The notion made Rafe sick to his stomach. She was too smart for the rancher and far too independent to put up with his high-handed ways. Rafe knew what he had to do. Come hell or high water, he intended to set Susanna straight about men in general and Duke in particular. He'd had seen it happen before. Women confused nature's urges with love all the time. Men didn't think the same way. They scratched what itched and went on their way.

Right now, what itched the most was Rafe's temper. Knowing that a tongue-lashing wouldn't help Nick, he pushed to his feet and looked down at Duke. "If you don't mind, I'd rather hear the news from Dr. Leaf."

"Suit yourself. She's down by the stream."

Rafe strode out the back door and headed along the dirt path he'd taken the afternoon he'd kissed Susanna. He took the coincidence as a good sign but changed his mind when he heard feminine laughter. Peering through the trees, he saw Susanna and Emily gathering purple flowers from a bush by the stream. A wicker basket sat between them as they worked in the pale sunlight.

Rafe had eavesdropped before and it had paid off. Staying in the shadows, he listened as the women talked about dresses and the upcoming dance Susanna had mentioned to Duke.

"I wish I knew how to dance," Emily said.

Rafe watched as Susanna dropped a handful of flowers into the basket. "Your mother loved to dance. I remember seeing her with your father at socials. Why don't you ask him to teach you?"

Emily heaved a sigh. "He'll tell me I'm too young."

Rafe frowned at the thought. At fifteen, Emily had to be prepared, not just protected. Dancing was harmless as long as she knew the rules. Susanna had stood and turned to the girl. Even from the distance, Rafe could see that she was troubled by Emily's comment.

"Dancing's not hard if you know a few steps," she said. "I'll teach you right now."

"Really?"

"Sure. It'll be fun."

Now this Rafe had to see. Leaning against a tree, he watched as Susanna led Emily into the middle of a grassy circle. She positioned the girl's hand on her shoulder, gave some basic instructions and began to count out the steps. When Emily could manage the simple box step, Susanna began to ta-da a tune, widening the circle until they were whirling in a full-scale waltz. Rafe felt a smile on his lips as the humming filled the air with bittersweet needs. Emily had to find her confidence, and Susanna needed a dance partner who wore trousers instead of a pinafore. Rafe knew just the man for the job.

He stepped to the edge of the meadow but stayed

out of view until Susanna was close enough to touch. Then he stepped forward and tapped her shoulder.

At the sight of him, Emily gasped and stepped back. Susanna turned into his arms. Putting his hands in place, he said, "May I have this dance, Dr. Leaf?"

Her eyes widened with a mix of surprise and longing. "I don't know."

He smiled at Emily to include her in the banter. "Would you mind, Miss Duke?"

Wide-eyed and blushing, Emily said, "Go ahead. I'll head back—"

"You can stay and watch," Susanna said hurriedly.

Rafe didn't want a chaperone, but dancing with Susanna was more than he'd hoped for and he planned to enjoy it. After taking her in his arms, he picked up the ta-das and swept her in circles to the "Blue Danube."

The last time he'd heard the music he'd been in Boston and lusting after a debutante whose name he'd long since forgotten. Looking into Susanna's brown eyes, he knew that he'd never forget anything about this moment. Warm in his arms, she added her voice to their makeshift music, matching him step for step. Forward and back, around and around... they danced with their eyes locked and their hands entwined. Even with a respectful cushion of air between them, Rafe felt as if they were one body. Knowing that Susanna was feeling the same pull, he drew her close enough to kiss.

If Emily hadn't been watching, he'd have done it. With the morning sun pale in the sky and the grass still damp with dew, he'd have brushed Susanna's lips with his, teasing her until she pushed him away or asked for more. He didn't know which one she'd choose, but he wanted to find out. The trick was getting rid of their chaperone.

With a final flourish, he ended the waltz and stepped back. "Thank you, Dr. Leaf."

"The pleasure was mine, Mr. LaCroix."

The formality, he realized, was for Emily. The girl was standing at the edge of the clearing with an almost worshipful look in her eyes. Seeing a chance to charm Susanna, Rafe tipped his hat to the girl. "You have a good teacher, Miss Duke. I hope you have a wonderful time at the dance."

"Thank you," she answered shyly.

Rafe remembered being fifteen all too well. He'd endured pimples, a cracking voice and clumsy moments with girls. He'd also been an outcast— the bastard son who didn't belong in high society but had a claim to a fortune. Emily wasn't alone in her nervousness.

"Want to know a secret?" he asked the girl.

When she blushed, Susanna answered for her. "Sure."

"The boys are more nervous than you are. I'd bet money that a few of them are dancing with broomsticks right now."

Emily looked doubtful. "Not Clint Morgan. He's eighteen."

Rafe glanced at Susanna, who looked torn between warning the girl and encouraging her. Taking the matter in hand, he lowered his chin and tried to sound like an uncle.

"Here's what you do," he said. "If this Clint fellow asks you to dance, say yes. If you like it, smile at him. When he asks again, tell him you're thirsty. If he offers you a cup of punch, you can talk awhile and then dance with him again. But not more than once."

"Why is that?" Susanna asked.

"You should know, Doc." Rafe flashed a smile. "It's biology. Men like the chase."

Emily blushed six shades of red. After stepping to the basket, she lifted it and stepped toward the trail. "I better take these inside."

"Can you set the leaves to dry?" Susanna asked. "I need to talk to Mr. LaCroix."

"Sure."

As the girl ran off, Rafe turned to Susanna. He intended to share a smile, but instead he had a sudden vision of her blue dress baring her shoulders. He blinked and she was dancing with Duke. He'd come to talk about Nick, but the boy could wait a few minutes.

Rafe gave Susanna a stern look. "That advice goes for you, too. Two dances with one man and that's it."

"Absolutely not," she countered. "I'll dance as much as I want and with whom I please."

Rafe didn't care for the idea at all. "If you look half as pretty as you do now, every man in Midas is going to be waiting in line."

She smiled at him. "Isn't that the idea?"

Yes, but Rafe didn't like the pictures in his mind. Old men. Young men. Every one of them enjoying her company while he read stories to Nick. Needing to think, he ambled to the stream and watched the current batter the rocks. If she was going to the dance alone, maybe she wasn't as keen on Duke as he'd thought. From the moment he'd walked into her bedroom, he'd sensed a loneliness about her. But neither was she the kind of person who'd compromise.

She stepped to his side and stood with her arms crossed. "You're starting to sound like my father. He's a bit too protective."

Rafe gave a dry laugh. "A preacher with a shotgun—now there's a picture."

"He's not shy about it, either. The talk goes something like, 'Treat her right or you'll be answering to Smith, Wesson and me.' After one Sunday dinner at the parsonage, most men are gone for good."

Rafe huffed. "If a man's too pitiful to stand up to your pa, he's not worth spit."

"Maybe so."

Rafe saw an opportunity and took it. "If the old goat talked to me like that, I'd tell him to butt out of my business. Then I'd invite you for a walk so we could smooch."

Rafe gave her his best smile. She didn't look bored this time, but neither did she seem impressed. "And do you know what I'd say?"

"Yes?"

"No."

But her eyes were bright and he didn't believe her. Before he could say so, she turned back to the bush with the purple flowers and then glanced along the edges of the meadow. "I was hoping to find autumn crocus," she said. "Horace Little is sure to find me at the dance and ask about his gout."

The shift in topic jarred him. Then he realized what she'd said and scowled. "No man should do that. I don't care if he's ninety years old."

Susanna kept her back to him. "I'm used to it."

"You shouldn't be."

"It comes with being a doctor."

But Rafe had seen her long legs and he'd tasted her lips. Sometimes he thought of her as Dr. Leaf, but right now, she was just Susanna—the woman who'd been haunting his dreams with bare skin and wicked requests. She deserved to know that she had that power over him, so he ambled up behind her and tugged gently on her braid. As her head tilted up, she faced him with her mouth gaping.

"What was that for?" she said.

"To show you that not all men are Horace Little. I'd finish the job by kissing you, but that's not why I came out here."

Rafe tried to read her expression, but she'd put on her doctor face—the blank one that looked at facts and made decisions.

"So why *are* you here?" she asked.

"You told Duke that Nick could be moved today. I'm hoping you'll take a second look at the leg and change your mind."

"Why?"

"I need a place to stay for a few weeks. If you decided that Nick can't be moved after all, Duke might let us stay."

"But it's not true," she answered. "He'd be fine in

the surrey, and I can take better care of him in town. It's been three days. I have to get back."

Rafe held in a cuss word as he stared at the pines. Colder weather was coming, but the cave seemed like the only place they could go. "I guess I'll have to borrow your buggy, but just for a day."

"Where are you going?"

"Back to the cave."

"Absolutely not!"

"Do you have a better idea?"

"As a matter of fact, I do. My parents are back East, which means the parsonage is empty. They boarded the horses before they left, so I'm the only person with a key. It's very private, but you have to promise something."

Rafe wanted to hope, but experience had taught him to be doubtful. He narrowed his eyes. "What's the catch?"

"No smoking in the house. My mother hates tobacco."

Rafe liked a cigar as much as any man, but he could do without them and not think twice. "Are you sure about this?"

"No, but it's best for Nick. I've seen how you are with him, so I'm trusting you."

Even so, her eyes held questions. *Where are you from? Why are you on the run?* Rafe didn't understand how a poultice drew an infection from the body, but he felt that pull on his soul. He wanted to tell her the truth, a dangerous urge because he'd learned never to trust anyone with his secrets.

"I don't know," he said. "Being in town is risky."

"For you, maybe. But not for Nick." Dr. Leaf put on her sternest expression. "The house is stocked with food and wood and has a water closet. Unless you're careless with the lamps, no one will know you're there."

"But what about Nick? People will see you coming to the house."

"I could visit at night, but I'd rather keep Nick with me."

The benefits of the arrangement outweighed the risks. In addition to privacy, he'd have a soft bed, clean sheets and a room all to himself. Even better, the house would be filled with Susanna's secrets. A late-night visit could lead to something fun, maybe a late-night rodeo. Rafe gave her a sincere smile. "Thank you, Doc. I appreciate what you're doing."

"It's for Nick."

"Of course."

"Are you packed? We can leave this morning."

As ready as he was to see the last of Duke, Rafe shook his head. "We'll go this afternoon. I want to arrive in town after dark."

Curiosity filled her eyes, but she didn't waste her breath asking why. "I guess that's all right. There should be a full moon tonight."

He was hoping for clouds but said nothing. As they turned up the trail that cut through the grass, he thought of holding her close and the way she moved, the look in her eyes and Horace Little's gout.

Rafe wasn't cautious by nature. If he cut his hair and wore a suit, he could take Susanna to the dance. People would assume he was a visitor from out of town. He'd be hiding in plain sight where he could listen for news of the Bentons and his guardian angel. But even better, he'd have a night with Susanna.

When he turned in her direction, he saw the sun bright on her face. Her cheeks glowed as if they were dancing again. "I enjoyed dancing with you," he said. "How would you like to do it again?"

She blushed. "Now?"

As tempting as it was, Rafe was hoping for bigger things. "I was thinking of that dance you mentioned to Duke. I'd be happy to take you."

Her expression froze. "I can't. Tim asked last night and I said yes."

Well, hell. Rafe didn't like that turn of events at all. "So tell him you changed your mind and go with me."

When she looked up at the trees, he knew she was

thinking about it. Good, he thought. Feeling naughty would make her blood race. But instead of turning to him, she shook her head. "I won't go back on my word."

Rafe decided to push. "If Duke has to wear a neck tie, he might be glad to get out of it."

"It *is* formal," she answered. "The Santa Fe Railroad picked Midas for their new headquarters. The new train station is opening and so is a hotel. The railroad's shipping in everything—the food, the music, even flowers. It's the biggest thing that's ever happened in Midas."

Rafe held in a curse. He knew the brand of champagne that would be served and how the flowers would be shipped. The train would take on ice near Raton and arrive exactly on time. A railroad depot was the last place he wanted to be seen. But instead of being relieved, he felt cheated. Susanna in blue satin would have been a vision—one that Duke wouldn't appreciate.

He toyed with the idea of talking to her about the man, but the house was in sight and the rancher was standing on the porch with his hands on his hips. That talk about men would have to wait...but not too long.

Chapter Eleven

Three hours later, Susanna was sitting next to Rafe in the surrey with Nick in the back seat. The temperature had dropped by twenty degrees, and the clear sky had turned to silver. She smelled snow in the air and huddled under the blanket Rafe had offered from his things. Behind her, Nick was wrapped up in a wool cocoon and talking so much that she wished she'd given him a dose of chamomile to make him sleep. It was painfully obvious that he wanted a mother, and he'd figured out a way to make that happen.

Rafe, tell Dr. Sue about how you captured Frank Benton....

Rafe, tell her how you found me....

Dr. Sue? Did Rafe show you the engraving on the carbine? He draws roses.

Her heart ached for the boy, but she'd endured enough matchmaking to last a lifetime. Every time an eligible bachelor showed up at church, her mother jabbed her in the ribs. As annoying as Abbie could be, Susanna didn't mind. Her parents had worked hard for their marriage and they wanted her to have the same happiness.

"Dr. Sue?"

She clenched her teeth. "Yes, Nick?"

"Did you know that Rafe can recite whole poems?"

"Is that so?" She tried to sound disinterested, but she glanced at the man sitting next to her. He'd turned up his collar against the cold, but she could see a hint of a smile. Far from being annoyed, he was enjoying Nick's matchmaking. He'd even winked at her, a sign that he knew what Nick was up to, and that had made her even more uncomfortable.

But why? Rafe LaCroix was all charm and no substance. Never mind that dancing with him had been a joy and his kiss still burned inside her. She had to forget the way he made Nick laugh and the shiver she'd felt when he'd tucked the blanket around her hips. There was no point in losing her heart to a man destined to leave. Except he'd already taken a piece of it. She'd yearned to say yes when he'd asked her to the dance, mostly because she understood the offer for the gift it was. He'd been willing to risk himself for her. It was far more than Tim would ever do. Solid and steady, the rancher would never change.

But Rafe could if he wanted to. It was a matter of facing the past. Her parents had done it, and like them, Susanna believed in a God who offered second chances. If Rafe would tell her the truth about who he was and what he'd done, she could help him set down the chip on his shoulder. It was time to ask a few questions of her own.

"Which poems do you know?" she asked.

Nick piped up. "Do 'Charge of the Light Brigade.' That's my favorite."

Rafe shook his head. "I've got something better for Dr. Sue."

"Go right ahead," she said.

"It's Shakespeare. Sonnet One Hundred and Thirty." He gave her a long look. "Do you know it?"

"Not offhand."

With his gaze locked on hers, he made his voice low. "'My mistress' eyes are nothing like the sun; Coral is far more red than her lips red; If snow be white, why then her breasts—'"

"Talk louder," Nick insisted. "I can't hear you."

But Susanna had heard every word. "That was rude."

Rafe put his hand over his heart in feigned shock. "What? Shakespeare? It's poetry, Dr. Leaf. The finest kind."

"You're trying to annoy me. Stop it." As soon as

the command left her lips, she knew he'd take it as a challenge to do the opposite. She needed to turn the tables. "Where did you go to school?"

"Here and there."

"New York?"

He sealed his lips.

"Was it Boston?"

His expression hardened. Boston meant something to him but what? Before she could probe, Nick piped up again. "Dr. Sue? What's your favorite book?"

She answered without thinking. *"Huckleberry Finn."*

"I ain't read that one."

"Haven't read," Rafe said. For the first time, he'd snapped at Nick.

Susanna wanted to ask more questions, but she wouldn't get anywhere as long as the boy was awake. She turned and tucked the blanket higher on his chin. "We can read some of it tonight."

"I'd like that." Nick snuggled down in the blanket and took a deep breath. Susanna hoped he'd fall asleep, but instead he wrinkled his brow. "Rafe?"

"What is it?" The man glared at the road.

"Did you know that Dr. Sue doesn't like peas?"

Heat crept up Susanna's neck. She and Nick had spent hours talking about nonsense. What else would he blurt?

She glanced at Rafe, who seemed relieved to be talking about vegetables instead of himself. "As a matter of fact I did."

Susanna frowned. "How did you know?"

"Last night at supper. You took a bite to be polite, but that was all." Rafe gave her a wily smile. "Do you know what else I've figured out?"

"I'm afraid to ask."

"Blue's your favorite color."

He was right and it irked her. "That was a lucky guess."

"Not at all. I saw your ball gown in the wardrobe." Rafe's gaze lingered on her face, but he spoke to Nick. "It's your turn, kid. Can you name Dr. Sue's favorite candy?"

"Peppermint."

"No, it's Tootsie Rolls. I bet she has some in her pocket right now."

She'd taken a handful for the trip. That knowledge meant that he'd been watching her, noticing things that shouldn't have mattered but were somehow important. Tim didn't even know how she took her coffee,

Rafe smirked at her. "Am I right?"

"I brought them for Nick." She reached into her pocket and gave the boy a piece of candy. She would have taken one for herself, but she didn't want to share with Rafe.

The boy was wide-awake and looking for more questions. "You both saw the angel, didn't you?"

The man hesitated. "I saw Dr. Leaf's shadow."

"It was an *angel,*" Nick insisted. "She had dark hair like my ma, but her eyes were blue like yours."

"I don't know, kid."

When Nick sighed, Susanna turned and adjusted his blanket. The sadness in his eyes broke her heart. "Your ma's still with you, Nick. She's in your heart and she's in heaven. So is the angel."

"Then you believe me?"

"Absolutely." In Susanna's experience, medicine and miracles went hand in hand. When Nick's eyes closed, she faced forward and saw that they had crested a hill. Clouds filled the valley below them, but she knew the mist hid a line of pines and the stream that led to the parsonage. It was a lovely place, but none of that beauty was visible. Susanna had no difficulty in believing in things she couldn't see.

But now we see through a glass darkly...

She loved the old Bible verse. She felt that mystery when looking at a sunset or feeling the sun on her face. A mother giving birth filled her with the same awe, and so did looking into Rafe's eyes. How many bounty hunters could quote Shakespeare? Not many, she guessed. Nor had she ever seen such fine engraving on a gun. Beyond the chip on his shoulders, he had an agile mind and a good heart. Who was he fighting and why? Even hunkered against the weather, he looked like a man staring down an enemy.

"Jeez, it's cold," he muttered.

Susanna didn't want to give him ideas, but she felt bad about hogging his blanket. "If you keep your hands to yourself, I'll sit closer. We can share the blanket."

"You've got a deal."

Being careful to keep air between their hips, she positioned herself next to Rafe and opened the blanket so it would reach across his knees. He took the edge and tucked it under his thigh without saying a word.

They had come a long way since he'd dragged her out of the clinic. Instead of wanting to push him off the seat, she had to resist the urge to scoot closer. His body heat was building under the blanket and curling around her hips. If she touched him, sparks would fly and light a fire. But that couldn't be. She wanted a husband and a family. Rafe LaCroix wanted a night in her bed.

But God help her, she was tempted to touch him.

What would it be like to feel his hands on the secret places of her body? To lie with him on a dark night? Susanna had come to grips with her longings back in Baltimore. Sex was natural and necessary, but she also believed that it was meant to be special. As her father once told a blushing congregation, "Animals mate. People make love. If you don't know the difference, I can't help you."

A smile curled on Susanna's lips. He'd created quite a stir that Sunday. But what about a woman like herself? The hope of marriage faded a little each day, while her desire for a man grew stronger. She felt it most at night when the moon was full and spilling through her window. She wanted to be kissed and held, cherished…possessed.

Rafe's voice cut through her thoughts. "Nick sure can chatter."

"Nick?"

Rafe gave her a peculiar look. "The kid in the back seat. Remember him?"

"Of course," she said, blushing. "Yes, he talks a lot. Most kids do."

"What do you make of his angel?"

Considering her mind had just been in bed with Rafe, it wasn't easy to focus. The moist heat of her thoughts was spreading through her middle and his hard thigh was close enough to touch. She could imagine her fingers on the muscle, traveling from his knee to his… Swallowing hard, she concentrated on the cold mist clinging to her face.

"It could have been the fever," she said. "But I've seen too many miracles to be a skeptic. If Nick says he saw an angel, I believe him."

Rafe shifted his leg so that their shoes touched. "He's got a crush on you, you know."

Common sense told her to move her foot, but she liked the closeness, and she didn't want him to realize that she'd noticed him. "He wants a mother. It's normal."

"What about you, Doc? I bet you want kids."

"A little girl would be nice."

"I can see that. If she's at all like you, she'll be a treasure."

Susanna was imagining a child with Rafe's eyes when he pulled back his foot. "Can I give you some advice?"

"Sure. But I might not take it."

"Don't fool yourself about Duke."

She bristled. "What do you mean?"

"You're too smart for him. Sure, he could give you babies, but the man's a mule."

She felt as if she'd been punched in the chest. She'd already figured that out for herself. "You should mind your own business."

"I'm just telling the truth. He's not right for you."

What could she do? She had to agree or argue. "You're jumping to conclusions. You have no idea what I feel for Tim."

"It's written all over you." Rafe stared straight ahead. "Has he ever kissed the wind out of you?"

She sealed her lips.

"Do you lie awake, thinking about—"

"No!"

"That's what I thought." Rafe lowered his chin. "I've been watching you, Dr. Leaf. You're all mixed up. You don't care about Duke. You're just hungry for a man."

"You're being ridiculous."

"It's the truth." He looked into her eyes. "But Duke doesn't come close to making your toes curl."

Not like I do.

He'd left the words unsaid, but she felt them low in her belly. She respected Tim, but she felt no sparks. Rafe sent flames licking up her spine, but he was a drifter with his eyes on Mexico. Midas was home and she'd never leave. She loved her parents and her brothers. Someday she'd be an aunt.... It would be enough. It had to be.

She was focusing on the empty road when Rafe tugged Lightning to a halt. "What are you doing?"

"I like you, Susanna." His voice was a rumble. "I don't want to see you make a mistake."

A smart woman would have ordered him to get going, but Susanna was feeling a little bit crazy. Her pulse was racing and she could see a matching throb in Rafe's throat. But even more alluring was the caring in his eyes. She slipped off her glove and touched his cheek. In a near whisper, she said, "Who are you?"

"Don't ask."

He reached for the reins, but Susanna had no intention of letting him slip away. She grabbed his wrist. "I'll make you a deal."

His eyes turned fiery. "What do you have in mind?"

"You tell me where you studied Shakespeare, and I'll tell you a secret of my own."

"The biggest one?"

"Yes."

"Forget it, Doc. I already know it."

Susanna squeezed tighter. "I bet you don't."

He took off his glove and touched her chin. His fingers felt hot against her chilled skin, and his eyes burned into hers as he tipped her face to his. "It's obvious, Doc. You want a man in your bed."

Susanna wasn't bothered by frank talk. "That's exactly right. And I want him to be my husband."

He moved an inch so that his breath warmed her face. "You're a demanding woman, Dr. Leaf."

"Do you know what else I want?"

He moved closer still. "Tell me. Or better yet, show me."

Susanna forced herself to breathe. "I want to sleep with my husband like spoons in a drawer. That's my secret."

He lowered his hand, but not before she saw a glimmer of longing in his eyes. But instantly his expression shifted into the mask that belonged to the man who'd offered her money for a night in her bed. Compared to the price she'd named, a thousand dollars was cheap.

He focused his eyes on hers. "If you want a man, I'd be glad to oblige. But it's a one-time event."

Susanna had no intention of saying yes to such a proposition, but neither could she let him win. "I'll keep it in mind."

"Anytime, Doc. Satisfaction guaranteed."

"Is that so?"

"Absolutely. We'll do it all night—kissing, touching, things you've never heard of."

Snakes of desire uncoiled in her belly and slithered down her thighs. Her breasts throbbed and so did her womb. She wanted to taste and touch and experience all the pleasure he promised, but she had meant what she'd said about sleeping like spoons. A single night wasn't enough. Never mind that her insides were burning and she could barely sit still. She wasn't a mare in heat. She had a mind and heart to go with her traitorous body, and she wanted a man who would respect her feelings. Rafe LaCroix wasn't that man. He didn't respect anyone, not even himself.

"Don't hold your breath," she finally said.

His blue eyes stayed locked on hers for a full five seconds, then he broke the stare and picked up the reins. "The offer stands, Dr. Leaf. Just let me know when you're ready."

While sipping bourbon in his hotel room, Garrett thought about the wire he'd just received. It had come from the boss and said, "Please send news."

For the boss's sake, Garrett wanted to reply that he'd found Rafe, but where did a man start looking? Garrett had dropped greenbacks in every shady saloon in Green River, but all he'd learned was that Rafe had left Colorado with a load of money. Some said he'd turned in Frank Benton for the bounty. Others said he'd betrayed the brothers and had made off with their booty.

Garrett didn't know what to make of the news. With Rafe, anything was possible. With his taste for fine things, he might have headed for San Francisco with its dance halls and streets of gold. Or perhaps he'd chosen to ride south. Garrett raised the glass to his lips, then he took a coin from his pocket and tossed it. Heads would send him to California. Tails meant Mexico. He caught the quarter in midair and slapped it on his wrist.

After looking at the result, he put the coin in his pocket and sipped his bourbon. Knowing the boss would be waiting for an answer, he opened his briefcase, withdrew a sheet of paper and wrote out the wire he'd send tomorrow.

Am headed south. Will keep you advised.

Chapter Twelve

By the time they reached Midas, Rafe was hard and angry. The hard part he could understand, but he didn't know why he was angry. Susanna had matched him barb for barb. He enjoyed that kind of sparring with a woman. It was a game he usually won, but Susanna had bested him. He'd spent the past two hours being lonely with an erection that wouldn't go away.

The only consolation was the night sky. Clouds shrouded the moon as he turned down the alley behind her apartment. They had already stopped at the parsonage where he'd left his horses. Now he intended to carry Nick up the stairs, get the key and go back to the house alone. After that, he'd crack open a bottle, get drunk and sleep without dreams of Susanna spooned against him.

"Nick, wake up." She jostled the boy's shoulder.

When he didn't stir, Rafe jumped down from the surrey. "I'll get him. You go on ahead."

As she headed for the stairs, Rafe lifted Nick. The boy mumbled something, but he didn't wake up as Rafe followed Susanna. He paused on the landing while she lit a lamp and then stepped into the entry. The apartment smelled like her, and he could see the wrinkled bed through the rear door. Before this afternoon's conversation, he would have made a racy joke. Instead he followed her into the front room where she was spreading a coverlet on the divan.

"You can put him here," she said.

Rafe lowered Nick to the cushions and then faced her. "I'll see to your horse and then head to the parsonage."

"You'll need the key." She opened a desk drawer and handed him a brass ring. "You can use any of the bedrooms on the second floor."

"Thanks."

Eager to be alone, he put the key in his pocket and turned to leave. He was almost to the door when he heard her let out a breath. "You must be as hungry as I am. I'm going to heat some soup. Would you like some?"

Rafe's stomach growled, but a man ate soup with a spoon and he didn't want to think about it. "I've got jerky. That's enough."

Before she could tempt him more, he strode out the door and down the stairs. Grateful for the darkness, he hurried to the edge of town where he took a muddy path that led to the parsonage. After collecting his saddlebags from the stable, he climbed the back steps to the house and let himself in.

Even in the dark, the kitchen felt alive. He could imagine Susanna's brothers eating breakfast before school, making jokes and kicking each other under the table. He smelled traces of yeast and apples coming from the stove, and someone had left the pantry ajar.

Rafe couldn't remember the last time he'd set foot in a real home. He didn't count the mansion that had belonged to his father. As for the boardinghouses where he'd stayed with Lem, they had provided shelter but nothing more. Even when he and Lem had taken their meals at crowded tables, Rafe had felt like an outsider.

He didn't feel that way in the parsonage. As he lit the lamp on the kitchen table, the house seemed to breathe a welcome, pulling him upstairs where he found four bedrooms. Judging by the toys, the two closest to the stairs belonged to her brothers. He ruled out the first one because it held a set of bunk beds that wouldn't hold his long frame. The second room offered a decent-sized bed, but it felt too much like his boyhood room in New Orleans.

Rafe poked his head into a third room. It looked

like a guest room, but the rope bed frame didn't have a mattress on it. Fearing what he'd find, he walked to the end of the hall and stepped into the last room.

Susanna was everywhere—in the books on the shelves and the pictures on the walls. In the collection of horse carvings on the bureau. But most of all, she was in the bed where he'd be sleeping for the next few weeks. He turned to go back to the bunk beds but changed his mind. What the devil was he running from? Certainly not a red-and-blue log cabin quilt.

He dropped his saddlebag on the floor and set the lamp on the nightstand. After retrieving his whiskey flask, he shrugged out of his duster, sat on the bed and took off his boots. How long had it been since he'd slept in his long johns or nothing at all? Months, he figured, but he would tonight.

At least he hoped he could sleep. He couldn't escape the sense of Susanna. The room held her childhood treasures, but Rafe had seen a wildness in her eyes when he'd offered to take her to bed. The woman was itching for a long, hard ride and so was he. He thought briefly of a late-night visit to the saloon and an upstairs room, but it held no appeal. Not when he compared it to being Susanna's first lover. What would that be like? To feel her body shaping itself to him, to see the discovery in her eyes and to hear soft cries coming from her throat?

He was dead sure that she'd be enthusiastic, even demanding. That was fine with Rafe. He rather liked the idea of getting her all stirred up and then making her wait for just right moment.

Rafe grabbed the flask and pulled the cork. If he kept thinking this way, he'd be tossing all night long. Instead he raised the bottle to his lips and took four long swallows. When the picture of Susanna blurred, he stripped down to his long johns. By the time he pulled back the quilt, his mind had slowed to a crawl. He was grateful for the haze, but the clean sheets brought Susanna back into the bed. He wanted to hold her close and lose himself inside her, to taste her skin and suckle her breasts. To go to the place where he could feel good and not be on edge. He rolled from his back to his side, and then flopped onto his belly.

He thought about taking care of the problem himself, but he feared that the physical release would make him feel worse. He could stand being lustful. Admitting that he'd fallen in love was another matter. Annoyed, he pushed up on one elbow, drained the flask and dropped back down on the mattress. Feeling foolish, he wadded up the quilt and pressed it to his belly. Then he bent his knees and hugged it. It wasn't the same as spooning Susanna, but tonight it would have to do. Contented at last, he closed his eyes and slept.

* * *

Susanna heard three sharp raps on the apartment door and wished again that she'd canceled the evening with Tim. She'd known it was a mistake since she left the ranch, but she had no way to get word to him. She also had an obligation to Emily, who had come to the clinic this afternoon for a last-minute dance lesson.

As nice as it felt to be dressed up, she would have preferred a night in her apartment with Nick and the checkerboard. Sometimes Rafe joined them later in the evening. After eating a bite of supper, he'd read Nick to sleep while she pretended to be studying a medical journal. When the boy dozed off, he'd turn down the lamp and ask her about her day. Seated on opposite sides of the room, they sometimes talked through the night. She told him about her work, her family, her dream of building an up-to-date clinic. She even had the land picked out and a sketch of the floor plan.

She still didn't know why Rafe was on the run, but he'd entertained her with tales about Lem and their bounty-hunting days. Once he mentioned growing up in New Orleans, but the middle years were lost.

A fourth knock interrupted her thoughts. "Just a minute."

The plan for the evening included Rafe sitting

with Nick, but he'd been adamant about arriving after she'd left with Tim. He'd made a joke of it, but Susanna had seen heat in his eyes. She wasn't foolish enough to think Rafe was jealous, but the thought gave her a bit of satisfaction. He'd been a perfect gentleman since their go-round in the surrey, but she hadn't forgotten how he'd made her feel.

Pushing back the memory, Susanna opened the door and smiled at Tim. "Come on in."

The instant he stepped into the light, she wished that she'd feigned a headache. His suit was dull brown and a size too small. His hair, slicked back with pomade, made his forehead look bulbous. Susanna held in a sigh. Tim was trying as hard as she was. She felt sorry for them both and forced a smile. "I'll say goodbye to Nick and then we can go."

She had placed her wrap by the door, but Tim didn't notice it. Empty-handed, he followed her into the front room where Nick was on the divan with *Kidnapped*. Rafe had found the book in the parsonage and loaned it to Nick with her permission.

"Where's your friend?" Tim asked the boy.

Nick looked at Susanna for guidance, so she answered for him. "He's staying in town until Nick can ride. Then they'll be on their way."

"That's good news." Tim gave Nick a nod. "I'm glad you're better."

"Thank you." The boy had sounded polite, but his face drooped with disappointment.

Tim led the way to the door. As he held it open, Susanna lifted her wrap off the coat tree and draped it over her shoulders. When he offered his arm, she took it and they walked down the stairs. With each thud of his boots, she felt more depressed. By the time they reached the boardwalk, she had forgotten about dancing entirely. With a little luck, Horace Little would ask her about his gout.

As soon as Susanna and Duke rounded the corner, Rafe made a beeline for her apartment. He'd arrived early and had been lingering across the street where he had a view of the stairs. He'd wanted to see her in that blue dress, and he'd enjoyed a long look.

She had been as lovely as he'd expected. A fringed shawl had hidden her shoulders, but the gown hugged her waist and flared over her hips. It wasn't hard to imagine a satin corset cinched tight. As for her stockings, he'd seen white ones in her bureau, but she probably had something fancy for a dance. Maybe black silk with roses embroidered on the ankle.

Rafe had gotten a glimpse of Duke, too. The man had as much style as an old saddle, but Rafe had decided last week to keep his mouth shut. Susanna was right—her personal life was none of his concern. Never mind that he would have shown her the time of her life. He'd have brought her flowers and told her she looked beautiful. They would have danced all night and walked in the moonlight. He'd have kissed her at the bottom of the stairs and again on the landing.

Rafe blew out a breath as he trotted up the steps. He let himself inside and found Nick in the front room with the checkerboard on a low table. After hanging up his hat, he pulled up a chair. "Red or black?"

Nick grinned. "Black."

The color of Susanna's stockings. Rafe clenched his jaw. He was going to be thinking about her all night. "Fire before smoke," he said as he arranged the disks. "I go first."

A first kiss...a first dance...her first time... Rafe tried to block his thoughts by sliding a checker to the center of the board.

Nick made a move and then sighed. "She sure looked pretty."

"I bet so." Rafe took his turn and waited for Nick to reply, but the boy slid a checker without another word.

He'd gotten a glimpse of Susanna, but he wanted to know more. Had Duke told her she looked pretty?

Had she been smiling? A gentleman took charge and made a lady feel safe, at least that's what Mimi had taught her son. It was also a lesson Nick would need when he grew to be a man. Rafe moved a checker. "There are things a gentleman does when he takes a lady to a dance. Did Duke bring her flowers?"

"Nope."

"He should have." Rafe would have brought her roses.

The boy couldn't have cared less, but Rafe wasn't finished. "How did Duke look? Did he dress up?"

Nick wrinkled his nose. "His hair looked funny. It was slicked back."

Rafe stifled a groan. Stylish or not, pomade was an abomination. No woman wanted to run her fingers through a head full of grease. He slid another checker into place. "Did he tell Dr. Sue she looked nice?"

"Nope," Nick answered. "But *I* thought she was pretty. I told her so, too."

A slow burn started in Rafe's belly. Duke should have showered Susanna with compliments—and not just for her looks. She had a presence that filled a room, a smile that put everyone at ease. She deserved a night of fun. Instead she'd be dancing with a pomade-covered mule.

When Rafe moved a checker without thinking, Nick jumped five of his men. "King me!"

That did it. King Henry had better watch out, because Rafe wasn't about to let Susanna spend the night dancing with a man who didn't appreciate her. If he put on his best clothes, he'd blend in with the crowd. And if he cut his hair, he'd be even harder to recognize. He looked across the board at Nick. "How are you doing on those crutches?"

"Pretty good. I can move around the apartment now." Nick looked up. "Why are you asking?

"I have to go somewhere, but I don't like leaving you alone."

"Heck, I lived alone for a whole month." The boy's eyes lit up. "You're going to rescue Dr. Sue, aren't you?"

"That's right, kid. She deserves a good time, and I'm going to give it to her."

After a single polka, Tim escorted Susanna to the sidelines and offered her a cup of punch. She accepted it with a smile, but it was Rafe's face that shimmered in her memory, along with his advice to Emily.

If he offers you a cup of punch, you can dance with him again.

Only Susanna had no desire for another turn

on the dance floor with Tim. He was a competent dancer, but he didn't enjoy it like Rafe did. As hard as she tried, Susanna couldn't shake the memory of their dance in the meadow and the knowledge that he moved as she did. The rhythm of that waltz had soaked into her body and touched her soul, taking her to the edge of the mystery of a man and woman moving in perfect time.

"Susanna?" Tim's voice broke into her thoughts. "This is Charles Logan. He's my neighbor to the east."

Susanna offered her hand and realized that she'd broken a rule. Women didn't normally shake hands, but she had insisted on that equality at Johns Hopkins.

Looking surprised, Charles Logan shook and introduced her to his sister, a woman named Eleanor who was about Susanna's age. Small talk revealed that the woman had come from Ohio and would be keeping house for her brother. When Susanna mentioned she was a doctor, Eleanor raised her eyebrows.

"Isn't that disturbing work for a woman?"

"Not at all," Susanna replied.

"But it's so unladylike."

"Perhaps, but I like helping people." Having endured this conversation before, Susanna met the woman's critical appraisal. "I'm also in favor of women's suffrage and changing divorce laws. Have you read anything by Susan B. Anthony?"

"No, I certainly haven't." Eleanor offered a faint smile, then turned to the men and pretended to be fascinated by a discussion of cattle prices.

Susanna wanted to plead a headache and leave, but it was too soon. Instead she excused herself from Tim and looked for Emily. She spotted the girl looking lovely and excited as she sipped punch with Clint Morgan. When they left to dance, Susanna ambled to the refreshment table. She was about to help herself to a chocolate biscuit when the orchestra struck the first notes of "The Blue Danube."

The music spread through her veins, bringing with it a sense of Rafe. She could smell his skin and hear the rhythm of his breath. With that awareness came the sense of a man standing behind her. The bay rum belonged to Rafe but not the soap. And yet it was familiar...a mix of lilac and witch hazel, like the brand her mother kept in the parsonage.

Before she could look, Rafe's deep voice reached her ear. "Good evening, Dr. Leaf."

With chills shimmering down her spine, she turned and studied the stranger behind her. The blue eyes belonged to Rafe, but everything else about him was brand-new. Instead of denim, he was wearing a black suit with an ascot tie that made him both sophisticated and rakish. Even more eye-catching was his hair. He'd cut it short and combed it away from his face. The new cut showed off his fine cheek bones and the warmth of his smile.

He held out his hand. "May I have this dance?"

Yes... Yes... Yes...

But Susanna felt a flutter of warning. She could say no to the bounty hunter who made rude propositions, but this man had the power to break her will. Not because he was poised and polished—she wasn't fooled by his fancy clothes. What made her blood race was the knowledge that he'd cut his hair for her. Why was he taking this chance? What did he want? She didn't know, but she could guess, mostly because she couldn't look at him without thinking of forbidden things. She'd have to be crazy or stupid to dance with this man. She wasn't stupid, but crazy was another matter.

Rafe took her hand and kissed the top of it. "Say yes, Susanna."

When his eyes found hers, she saw a mix of challenge and mirth. He'd enjoyed surprising her. Another shiver ran down her spine and into her toes. The night was alive and full of possibilities. Maybe she'd offer a surprise of her own. Or maybe not. She didn't know what she wanted, so she smiled at him. "It's 'The Blue Danube.'"

His voice turned husky. "It's for us."

As Susanna stepped forward, Rafe swept her onto the dance floor and into the music. Her blood thrummed with the rhythm and pleasure of matching his steps. With each turn he pulled her closer until his arm was around her waist and her skirt was tangling with the wool of his trousers. Even with their straight-backed posture, she felt as if they were molded together. Yet the distance between them was perfectly respectable.

Rafe brought his mouth to her ear and whispered, "You're even more beautiful than I imagined."

Heat raced to Susanna's cheeks. "And what have you imagined?"

A low hum had spilled from his throat. "Since I'm being a gentleman tonight, I won't answer that."

They should have been on familiar ground—the place where Rafe pushed and she said no—but this man was a stranger. Needing answers, she tipped her face up to his. "You bear a striking resemblance to a bounty hunter I once met."

His eyes burned into hers. "I know him well."

"Is he a friend of yours?"

"More like a distant cousin."

"Tell me more."

A wry smile curled his lips. "He's a dangerous man, Dr. Leaf. You should keep your distance."

Susanna shook her head. "The man I know has a good heart. He's not nearly as tough as he wants me to think."

Refusing to look away, Susanna waited for Rafe to reply. Slowly she became aware of his hand on her back, sliding from a respectable position on her waist to the bottom of her corset and finally to the upper curve of her bottom. The heat of him passed through the silk and into her skin.

Desire filled his eyes. "Do you still think LaCroix's harmless?"

"Absolutely."

But she had lied. Desire was slithering around her hips and up through her chest. It traveled higher still to her imagination—the most dangerous place of all. She blinked and saw them together in her bedroom. She inhaled and felt Rafe breathing with her.

Challenging her with his eyes, he pulled her an inch closer. His touch was commanding, even possessive, and she flushed in his arms.

A night with Rafe...mysteries revealed.

Susanna knew what she wanted—flowers and courtship, a gold band—but what if love wasn't in her future? What if tonight was her only chance to cross that line?

With the music rising and Rafe's eyes on hers, Susanna weighed the risks. She'd been born because of a night of passion and her parents had paid for that choice. But Susanna knew her body and how to avoid conception. Her monthly was due in two days. As far as a woman could be certain, this was a safe time of the month.

Shaking inside, she raised her fingers to the nape of his neck and caressed the strip of warm skin between his collar and hairline. When his muscles tensed, she smiled and stroked him again.

Rafe's eyes burned into hers. "I've been having dreams."

Me, too.

But she couldn't find her voice. So much was at stake. If she let Rafe take her to bed, she'd never be the same. But wasn't that the point? She was tired of being curious. She wanted to experience passion for herself. But she also wanted forever and not just a night. As the waltz came to an end, the violinist held a high note until it quivered to silence. All around them couples were linking arms. Some were strolling to the sidelines, while others gazed at each other in anticipation of another dance, a kiss, maybe a lifetime together.

Susanna pushed back a swell of envy and faced a simple truth. She was tired of being naive and sick of being alone. Knowing she couldn't go back, she reached for Rafe's hand and said, "Take me home."

Unless Rafe had lost his knack for reading women, "Take me home" had meant "Take me to bed." He wasn't sure what to make of Susanna's request. He'd come tonight with the best of intentions—to rescue her from Duke and protect her from a pack of wolves. Instead she was flirting with the biggest wolf of all.

He should have been eager to whisk her out the door, but he'd come to waltz with her and treat her right. A few more turns around the dance floor wouldn't hurt at all. In fact, dancing close would make the rest of the night even better. As the orchestra began to play, he smiled at her. "I like dancing with you. Let's stay a bit longer."

She shook her head. "I want to leave right now."

Rafe didn't understand the hurry, unless it had something to do with Duke. Cold fury settled into his belly. "Did Duke do something? Did he—"

"Not at all," she insisted. "I just want to leave. I'll make an excuse to Tim and meet you outside."

Who was Rafe to argue with a lady? Besides, every minute he spent at the dance brought him closer to being recognized. "I'll wait by the door."

"I'll be there in two minutes."

The promise in her voice gave him ideas, but Rafe couldn't shake the sense that something was wrong. She was in too much of a hurry—like a person mustering the courage to jump off a cliff.

When the orchestra struck up a reel, Rafe guided her into the crowd where he spotted Duke approaching them with his youngest daughter in tow.

After a snide glance at Rafe, he spoke to Susanna. "We have to go. Bonnie's not feeling well."

Susanna put her palm on the child's forehead. "What's wrong, honey?"

"Noth—"

"She ate too much candy," Duke said. "I'm taking her to my sister's house. Sorry to cut things short, but I have to take you home."

Over Rafe's dead body. Using his best manners, he addressed Duke. "If Dr. Leaf agrees, I'd be glad to look out for her."

"This conversation isn't necessary, " Susanna said archly. "I can take care of myself."

"I can't allow it," Duke insisted.

Rafe wanted to throttle the man, but it wasn't his place. Instead he glanced at Susanna whose eyes had filled with pity. "I'm sorry, Tim. I encouraged you, but tonight was a mistake."

Duke huffed through his nose. "You're right about that. You're too uppity by half."

"Hold it right there." Rafe's voice was a growl. "You owe Dr. Leaf an apology."

Duke saw Rafe's fury and relaxed his stance. "I'm sorry, Susanna. That was uncalled-for."

"Apology accepted," she answered. "I hope we can be friends."

After a grunt, the rancher muttered, "I guess." Then he lifted Bonnie and headed for the door.

Rafe turned to Susanna and took her hand. "Do you still want to leave?"

"More than ever."

So did Rafe. The argument with Duke had drawn a handful of curious spectators, mostly biddies with nothing better to do. Gossip was the last thing he needed. Nor did he want Susanna to be the focus of worthless talk.

He held out his arm. "Let's go."

She took it and followed him to the cloakroom where he tipped the clerk and then helped her with the shawl. The back door was closest, so they slipped outside and walked through an alley to the main street. As soon as they reached the boardwalk, Susanna picked up her pace.

Rafe figured she was either eager to be alone or freezing to death. He wasn't in the mood to hurry, so he clasped her elbow and slowed her to a halt in front of a dress shop. The black glass caught their reflections as she pivoted and faced him with her chin tilted up and her eyes ablaze. He could see the creases at the corners of her mouth, the powder she'd put on her nose and a faint sheen on her lips because she had just licked them. Wanting to make the night last, he shrugged out of his coat and held it for her. "Put this on."

Smiling at him, she slipped the shawl off and put her arms through the sleeves. When she straightened the jacket, her dress pulled tight across her breasts, revealing their fullness and the cleft between them. Rafe took the shawl from her hand and draped it around her neck, freeing her hand so he could hold it. She looked beautiful and eager, but he couldn't forget the expression he'd seen in her eyes at the dance. He wasn't sure what she needed tonight, but he was determined to give it to her. "Let's slow down," he said.

When she nodded, he put his arm around her waist and tucked her against his ribs. Side by side, they walked past storefronts until they reached the front of her office. A cloud shifted over the moon, turning the night even darker. When Rafe squeezed her hand, she squeezed back—a silent acknowledgment that she wanted more than a kiss good-night.

So did Rafe. Not once in his life had he said no to a woman and he didn't want to start tonight. At the base of the stairs, he pulled Susanna fully into his arms. Looking into her eyes, he matched his mouth to hers and kissed her as if they had all night. She wasn't the least bit shy. For every glide of his lips, she matched him with a demand of her own. He felt her hands in his hair and then on his back, exploring his muscles and holding him close.

Wanting to feel more—needing her—he slid his hands inside the coat and caressed her shoulder blades, her spine, the curve of her waist. As the silk turned hot beneath his hands, their kiss caught fire all over again. She wanted him in her bed. He was sure of it, but he couldn't shake a sense of worry.

With the taste of her on his lips, he eased the kiss and looked into her eyes. The clouds had drifted by, giving full glory to the moon and the dazed expression on her face. Rafe felt his stomach twist into a knot. They were back on the cliff and she was mustering the courage to jump. He knew it would be a thrilling fall. They'd plunge together into a lake of pleasure. The water would engulf them and they'd gasp for air. Then they'd surface together and jump again.

It sounded like pure pleasure—except the water was deep and Susanna didn't know how to swim.

Instead of asking her if she was sure, he tucked her head under his chin and stroked her hair. He noticed the blackboard where she'd written "At the train depot." Those chalky letters said everything about the differences between them. He never told anyone where he was going, and she always left a note.

Still holding her close, Rafe imagined swimming in that lake of fire. But he knew in his gut that part of her would drown. She wanted to sleep like spoons and he'd be gone in the morning and again in a few weeks. Then there was the matter of babies. He was careful when it came to sowing his wild oats, and he didn't have a French letter. But even if he'd had one, it wouldn't have mattered. He couldn't imagine barriers with Susanna. Sex was supposed to be wet and messy. Couples tasted and touched and forgot about everything but each other. A least that's what Rafe had in mind.

Knowing he'd feel like a fool and that she might hate him for it, he tipped back her head and kissed her forehead. "Good night, Dr. Leaf."

Her mouth gaped. "You're *leaving?*"

"That's right."

She grasped his shirt. "But I want you to stay."

Her breath warmed his face and weakened his knees. He told himself to let go of her, but instead he caressed the shell of her ear with his fingers. "Go on, Doc. Get upstairs before I change my mind."

A slap to his face would have been kind. Instead she tangled her fingers in his hair and gave him a tender kiss. The sweetness was cruel to the extreme, and the press of her breasts was added torture. But it was nothing compared to his awareness of her hips. Rafe pulled his mouth from hers and moaned into her ear. "Don't tempt me, Susanna. I'm trying to do the right thing."

She went still in his arms, murmured something and stepped back. Huddling in his coat, she looked into his eyes. "Why now?"

Rafe clenched his jaw. "I think I…" *Love you.*

Hell would freeze before he'd say those words to her. His life was a mess and he didn't want to hurt her. She belonged in Midas and he was headed to Mexico. But neither could he say something mean just to push her away. His conscience was gossamer thin, but it saved him now. "As much as I want you right now, I don't think it's right for either of us. I'm trying to protect you."

She took his hand in both of hers, raised it to her lips and kissed his knuckles. It was a blessing of sorts and he felt proud. He also needed to get away from her before he changed his mind.

"Go on," he said. "Get inside before you catch a chill."

He saw a twinkle in her eyes and felt like a fool.

When had he become the doctor? He never talked about things like chills. Nor had he ever turned down a willing woman.

Susanna gave his hand a squeeze and then started to remove his coat. "You'll need this back."

"Keep it," he said. "I'll get it later."

He watched as she walked up the stairs. When she reached the landing, she smiled at him.

"Good night, Rafe."

"Good night, Doc."

As she lingered on the landing, moonlight stretched her shadow across the wall. Rafe thought of Nick's angel—tall and strong in the middle of the night. He didn't want to believe in miracles, but something had happened to him tonight. For the first time, he'd done the right thing. Was it a miracle? It had to be. The other explanation was to believe in his own good intentions, and that was more ridiculous than believing in angels.

As soon as Susanna shut the door, Rafe took off for the parsonage. Whiskey was a poor substitute for holding her in his arms, but tonight it would have to do.

Being careful not to awaken Nick, Susanna stood at the window overlooking the street and watched Rafe walk away. She wanted to be disappointed in how the evening had ended, but she couldn't deny the relief that had come when he'd refused her. She wasn't afraid of making love—she could hardly wait—but she also knew that she'd been settling for less than she wanted. As surely as Tim was less than the man she wanted for a husband, a single night was less than she wanted from Rafe.

Hugging herself inside his coat, she breathed in his scent and recalled the taut muscles in his back. She'd kissed him and knew how he tasted. Was a night better than nothing? She didn't know, but another truth fell in her stomach like a stone. Rafe was two men. The rogue at the dance had broken her will. In spite of her dreams of a husband, she had been ready to go to bed with him without the benefit of marriage. The gentleman who'd just left had been just as dangerous, maybe more so. When he'd left, he'd taken her heart.

Clutching the lapels of the coat, Susanna closed her eyes and sighed. Tonight she'd fallen in love with Rafe LaCroix and there wasn't a thing she could do about it. He was a man with secrets and he was headed to Mexico. Tonight had ended for the best.

Susanna went into her bedroom and closed the door. Using a buttonhook, she undid the back of her dress and let it fall to the floor. Then she tugged on the ribbons to the corset and peeled it away from her skin. Her camisole and stockings came next. Shivering, she put on her flannel nightgown and pulled the covers up to her chin, wondering what she would do if Rafe came back.

Chapter Thirteen

"Rafe? I've been thinking."

The kid had been doing a lot of it lately. That's why Rafe had taken him fishing in spite of the nip in the air. The stream behind the parsonage still carried a few trout, and the cottonwoods had turned bright yellow. It was a perfect place for a man to sit and let his thoughts unfold.

Rafe had discovered it after the dance. Instead of holing up in the parsonage with a bottle, he'd walked toward the rushing water and sat on a rock, shivering because Susanna had his coat. The cold air had cured what ailed him and he'd felt better than he had in years. For both their sakes, he'd vowed to keep away from Susanna.

As much as he missed her, he had no regrets. Getting tangled up in his life could only bring her heartache. He also had to consider Nick. The boy had fallen for her as hard as he had. Neither of them had mentioned Mexico in days, but the circumstances hadn't changed. Rafe would be leaving soon. The choice to go with him or stay in Midas would be Nick's.

Rafe looked upstream where the boy was perched on a slab of granite with his crutches propped at an angle. The pole in his hand belonged to one of Susanna's brothers and made him look carefree. Rafe envied that innocence. For himself, he had taken a longer pole with a thick handle and a fancy reel.

As a fish swam past his hook, he answered Nick. "So what's on your mind, kid?"

"Do you think you're still being followed?"

"I'm sure of it."

"When do you think we'll have to leave?"

Rafe heard the *have to* and felt bad. He'd enjoyed living in the parsonage. Between the bookshelves and John Leaf's gun cabinet, he had spent hours speculating about Susanna and her family. He'd even skimmed through the family Bible where he'd seen a genealogy. On Abigail's side, the family tree stretched back for five generations. But the Leaf side started with John, as if he had no mother or father.

As he watched the fishing line bob in the current, Rafe wished his own father was that easy to forget. Without his guardian angel hunting him down, he could have settled in Midas and started a new life. But that wasn't possible.

"It depends on your leg," he said to Nick.

"Can we stay for Thanksgiving?"

November had arrived a few days ago. Rafe blinked and imagined the three of them sitting at Susanna's table with pies and platters of food. They'd play checkers and tell silly stories, then Nick would go to sleep and he'd kiss her for the last time. What harm could there be in making a memory? "Turkey sounds good."

"That's great," Nick declared. "They make a turkey *and* a ham."

Rafe's nerves prickled. "Who are 'they'?"

"Her parents. They're going to be back in two weeks."

Rafe felt like a fish that had taken the bait and been jerked out of the water. "This may not work."

"It'll be fun," Nick insisted. "Reverend Leaf and J.J. hunt for the turkey, and her mother makes the pies. Susanna makes fudge and everyone eats and plays games. I bet I can win at checkers."

"You probably could."

Rafe nearly strangled on the words. He'd spent hours studying the Leaf family photographs on the hearth. A double frame held pictures of Susanna and her father, while a row of others showed Abigail in her wedding gown, Susanna's half-brother who was away at college and poses of the three boys looking rascally.

Nick's smile lit up his face. "Did you know that she has four brothers and three of them are my age?"

Rafe knew their names and more. The twins were called Silas and Law and collected toy trains. John Jr. devoured detective stories. The oldest brother, Robert, was listed in the family Bible but had the last name of Windsor. Rafe guessed there was a story to tell.

"I know all about her family," he said mildly.

Nick jiggled the line. "I wish I had brothers."

"I know how that is."

"Do you think I might have one someday? Not a blood brother, but maybe... I don't know."

Hoping to stop Nick's train of thought, Rafe pulled his line out of the water and checked the hook. The worm had wiggled away, so he put on another one and reset the line. "The fish aren't biting, are they? I guess it's late in the year."

"Uh-huh."

He tried again. "I bet the fishing's good in Mexico."

When the boy looked up, Rafe saw a world of hurt in his eyes. "You like Susanna a lot, don't you?"

"I do."

"She likes you, too."

Rafe heard the question Nick didn't have the heart to ask. "I have to leave, kid. But if you want to stay, I understand."

"But you're my best friend."

"And you're mine." Rafe swallowed back a lump. "Nothing will change that."

The boy looked to the stream. "Can I think about it?"

"Of course."

Rafe had no doubt which road the boy would choose. He knew what *he* would have done. He'd have courted Susanna properly, opened a gunsmithing business and made her proud. As for those brothers Nick wanted, Rafe imagined a little girl with her mother's brown eyes.

The thought sent him down a lonely road that ended in saying goodbye. He'd rarely done it in his life and decided he wouldn't do it now. When the time was right, he'd leave a letter and disappear. Rafe was dreading that moment when he felt a tug on the line. As soon as the fish took the bait, he reeled it out the water. He'd clean it and give it to Susanna to cook for supper, but he wouldn't be sitting at her table. Never mind that she had him hook, line and sinker...he couldn't stay.

* * *

"The baby's due in June," Susanna said to Melissa.

She had just finished examining the girl and the two were talking in the back office. The room had once been a haven for Susanna, but now it held the memory of her first encounter with Rafe. For the past week, he'd avoided her and she'd been grateful—almost.

She pushed the candy jar toward her patient. "Try a lemon drop. Sour things might settle your stomach."

Melissa did as Susanna urged, but they both knew a piece of candy couldn't touch her real problem. As she popped the sweet into her mouth, she slumped in her chair. "My father thinks I should go away for a while."

"It's an option." Susanna's heart broke for the girl. At seventeen, she had no resources of her own. "How do you feel about it?"

"I don't know. If I keep the baby, it won't have a father. I'd be so ashamed. I could live somewhere else and say I was a widow, but where could I go? I don't know how to do anything but housework. Besides, this is my home. I don't want to leave."

Susanna understood how Melissa felt. She couldn't imagine leaving her family and living on letters, or worse, having no contact at all. "That's true."

"There's something else." Melissa lowered her eyes. "I can't stand the way people stare at me. They know what happened."

Sympathetic or not, people liked to gossip and Melissa had endured everything from curious stares to pity. "I wish I could fix it," Susanna said. "Someday it'll pass, but right now it's hard."

Melissa twisted the hankie in her lap. "There's something else, but I can hardly say it."

"Whatever it is, you need to get it out." Susanna spoke gently but with authority. Sometimes being a doctor meant causing pain to find the source of it.

"I *hate* Zeke Benton." Sobs racked Melissa's thin body as she squeezed her hankie. "How can I love his baby? Or maybe I *do* love it. I want it to have a good home with nice things, but I can't buy her clothes or even feed her without help from my pa."

Back in a Baltimore clinic, Susanna had helped other women with Melissa's burden. The circumstances always broke her heart. "Have you thought about adoption?"

The girl took a deep breath and sagged with relief. "I don't know what else to do."

"Maybe I can help you," Susanna said. "Do you have family outside of Midas?"

"Only an aunt, but I don't like her."

"Any cousins?"

"No one."

Susanna knew of a home for unwed mothers in Baltimore, but New Orleans was closer. She'd been avoiding Rafe since the dance, but the time had come to pay a call on him at the parsonage. She wasn't sure what to say about the aftermath of the dance, but his absence was hurting Nick. The boy hadn't been himself, and that fishing trip had made him even more silent. Melissa's situation was the final excuse Susanna needed to confront him, and she decided to go tonight.

"There's a home in New Orleans that's run by nuns," she said. "I'll found out more about it."

"I'd appreciate it."

As Melissa pushed to her feet, Susanna walked around her desk and gave her a hug. Together they walked to the street where Melissa's father was waiting in the family wagon. After a round of promises to visit, Melissa's father steered the wagon down the street.

"Dr. Leaf?"

Susanna looked to her right and saw a man in his thirties. He was dressed in an expensive suit, but life hadn't been kind to him. A scar ran across the orbit of his right eye and down his cheek. The eye itself was lazy, a sign of blindness, and he was carrying a cane. Without the scars, he would have been a handsome man with sandy hair, hazel eyes and a square jaw.

"Can I help you?" she asked.

"I hope so." The stranger handed her a photograph. "Do you recognize this man?"

There was no mistaking the angry slant of Rafe's mouth and his pale eyes. Judging by the crest on his coat, she was looking at a graduation picture from Hamptonshire, a distinguished boys' academy in Boston. A classmate at Hopkins had attended the school and bragged about it. Susanna blanked her expression. She wasn't about to reveal Rafe's where-abouts to a stranger, but she also saw a chance to glean information. She handed back the photograph. "I saw this man two weeks ago."

"Is he still in town?"

"I doubt it. I figured he was a drifter."

"Why did he come to you?"

Susanna gave him the look she used on stingy bankers. "I don't gossip about my patients."

The stranger frowned. "Did he mention where he was headed?"

"No, and I didn't ask."

"What about his name. He goes by Rafe LaCroix. Is that familiar?"

"I don't recall."

As the man leaned more heavily on his cane, Susanna glanced at the handle where she saw a silver casing studded with three rubies. Her visitor wasn't a lawman or a Pinkerton's detective. Wealth oozed from his pores. Wanting information but afraid of revealing her connection to Rafe, Susanna tried to appear casual. "Why are you looking for him?"

The stranger forced a smile. "Excuse my lack of manners. My name is Thomas Smith. Mr. LaCroix has inherited a large sum of money. I was asked by the family to locate him."

The cane gave credence to the man's claim, but Susanna suspected he'd made up the story on the spot. An inheritance struck her as too convenient, a device designed to tug on her goodwill. Even his plain name had a false ring to it.

Susanna considered quizzing the man, but she wasn't a good liar. With a false word she could give away Rafe's presence without understanding the cost. Before she said anything else to Thomas Smith, she wanted to hear the truth from Rafe.

To end the conversation, she stepped to the clinic door. "I wish I could help, but that's all I know."

The stranger moved the cane so that the rubies caught the light. "You should know there's a reward for information regarding Mr. LaCroix."

Susanna could only stare. "How much?"

"A thousand dollars in gold."

The sum was huge by anyone's standards, but the thought of money for betraying Rafe was repulsive to her. Still, she had to wonder what he had done. Susanna forced herself to shrug. "Like I said, I don't know anything else."

Thomas Smith had cat eyes and they were glimmering. "If you think of something, I'll be at the Midas Hotel."

"For how long?" she asked, thinking of Rafe.

"As long as necessary." After a tip of his hat, Thomas Smith turned his back and limped down the boardwalk.

Melissa had been her last patient, so Susanna fled to the privacy of her apartment. Butterflies were beating in her stomach, and she wanted to talk to Nick about Thomas Smith. Having traveled with Rafe, the boy might have heard of the stranger. She stepped into the front room and found Nick sitting by the window with *Kidnapped* in his lap.

As Susanna approached, he looked up with a troubled expression. "I think he's gone."

"Who?" she asked. "The man I just saw?"

"No, Rafe."

Susanna's stomach knotted. "But why?"

"Because of what I said when we went fishing."

She didn't have to ask Nick for an explanation.

With Rafe keeping his distance, she'd taken his place at the checkerboard and they had talked about the possibility of Nick staying in Midas. The boy had come to love her and she loved him. With the added appeal of school and the promised friendship of her brothers and the Duke girls, Nick had found a home.

Susanna patted the boy's shoulder. "I don't think he'd leave without saying goodbye."

Nick's fingers curled on the cover of the book. "Someone bad is after him. Maybe he *had* to leave."

But without a goodbye? Susanna wanted to reassure the boy that Rafe wouldn't do such a thing, but she couldn't. He had a knack for doing the wrong thing for the right reasons. Or the right thing at the wrong time as he had on the night of the dance. Susanna felt a throbbing in her chest. In spite of telling herself that his rejection had been for the best, Rafe haunted her thoughts. Her feelings went deeper than mere desire. She saw blood on his soul, a gunshot wound that needed to be cleaned and stitched. For all his bravado, he was as lost as Nick.

If it hadn't been for Thomas Smith, she would have left for the parsonage immediately. Instead she rubbed Nick's shoulder.

"I'll visit him tonight," she said. "At least we'll know for sure."

* * *

Garrett trusted his instincts, and they were telling him to keep an eye on Dr. Leaf. She had held Rafe's photograph a little too long, as if she were looking for clues of her own. And even more revealing, she hadn't shown interest in the reward money. Certainly not as much as the other business people he'd visited this afternoon. At the mention of a thousand dollars, everyone else had found more to say. But not Dr. Leaf. Garrett was sure that Rafe meant something to her, but what?

As he headed for the Midas Hotel, he decided a late-night walk would be in order. He'd enjoy a good supper, smoke a cigar and then take a stroll when the town had settled down. With a little luck, Dr. Leaf would leave her apartment and lead him to Rafe.

Garrett hoped it happened soon. Back in Raton, the first city over the New Mexico territorial line, he'd received a wire from the boss. The old man was growing more impatient and Garret knew why. Poor health had a way of putting things in perspective. The hurts a man had suffered stopped being important, while the ones he'd inflicted haunted his sleep. Garrett had a few regrets of own.

Limping down the street, he wondered if Rafe felt the same way.

Chapter Fourteen

Grateful for a moonless sky, Susanna put on her duster and hurried to the parsonage. She thought of glancing in the stable to see if Rafe's horses were gone, but she didn't want to cross the yard. Instead she climbed the back steps and let herself into the house where she scanned the kitchen for a sign of him—a coffee cup, a dirty plate—but the counters had been wiped clean and the stove was cold.

Her heart sank, but she couldn't believe he'd gone without saying goodbye. She glanced at the table, dreading the presence of a letter. When she didn't see one, she didn't know whether to be relieved or angry.

With her hope fading, she climbed the stairs and turned down the hall where the bedroom doors were closed except for hers. Other than a gray square of light, the hall was pitch-black. She paused to listen for Rafe's breathing but heard only silence.

Accepting that he'd left, she walked toward her old room. Perhaps he'd left a letter on her bureau.

"Don't move."

The gun at her back was no laughing matter, but she knew that voice. "Darn it, Rafe! Put that thing away."

"Susanna?"

As he lowered the gun, she turned and glared at his shadowy outline. Traces of light gave shape to his white undershirt, revealing his muscled chest and tense shoulders. She smelled soap and realized he was freshly bathed. He'd also washed his clothes with her mother's blend of ash and lye. She realized that he'd gotten ready to go, but the effort had made him belong in her life even more.

"Where have you been?" she asked. "Nick thinks you left without him."

Rafe answered with silence, a sign that he'd considered doing just that.

"Why?" she demanded.

A low growl came from his throat. "I'm still here, aren't I?"

"Yes, but—"

Before she could say another word, he cupped her face between his hands. His eyes lingered on hers, then he brushed her lips with a kiss. In a blink, they were back on the street after the dance—taking from each other and giving everything. Susanna knotted her fingers in his shirt and vowed to herself that she'd never let go. Tonight the truth would be told.

Rafe eased the kiss to a memory but kept his lips a whisper from hers. "God, I've missed you."

"I've missed you, too."

As he stroked her back, she nestled against his throat and listened to the pounding of his heart. He was kissing her temple, murmuring sweet things as they clung to each other, but the touching wasn't enough.

"We need to talk," she said.

"I know."

Tucking her against his ribs, he guided her down the hall to her old bedroom, where he lit the lamp on the bureau. As he trimmed the wick, she saw her diary poking out from under the bed. She'd started it the day she'd arrived in Midas, and it held the best and worst of her past—including the details of her first kiss.

What's all the fuss, I wonder?

She hoped he hadn't gotten that far, but his half smile told her that he had. As she sat on the unmade bed, he pulled up a chair. "I've had a rough few days."

"Tell me about it."

As she took Rafe's hand, Susanna studied his face.

His chin still had an arrogant jut, but the creases around his mouth had softened and his blue irises had a spark she'd never seen before. He looked almost relieved, but the tension in his shoulders told her he was still carrying a weight. She needed to tell him about Thomas Smith, but the news could wait.

Holding her hand, Rafe looked straight into her eyes. "I almost left last night."

"Thank God, you didn't." She squeezed his hand. "What stopped you?"

"A two-bit piece of metal." He lifted something off the nightstand and held it carefully by the end.

Susanna saw the barbed tip of a fish hook. "I don't understand."

"I'm not sure I do, either." Rafe stared at the hook as if it were magical and then looked back at her face. "I was about to ride out when I remembered the fishing poles. I'd left them propped by the door. I didn't want anyone to know we'd used them, so I went back to put them away."

Susanna knew every nook and cranny in the stable. The fishing poles were kept in a cabinet on the back wall. Each of her brothers had his own pole and her father had a bigger one.

Rafe rolled the end of the hook between his fingers and held it to the light. "This thing got caught in my sleeve. The next thing I knew there was fishing line all over the place. I tried to wind it back up and ended up nearly hog-tied."

Susanna smiled. "It must have been my father's pole. The reel's imported from Germany. I gave it to him for Christmas."

A wry smile curled Rafe's lips. "It's quite a device. There I was—tangled up in fishing line with a hook in my sleeve. I tried to get it loose and ended up with it stuck in my finger. It hurt like the dickens, but that wasn't the awful part."

"Tell me," she said.

"I was happy about it."

Rafe decided not to tell her about the five minutes between getting caught and the realization that he had to see her again. He'd cussed out the fishing pole and the darn thing had listened. Bitter words had spewed from his lips like lava, but that feeling had cooled into the black rock of remorse. Before he knew it, he'd hit his knees.

Please God, don't let me hurt Susanna....

With the fish hook woven into his shirt, Rafe had thought about love and angels on walls. By some mysterious hand, Nick had been spared a crippling blow. Was it possible for Rafe to find that same mercy? Sitting on the stable floor, he saw himself for what he'd become—a man who had run too far and too long. He was sick of his life, but he didn't see a way out of the muck. The Leaf family tree had flashed in his mind, but he'd found no hope in it. The Reverend had found a way to become rootless. Rafe wanted the same fresh start, but his father wouldn't let him disappear.

Was a second chance too much to ask?

He loved Susanna and wanted to make her his wife. But how could he ask her to leave her home and follow him to Mexico? He couldn't. But if he stayed in Midas, he was risking prison or even the gallows for the crime he'd committed in St. Louis. Blinking, he imagined Susanna seeing him hang. He refused to allow that misery, but neither could he stand the thought of leaving her.

She squeezed his hand. "I'm glad you got caught."

"You shouldn't be."

"But I am."

Guilt washed over him. "I've been sitting here all day deciding what to do. Disappearing seemed smart. At least you and Nick would have each other. But when it came time to saddle up, I couldn't do it."

"Because you care."

"No," he said. "Because I'm a selfish son of a bitch."

Her eyes filled with kindness. "You're human, Rafe. We all are."

Unsure of what to say, he looked out the window and saw the reflection of the lamp. The flame burned an orange hole through the black pane but only hinted at the tree branch that he could see during the day.

But now we see through a glass darkly...

He remembered the verse because someone had marked it with stars and it described how he felt. He was trapped behind a black window, unable to see what the future held. Experience had taught him his life was cursed, but the verse went on to say that men only partly knew what was beyond the glass. Nick had seen a full-blown angel in a shadow. Rafe had seen only gray light. But then he'd recognized Susanna and witnessed love at work. Things weren't always what they seemed to be, but he couldn't make himself believe that anything good lurked behind that black glass, not with his guardian angel hunting for him.

Even so, he owed Susanna the truth. His lips felt dry and his throat tightened, but he forced himself to look her in the eye.

"I killed my half brother," he said.

Worry filled her eyes, but she didn't recoil from him. "Are you sorry?"

"More than I can say."

"Then tell me what happened."

Rafe took her from New Orleans to Boston and back to St. Louis. By the time he led her into his father's study, they were curled together on the bed. She had placed her head on his shoulder and her hand over his heart.

"I'd been planning to leave for a while," he said. "Other than getting away I didn't care where I went, just so it was far."

Susanna stayed close. "What happened next?"

"My father's a wealthy man. I figured the money in the safe was my due so I took it. My half brother showed up at the wrong time and took a swing at me."

Rafe left out the insults they had hurled at each other. Rivals from the start, they had never gotten along. "What happened next is burned in my mind. I hit him so hard that he spun like a top before he smashed his head against the bricks. There was blood everywhere, all down the side of his face, and his eye was so messed up I couldn't see it."

Her fingers stiffened on his chest. "Which side of his head hit the bricks?"

"I don't remember. Does it matter?"

Her voice turned urgent. "Did you check his pulse?"

"Hell no, I ran." Rafe didn't understand her interest, but his nerves were jangling with alarm. "Why the questions?"

She pushed up on her elbow. "I think he's alive."

"*What?*"

"A man came to see me today. He had a facial scar and a blind eye on the right side. He showed me your picture—"

Rafe rolled off the bed and raked his hands through his hair. "Tell me everything."

As she described the photograph, the alleged inheritance and the reward money, Rafe realized that his guardian angel had found him. As for the man's identity, it was possible Garrett had survived the attack, but the head injury had left him with a weak left side. Even the name "Thomas Smith" made sense to Rafe. His half brother was clever. Knowing that Rafe was on the run, he'd travel incognito in order to lay a trap.

As Susanna ended the story, hope filtered into her voice. "Do you think this man's your brother?"

"It doesn't matter," Rafe answered. "Nothing good can come of it."

"But you wouldn't be wanted for murder."

"Attempted murder is just as bad."

"You're jumping to conclusions," she insisted. "You don't know what this man wants."

"Oh yes, I do. Garrett hated my guts to start with. If I left him blind and scarred, I don't want to think about what he'd do to me. And my father—I stole from him. Believe me, Susanna. He's not a forgiving man."

"How can you be sure?"

"Because his name's Walter Albright and he owns half of the Santa Fe Railroad. A man doesn't get to be that powerful by showing mercy."

Susanna looked skeptical. "You can't judge him without hearing what he has to say. What if you're running from nothing?"

"I'm not." Rafe tasted acid. "Aside from what I did to them, they wronged *me*. My mother *died* because of that man. And then he bought me off with an education I didn't even want."

"Oh, Rafe."

He tried to read her expression, but she'd put on her doctor face. "Don't get me wrong. I'm grateful for the schooling. But at the time I felt like a piece of trash. When his wife died and he moved me to St. Louis, I felt like a stray dog with fleas."

Some of the anger went out of him and he sat next to her on the bed. She took his hand and cradled it in both of hers. "That must have been hard."

"It was. But it's not as bad as what I'm feeling now." He turned and looked into her eyes where he saw pools of compassion and so much more—love, daring, even hope. She was a remarkable woman and deserved to know it. "I love you, Susanna. I can't stand the thought of leaving you, but I can't fix this mess."

"I love you, too."

Her eyes were brimming and so were his. But their feelings had nowhere to go. Even a kiss felt dangerous. Rafe knew what he had to do. All that mattered was protecting Susanna from the hell he saw in his future. "I should pack up."

"Oh no, you don't." With a swift turn, she pushed him to his back and rolled on top of him. In an instant he went from being half-dead with misery to being fully alive. Susanna had him pinned right where he wanted to be. "I don't want to lose you, Rafe. We'll figure this out together."

He wasn't used to feeling hopeful, but he'd never had so much to lose. "What do you have in mind?"

"For now, you're safe. No one knows where you are."

"As far as we know, that's true."

"You can stay here while I find out more about Mr. Smith."

The idea had merit, but then he recalled "The Blue Danube" and groaned. "Half the town saw me at the dance."

"You weren't there more than fifteen minutes."

"What about Duke?"

"He doesn't come to town very often. We'll have to risk it."

Rafe felt torn in two. He wanted to keep Susanna out of trouble, but she felt like heaven pressed against him. An hour ago she had shed her duster, revealing her office skirt and a shirtwaist with tiny buttons. They were begging to be undone, but Rafe knew he'd be opening a door that led to an uncertain future.

Instead he stroked her back and shoulders, moving lower until he found the sides of her breasts through the cotton. Soft and pliant, they made him yearn for sex and love and everything in between. Judging by the hum in her throat, Susanna felt it, too. Wanting to give her more, he cupped her breasts fully in his palms. A low moan escaped from her throat.

"There has to be a way," she said.

Rafe wanted to share that faith, but the only answer he could imagine was taking her to Mexico. *Come with me....*

Except the words caught in his throat. He'd be taking her away from everything she loved. It didn't seem right. Aching inside, he settled for rolling her onto her back and kissing her slow and deep. Desire hardened his body, but love made him see a painful truth. He couldn't stay in Midas, and he couldn't ask her to leave. One way or another, he was going to break this woman's heart.

Garrett looked at the moon and cursed himself for falling asleep after supper. His ten-minute nap had lasted two hours and he'd left the hotel later than he'd intended. By the time he positioned himself across from Dr. Leaf's clinic, the moon had risen and her apartment was dark.

Leaning against a splintery wall, he wondered if she'd left earlier or if she had already retired for the night. A cigar would have been nice, but he would have welcomed a bench even more. Glancing at the sky, he decided he'd been here long enough. Perhaps Dr. Leaf had been telling the truth and Rafe LaCroix was nothing to her.

Garrett shifted his cane to the other hand, but then he heard footsteps and froze in place. Cursing his poor eyesight, he watched as Dr. Leaf hurried up the stairs to her apartment.

Had she been on a late-night call? It was possible, but she hadn't been carrying her medical bag. It seemed more likely that she'd gone to see Rafe. As she closed the door with a click, Garrett weighed his options. If she suspected he was in town, she'd be careful. But if he told her he was leaving New Mexico, she might just lead him to his brother.

Tomorrow he'd pay her another visit. This time he'd leave a card with a St. Louis address and thank her for her time.

Sleep hadn't come easily to Susanna after her encounter with Rafe. With her body flushed and unsettled, she had lain awake in the dark, wondering if Thomas Smith was Rafe's brother. Susanna understood the force of hate and revenge. If Garrett and Rafe's father were truly evil men, she could understand running. But how could Rafe be certain of the man's ill intentions? Five years had passed since that night in his father's study. Susanna knew from experience that fathers weren't always the men they seemed to be.

With so much at stake, she decided to pay a call on Thomas Smith first thing in the morning. With a little luck she'd catch him in the café and join him for coffee. To hide her real interest in Rafe, she'd ask about the reward. If Smith wouldn't tell her more about his motives, she'd see what she could find out by offering information about Rafe and the Bentons.

Yawning, Susanna rose from her bed and put on a fresh skirt and shirtwaist. She was putting up her hair when she heard an urgent knock on the door.

"Doc? It's Howard Tucker. It's my wife."

Susanna turned the lock and saw a man in his

thirties. Judging by his worried expression, he was about to become a father. "Is it the baby?"

The man's head bobbed. "I think so."

"Is she having pains?"

"Like clockwork and she's terrified. Can you come right now?"

"Of course."

Susanna held in a sigh. Martha Tucker was a petite woman and this was her first child. Having breakfast with Thomas Smith would have to wait.

After waking Nick and telling him where she'd be, she retrieved her bag from the clinic and walked with Howard past the hotel. Maybe she'd be finished by lunch and could see Smith then.

But that didn't happen.

By the time Susanna left the Tucker house, the sun was high in the sky. She'd had the satisfaction of laying Alison Tucker in her mother's arms, but the effort had done them all in. The baby had been breech, and Susanna had used every bit of her skill to deliver the child. She couldn't confront Thomas Smith while looking disheveled, so she headed home to wash her face and change into clean clothes. She also needed to check on Nick and see if anyone had left a note on her chalkboard.

As soon as she saw the front of her clinic, Susanna's heart sank. Jayne Dawson and her three youngest children were standing at the door. Judging by the spots on the oldest boy's face, he had the chicken pox. Susanna invited them in and gave Jayne a special soap.

Roger Hardy showed up next. He had a boil that needed lancing. But mostly he missed his deceased wife and wanted to talk.

Ginger Abbott arrived with an embarrassing itch.

Priscilla Wayne had hot flashes and headaches.

Mayor Jenner's ulcer was acting up.

Three hours passed before Susanna dragged herself up the stairs. As she walked into the front room, Nick motioned toward an envelope on the side table. "Someone slipped that under the door this morning."

Susanna snatched it up and looked at the handwriting. When she didn't recognize the script, she tore open the envelope and read.

Dear Dr. Leaf,
Business has called me back to St. Louis. If you recall anything about Mr. LaCroix, please wire me at the above address. I repeat, it's urgent that I locate him.
Regards,
Thomas Smith

Needing to think, Susanna dropped down to a chair and rubbed her temples. She had missed her chance to glean information from Thomas Smith, but his departure made it possible for Rafe to stay without hiding. He could spend time with Nick during the day, and they could have suppers at night. Maybe in those cozy hours she could convince him to write to Smith.

She hoped so. Even now, she could feel his lips on her throat and his hands caressing her breasts. But desire alone hadn't caused her aching heart. He was intelligent and funny, a man with dark insights and a sharp wit. He respected her abilities and was even proud of them. He was the man she wanted to marry.

He hadn't asked her to leave with him, but she had seen the question in his eyes. Last night she'd imagined how it would feel to say goodbye to her family. Going away to school had been different. She'd come home for the summers and had always planned on settling in Midas. If she left with Rafe, she might never see them again.

Tears pressed into Susanna's eyes. She had lost the first fourteen years with her father and didn't want to give up the future, too. She and her mother were best friends. As for her brothers, she'd miss their jokes and the nieces and nephews she'd never see.

Closing her eyes, Susanna prayed for God's hand to touch her life with Rafe, but she felt no peace.

Whether Susanna chose Mexico or Midas, she knew that her heart would be torn in two. She could only pray she wouldn't have to make the choice.

Chapter Fifteen

"You're wrong. That's all there is to it." Rafe put the dinner plate on the shelf with a clatter. They were in Susanna's tiny kitchen where, for the third time, he had tried to explain why she couldn't send a wire to Thomas Smith. Other than the pleasure of a good supper and laughing with Nick, nothing about tonight had gone the way he had planned.

Three days had passed since Smith's departure. In spite of Susanna's confidence that they had been granted a reprieve, Rafe had laid low. Years on the run had given him good instincts, and his nerves were humming with the sense of being watched. She had visited a few times at the parsonage, and each visit had made him more nervous. He would have asked her to stay away, but he hated the loneliness. She had also asked him to help Melissa. Rafe had been glad to write a letter to the nuns in New Orleans who ran the home for unwed mothers.

When that task had been completed, he'd had nothing to do but think about the future. Every road led to disaster—except for one. Tonight he had come to Susanna's apartment to ask her to elope with him to Mexico.

He hadn't made the decision easily. He'd be asking her to give up everything—her friends, her practice and especially her family. In exchange she'd get a man with a past, but one who loved her and wanted to make her happy. Nick would benefit, too. Someday the boy would have brothers and sisters, and Susanna would have a dark-eyed girl. Rafe couldn't shake the worry that it wasn't enough for her, but it was the best he had to give. Surely that counted for something.

The other choice was to stay in Midas and face Thomas Smith. But Rafe saw that option as certain heartbreak. He'd go to prison or hang. The only thought more troubling than Susanna waiting for him for twenty years, was imagining her at the foot of a gallows. Either way, she would grieve. At least by taking her to Mexico, they had a shot at a life together, but first he had to convince her that contacting Smith was a fool's errand. So far, he'd failed miserably.

He was gritting his teeth when Susanna touched

his back. "We have to get more information," she said. "We don't really know what he wants."

"Like I said, I don't care."

"But it could change everything."

Not in Rafe's opinion. Alive or dead, Garrett was a ghost he didn't want to confront. As for his father, Walter Albright had ruled his home like he ruled the Santa Fe Railroad—with an iron fist and no mercy. Just the thought of the man sent bitterness coursing through Rafe's veins.

Susanna had wrapped her arms around his belly and was hugging him from behind. As she nestled closer, he thought about sleeping like spoons. They needed to talk, so he turned to hold her in his arms. As soon as Nick dozed off, he'd ask her about Mexico. Kissing her forehead, he decided to change the subject. "Let's go in the other room. I'll read out loud until Nick falls asleep."

Her eyes clouded with irritation. "All right, but you're not leaving tonight until we decide about contacting Mr. Smith."

"That's fine." The sooner they left for Mexico, the better.

Together they went into the front room, where they found Nick already asleep with the book on his chest. Susanna dimmed the light and then led Rafe into her bedroom where they could talk in private.

She lit a lamp and turned it low, while he pulled up a chair so she could sit on the bed. Moonlight fell across the floor, making the room as silvery as the night he had kidnapped her. When she sat, he took her hand. "I've been thinking about Smith a lot."

"I have too," she said. "Rafe, this is our chance. I know you think he wants to do you harm, but I'm not convinced. If Garrett's alive, you're not a wanted man."

Rafe couldn't believe his ears. "You forgot about burglary and attempted murder."

"You won't know unless you confront him."

"I won't do that."

"But I can do it for you."

"How?"

"I'll write to him. Maybe your father and Garrett want to bury the past. Just think—you could stay in Midas."

Her eyes glistened with excitement. "My parents are due back in a week. I can hardly wait for you to meet them. Nick could go to school with my brothers. Your engraving is beautiful. You could start a business. It would be perfect."

Rafe thought so, too. But he knew a false hope when he heard one. "What if you're wrong? What if Smith wants to haul me back to St. Louis for a trial?

That night was more of an accident than a crime, but we both know I was in the wrong."

Susanna nodded slowly. "You have to make amends. I know that."

"I'm as sorry as I can be, but I don't want to hang for a mistake."

When her eyes dimmed, he lifted her hand to his lips and kissed each of her knuckles. She smelled like cinnamon from the apple pie she had baked from her mother's recipe. When he looked up, he saw the wall calendar with her father's birthday marked for a Tuesday in November. Earlier she had told him how excited she was about a new stethoscope that had arrived and how someday she wanted a bigger clinic.

Rafe felt the call of Mexico in his belly, but Susanna belonged in Midas. Blinking, he flashed on the day he'd been ripped from New Orleans. He knew about roots and how it felt to be torn away like a weed. Was it right to ask her to come with him to Mexico, knowing she'd grieve for what she had given up? Or was it more loving to protect the life she had?

Last night he had read a story about two women claiming to be the mother of the same child. They had gone to the king and asked him to decide who was telling the truth. In his wisdom, the king had threatened to cut the baby in two and divide it between them. The real mother had given up her claim to save her child's life.

Until he'd met Susanna, Rafe couldn't have understood that sacrifice. But looking at her in the moonlight with her ivory skin and contented smile, he knew what he had to do to protect her. He'd leave just as he had arrived—alone in the middle of the night. At least she'd have Nick and the boy would have her. He'd leave them each a letter explaining his decision. It was cowardly to vanish without a face-to-face goodbye, but he wasn't strong enough to walk away with her broken heart in his hands.

Susanna dragged her fingers through his short hair and smiled at him. She had a way of making him hope for things, which meant he had to leave tonight.

"I love you," she said. "We'll find a way."

"I love you, too." Knowing it was the last time he'd say the words, Rafe kissed her mouth with tender longing. With the feel of her lingering on his lips, he pushed to his feet, pulling her up with him. "I'd better go."

"Are you sure?"

Her voice had turned seductive, but he didn't dare kiss her again. He wanted to make love to her all night long. He needed the release, both from the tension in his body and the pain of leaving, but making love was a promise he couldn't make. They'd end up sleeping like spoons and he'd never leave. Instead he kissed her forehead and whispered, "Don't tempt me, Doc."

Leaning against him, she laced her fingers behind his neck and smiled. "But it's so much fun. Are you sure you have to leave?"

Rafe managed a low chuckle, but a knife to the gut would have been kinder. After kissing her once more, he walked out the door.

Three hours had passed since Rafe's departure, but Susanna hadn't changed out of her clothes. Too restless to sleep, she was sitting by the window in the front room when she heard a squeak. It sounded like her office door. Chills shot through her body, but she wasn't foolish enough to rush downstairs. Her apartment was locked, so she stayed at the window where she could see the street.

She had never been burgled, but she'd heard of opium addicts stealing laudanum. After several minutes of silence, she decided it was safe to check the office. Not bothering with a coat, she walked down the stairs and saw that the door was ajar.

She considered fetching her Colt, but the office was dark and still. The intruder had probably heard the squeak when he entered and opted to leave the door open when he left. Confident she'd be safe, Susanna entered the office, lit the lamp and saw a sheet of paper tucked under the blotter. Someone had written, "Check the bottom drawer."

Susanna sat in her chair, opened the drawer and gasped. In addition to a white envelope, she saw a stack of hundred-dollar bills. It was enough for a new horse and buggy, a coat, everything she needed. With trembling fingers, she opened the letter and began to read.

For your sake and Nick's... You have a life... I want to spare you the sadness... The money is a gift... Tell Nick I care... I'll love you forever.

Susanna dropped the letter and bolted for the door. If Rafe thought he could leave now, he was crazy. Praying that he hadn't already vanished into the hills, she ran to the parsonage where she saw a beam of light pouring from the kitchen window. Chilled to the bone, she burst through the back door and felt a blast of heat from the stove. Rafe was sitting at the table with a fountain pen and another sheet of paper.

"How dare you leave like this!" she cried.

He pushed to his feet and stared at her. "It's for the best. You know it as well as I do."

"I don't know any such thing."

He turned his back and poured a cup of coffee at the stove. After gulping it down, he spoke to the wall. "It's freezing outside. Where's your coat?"

Susanna positioned hereslf between the lamp and the stove. She couldn't make Rafe look her in the eye, but he had to see her shadow. "You should have told me you were leaving."

"Why bother?"

"That was mean."

He set down the cup and glared at her. "I'm sorry, Doc, but this is all wrong. I'm headed to Mexico where the sun's warm and the women are willing."

Susanna saw red. "You're being a jackass."

"That's me, all right."

His voice rang with bravado. Praying that he'd stop her, she walked to the door. "You're a fool, Rafe. Enjoy the tequila."

"I will, thank you."

She gripped the knob and turned it. When he didn't move, she opened the door wide. Cold air blasted into the kitchen.

"Damn it!" he shouted. "Get a coat."

"No."

Leaving the door ajar, she stood shivering on the threshold. Fresh air made the lamp burn even brighter and caused him to pivot on his heels. His eyes burned as bright as a flame, glistening with a longing she felt in her own bones. Mercy made her step into the kitchen and close the door without being asked. "I'd like some coffee, please."

He turned back to the stove. "Help yourself."

It wasn't the welcome she wanted, but neither had he sent her away. After opening the cupboard, she picked a familiar mug, stepped to the stove and held it out so he could fill it. She saw him hesitate, as if by filling her cup he was promising to do it again, but then he picked up the pot and poured coffee into her mug. Steam rose in a mist and then vanished into the cold. Still chilled, she took a sip and swallowed, feeling the heat all the way to her belly.

Rafe broke the silence. "You shouldn't have come."

"You didn't give me a choice."

"That's true," he said. "I made the decision for us. Earlier tonight I'd planned to ask you to elope with me to Mexico. I had it all figured out. We'd find a church and get married on the way. But I can't ask you to leave Midas."

"Isn't that my decision?"

"Not entirely."

"But neither was it yours, Rafe. Not to make alone."

His eyes burned into hers. "What would you have said?"

Yes...no...maybe...

She'd been asking herself that question for days. Standing in the kitchen where she truly felt at home, she tried to sort her thoughts. They were a jumble, but one feeling was stronger than all the others. She loved Rafe and wanted him to know it. After setting down the coffee cup, she laced her hands behind his neck. "I just want you."

Her meaning wasn't clear. For tonight? For always? As he peered into her eyes, Susanna felt like a woman poised on a cliff. Another step and she'd be flying with him into oblivion.

He put his hands on her hips and held her a foot away. "I want you, Susanna. I have since I first saw you, but I'm leaving. If not right now, then soon. Do you know what that means?"

She forced herself to nod. "It means we have tonight."

"And nothing else."

He stayed still, giving her time to weigh the cost of giving him her body for a single night. Looking into his eyes, she couldn't think of a thing. Vaguely she recalled dreaming of a real wedding night and a lifetime with one man. Her mother had told her that sex was like glue. It bound a man and a woman in a way nothing else could, but it also had the power to shatter a woman's life. *It's a gift, Susanna. Enjoy it wisely.*

That's what Susanna had always intended, but she hadn't bargained on loving a man like Rafe. He was the husband of her heart. But the risk… Susanna knew she was gambling. Almost two weeks had passed since she'd had her monthly. Any day she'd feel a pinch in her side as her body released an egg. She hadn't felt the signs yet, but she would soon. In a week? An hour? She wasn't always regular, so she didn't know.

She took a breath to steady her nerves. What were the odds of conception? Not very good, but not as low as she would have liked. If she made love to Rafe, she'd be gambling. But if she didn't, she'd regret saying no for the rest of her life.

Crazy or not, she stepped into his arms. "Let's go upstairs."

"Are you sure?"

"I'm positive." But she had answered two questions. She wanted to make love to him, but she was equally certain of the risk.

With his hand on the small of her back, he guided her up the stairs and into her bedroom. Moonlight pushed through the window, giving the air a silvery glow. Leaving the door open, Rafe pulled back the blanket and faced her. Unsure of what to do, she raised her hands to the top button of her dress. By the time she reached the third one, her hands were shaking.

He covered her fingers with his. "There's no need to hurry."

"But I want to."

His focus felt warm on her face. "First times shouldn't be rushed."

One by one, he removed her hairpins until her braid tumbled down her back. Next he untied the ribbon holding the ends. Using both hands, he started at her scalp and worked his way down until her hair was loose and free. He gave her a lazy smile. "I've wanted to do that since the first night."

"I figured as much."

"You were furious with me."

"And with good reason."

But so much had changed. She loved this man. Truly she did, but the risk...*don't think.*

Satisfied with her hair, he went back to unbuttoning her dress. When the last button had given way, he pushed the garment off her shoulders so that she was standing in her chemise in the middle of the room. The air held a chill, but Rafe's gaze burned through the cotton. She felt naked and wished she was. Feeling brave, she untied her drawers and let them drop on top of the dress with Rafe watching her every move.

"You're not shy, are you?" he said.

"No, just a little nervous."

"Trust me, I like what I see."

He kissed her sweetly on the lips, then lifted the sheet and guided her under the covers. She rolled to her side, while he sat on the edge and tugged off his boots. Leaning forward, he blew out the lamp and then shimmied out of his clothes. Wearing nothing at all, he rolled her to her back and kissed her.

She felt his hairy legs against her calves and the heat of his bare arm against her side. Tantalized by the mix of muscle and skin, she stroked his back, slowly moving down his ribs. She'd seen plenty of male chests, but she had never explored with a woman's curiosity. With her fingers on the side of his waist, she brought her hand to his belly and followed the line of hair to the middle of his chest. What she found delighted her. He had a patch of silky hair, hard muscles and sensitive spots that matched hers. When a pleased sigh spilled from his lips, Susanna touched some more.

She wanted to feel free to enjoy this moment, but her thoughts were clanking like rocks in a can.

What if...what if...

To fight the worry, she concentrated on Rafe—the taste of him, the scent of his skin, the flex of his thigh as he draped his leg over hers. He was fully aroused and hard against her hip. She loved him. She wanted to show him how much. But all the desire in the world couldn't block out the simple truth that a child could come of this union. Still kissing her, he caressed the side of her breast. Susanna tried to relax into the mattress, but she couldn't. If she was going to change her mind, now was the time. Horizontal or not, a kiss was just a kiss.

"Rafe, I—oh Lord."

He had taken the tip of her breast between his fingers and was making exquisite circles, whispering sweet words in her ear. A moan hummed in her throat as he kissed her, caressing her relentlessly and making her squirm. She didn't want him to stop— not now, not ever. Tomorrow she'd think about the risk. Tomorrow...

"I love you," she whispered.

"I love you, too."

Lazy and sure, he tugged the chemise up to her waist, baring her hips as he caressed her thigh with ever-rising strokes. When she was writhing with need, he found her breast and suckled through the cotton as she clutched at his feather-soft hair. His lips demanded more, gave more, as he found her most private place and touched her on the inside. Her breathing went crazy, but her mind focused on the facts with a clinical detail. He was about to join his body with hers. Their cells would meet and mate.

A boy with Rafe's blue eyes...a girl with her brown hair. Susanna wanted to feel joy at the thought of such a gift, but instead she tasted bile. Choking back a cry, she clamped her legs together and hid her face against his chest.

Rafe froze. "Susanna?"

She could still feel him touching her, wanted to feel him, but she had to tell the truth. "I'm terrified. It's a risky time of the month."

He had every reason to be angry. But instead of muttering with frustration, he whispered in her ear, "Lie back, honey. I'll keep you safe."

Trusting him, she sank into the mattress with her nerves blazing and her muscles taut. He was kissing her and stroking her, caressing her innocence until the tension snapped in a blinding wave of tears and pleasure. Lights exploded behind her eyes and fell like dying stars, leaving her aware of Rafe's breath on her cheek, the tension in his arms and the aroused state of his body. She had never felt so stupid in her life.

"I'm so sorry," she cried.

He was still holding her, absorbing the last waves of her climax. "Don't you dare be sorry. I'm the one who should apologize. I should have asked if it was safe."

Susanna trembled in his arms. She had never been more afraid in her life—or more disappointed. The shivers of sensation had released the tension from her body, but she felt empty inside. This wasn't the union she had wanted.

Rafe pulled her higher on the bed and cradled her in his arms. "The last thing I want is to ruin your life, and I sure don't want a kid growing up like I did."

Susanna felt him shudder, from both fading desire and loathing for himself. She thought about offering what relief she could, but she knew it wouldn't be enough.

"Where do we go from here?" she asked.

"The same places we were going an hour ago. You're staying in Midas and I'm headed south. That's the way it has to be."

"But—"

"Go to sleep." His voice had a catch. "We'll say goodbye in the morning."

With tears welling in her eyes, Susanna stared into the dark. She couldn't see out the window, but somewhere in the heavens was the first star of the night. Closing her eyes, she made a wish.

Star light, star bright...

* * *

Rafe jolted awake but didn't know why. He usually dozed like a cat and had expected the dawn to wake him, but sunlight was already streaming through the window. Still curled in his arms lay Susanna, worn-out and breathing deep. Saying goodbye was going to be hell, but last night had carved his decision in stone. He wanted to do right by her and that meant leaving Midas.

Yawning, he rolled to his side and snuggled against her. Another minute seemed like a small thing to ask, but his skin was crawling with awareness. He couldn't escape the sense that he was being watched. He was about to grab his pants when a man's deep voice bellowed into the room.

"Who the *devil* are you?"

Rafe jerked upright and saw a man who had to be the Reverend John Leaf. Dressed in black and pointing a shotgun, he had narrowed his gaze to Rafe, waiting with a deadly calm for an explanation. Rafe had listened to Lem's wild tales with half an ear. Now he wondered if his friend had been holding back. The Reverend had an air of violence about him and he hadn't yet noticed Susanna. Scrunched on her belly in the tangle of sheets, she was hidden except for the hair fanned across her face.

Rafe heard a contented sigh spill from her lips

as she began to stir. Feeling the tension, she jolted awake and realized they had company.

"Pa?" Looking far too rumpled, she sat up with the sheet clutched to her chemise. "What are you doing here?"

He lowered the gun but didn't relax his stance. "I live here. So does your mother."

"But your train wasn't due for a week," she replied. "I wasn't expecting you."

"That's rather obvious. J.J. said someone had been in his room, so I came upstairs to check. It looks like he was right."

Rafe would have sold his soul for his pants. Instead he watched as a pretty woman in her early forties walked up behind the Reverend and touched his sleeve. "John, come downstairs."

"Hell, no!"

"Hell, yes," she countered. "They need a minute alone."

With that kindness, Abigail Leaf won Rafe's loyalty forever. He hoped the Reverend would listen to his wife, but Susanna dashed those hopes.

"Pa, it's not what you think."

The Reverend looked down his nose at Rafe. "Did I miss the wedding?"

Susanna answered. "No, but—"

"John, stop it," Abbie insisted.

"Not until I find out who this *gentleman* is."

Susanna bent over the side of the bed, snatched up Rafe's clothes and jammed them into his hands. As he wiggled into them, she picked up her dress and shrugged it over her shoulders. Sitting on the edge of the mattress, he tugged on his boots.

The Reverend watched Rafe's every move until he and Susanna both pushed to their feet. This wasn't the goodbye Rafe had envisioned. He'd intended to slip away at dawn, leaving Susanna free to live her life. Instead he'd left her with another mess. Determined to help her clean it up, he cinched his belt tight and addressed the Reverend.

"Sir, my name is Rafe LaCroix. I know what this looks like, but nothing happened."

"I find that rather hard to believe."

Rafe had been down this road before. Innocent or not, he looked guilty. He knew better than to argue, but he couldn't stop himself from mouthing off. "Then you're a fool."

The Reverend's eyes turned hard. "I want you out of here. *Now.*"

Susanna interrupted. "Pa, let me explain."

"I'll be glad to, right after Mr. LaCroix has found other accommodations."

That was fine by Rafe. He had nothing else to say. After grabbing his shirt and hat, he brushed past the

Reverend. He'd packed the horses last night and his duster was hanging by the back door.

The ordeal might have come to an end, but Susanna came charging up behind him. "Rafe, wait. I'm coming with you."

"Forget it, Doc." He trotted down the stairs and into the kitchen. When he stopped to button his shirt, Susanna's brothers raced in from the front room. The oldest one was Nick's age and the spitting image of John Leaf. The younger ones were mismatched twins.

"Go away!" she said to them.

The oldest boy pointed at Rafe. "He stole my books."

"He *borrowed* the books," Susanna declared. "They're at my house."

Rafe didn't know which bothered him more, being falsely accused by a kid or the fact that J.J. reminded him of Nick. Rafe was about to push through the door when Susanna grabbed his arm. "I have to put on my shoes."

He glanced down and saw the laces dangling from her hand. He'd once taken those shoes to keep her from running away from him. Now she wanted to stand by his side and he had to make her stay. He grabbed the shoes and tossed them across the room.

"You're not going with me, Doc. It's been a pleasure, but it's over."

Her eyes glistened with emotion. "You can't leave like this."

"Yes, I can."

He wanted to kiss her and tell her again that he loved her, but her brothers were standing guard and her father was thumping down the stairs. Rafe settled for lifting her hair and letting it fall in a wave. After a peck to her forehead, he walked out the door.

Standing at the window in her apartment, Susanna watched the sun dip below the mountain called Broken Heart Ridge. She had read Rafe's letter for the hundredth time and was on the verge of fresh tears. She hadn't felt this alone since she had arrived in Midas eleven years ago. Even then, she'd had Silas for a friend. Now she had no one.

After the disaster at the parsonage, her mother had made a pot of tea and asked her to sit down, but Susanna had refused it. Instead she had defended Rafe with the details of the past few weeks, gone home and left a note on her blackboard saying she was indisposed. As gently as she could, she had told Nick that Rafe cared for him, but that circumstances had changed and he had to leave immediately. The boy had accepted the news with a shrug that broke her heart. Then he'd picked up a book and started to read, leaving her free to hide in her bedroom.

Nick was accustomed to being left, but Susanna wasn't. She'd been trained to clean wounds and stitch them tight. Rafe had ripped out her heart and left her bleeding. She would have grieved through the night, but Nick had needed supper. Neither of them had tasted the canned stew. The boy had gone back to his book, leaving Susanna alone to stare at the sky.

A knock on the door pulled her out of her thoughts. "Sweetie? It's me."

Susanna could handle her mother, but she was in no mood to speak to her father. She had always counted on him to listen first and make judgments later. This morning he'd done the opposite. Praying Abbie had come alone, Susanna opened the door and breathed a sigh when she saw only her mother.

"Can I come in?" Abbie asked.

Her mother never asked permission. She had always made herself at home. Susanna opened the door wider. "Of course."

As she stepped into the front room, Abbie's attention shifted to Nick. "You must be the young man who borrowed J.J.'s, books. He's downstairs if you'd like to meet him."

Nick looked to Susanna. For the boy's sake, she tried to sound cheerful. "Nick, this is my mother."

"Hello, Mrs. Leaf."

"You'll like J.J.," Susanna said. "Plus I need to talk to my mother alone."

"Then I guess I'll go."

Using one crutch, Nick walked to the door. Susanna watched as he managed the stairs, waved to her brother and went back inside. Her mother was standing by the window, reading the letter Susanna had left in plain sight.

Abbie looked up with moist eyes. "This is heartbreaking."

"It's hard for Nick, too."

"So Rafe hasn't come to see you?"

"No, and I'm sick about it. You can tell Pa that he's gone." Bitterness had leaked into her voice.

"Sweetie, I'm so sorry."

When Abbie tried to hug her, Susanna stepped out of her grasp. "Right now, I'm so angry I can hardly talk. Rafe was telling the truth. In fact, he was smarter about things than I was."

Abbie touched the letter with her fingertip. "Your father reacted like any man would, but I was angry with him, too. He knows better than to cast stones."

Abbie didn't have to explain the Bible story about the adulterous woman. *Let him whose slate is clean cast the first stone.* Her father lived by that verse and so did her mother. Susanna understood why.

She was living proof that her parents were as human as anyone.

Abbie reached inside her pocket and withdrew an envelope that had yellowed with age. "Read this and then we'll talk."

Susanna recognized her father's handwriting, unfolded the letter and started to read. She skimmed it because she had lived through that day, but the final words grabbed at her heart.

> **Your happiness means more to me than anything, Abbie. That means protecting you at any cost and loving you with every breath I take. I pray that tomorrow ends well, but if it doesn't, know that I made the choice out of love and with the best of intentions.**
>
> **Your faithful husband,**
> **John**

Susanna would never forget the events that had led to this letter. Her father had offered a terrible trade to protect the people he loved. By leaving, Rafe had tried to do the same thing. After wiping her eyes, Susanna folded the letter and gave it back to her mother.

Abbie tucked it into her pocket. "Does Rafe love you like that?"

"He does. That's why he left." Susanna recounted the story of their meeting, including the kidnapping, the events at the cave and his arrival at the dance. When she explained the arrival of Thomas Smith, Abbie's expression turned grim. Having once been trapped by an evil man, she understood Rafe's plight.

"You know the rest," Susanna concluded. "After this morning, I doubt he'll be back."

Abbie took her hand. "I'm not so sure. Your father knows he overreacted. He's been looking for Rafe all day."

Susanna's heart swelled. "Do you think Pa will find him?"

"I hope so," Abbie said. "But I'm not sure that you and Rafe belong together, and not just because things happened fast."

Susanna moaned. "Ma, I'm twenty-five years old. I know my heart."

"I don't doubt that you love Rafe," Abbie said. "But do you love him enough?"

"Enough for what?"

"To leave with him."

Her mother was squeezing her hand with a keenness born of lost dreams. Abbie had once faced the same decision and made the wrong choice. Because of those regrets, she had a passion for independence and had made sure her daughter could stand alone. Susanna's father felt the same way. Her parents had given her wings and told her to fly as high as she could. And as far...

Susanna knew that leaving would break her heart, but she also believed that God had a plan for her life. She had been born to love and heal, and no one needed her more than Rafe. Clinging to her mother, she said, "I do, Ma. I love you all so much, but I love Rafe, too. We belong together."

Rafe looked at the shot of whiskey and felt more hopeless than ever. This morning he'd left Midas and ridden south. But he'd felt miserable and had turned west. When he'd stumbled into Needle Canyon, he had reversed his route and gone east. By the time dusk had settled, he'd arrived back in Midas where he'd sauntered into the saloon.

Half-starved and angry, he'd ordered a sandwich and a shot of Texas Gold. The food had eased the ache in his belly, but the whiskey had no appeal. Neither did the poker game in the corner or flirting with the girl serving drinks. Instead of making him laugh, the barkeep's bawdy jokes struck a sour note.

All he wanted was to see Susanna. Just one more time, he told himself. But he knew that once wouldn't be enough. The whiskey was sounding better by the minute. In fact, the shot glass was his only friend.

He was staring at the golden cure when a hush settled over the room. Hunched at the bar, he listened as boot heels tapped across the floor. When no one called a greeting, Rafe slipped his hand into his coat where a Remington hung heavy on his thigh. If the Bentons had tracked him down, he'd fight. A visit from Thomas Smith wasn't as simple. The boot steps halted a foot away, giving him a sideways view of worn black leather and a black coattail.

"Damn it, LaCroix. My wife's furious with me and it's your fault."

Rafe turned and saw Susanna's father wearing both a scowl and his preacher's coat. One suited him; the other didn't. After this morning's insults, Susanna's father was the last person Rafe wanted to see. Lifting the shot glass, he said, "You're an ass."

Reverend Leaf snorted. "Thanks for the compliment."

Rafe set down the whiskey without drinking it. "Do you know what really pissed me off?"

"No, but you're itching to tell me."

"It's not that you didn't believe *me*. Hell, I know what it looked like. But you didn't listen to your daughter. She's the finest woman I know. I swear to God, I'd never do anything to hurt her."

"Then why are you leaving?"

Glaring, Rafe told the truth. "Because I'm a first-class son of a bitch."

"Oh yeah?"

"Yeah."

The Reverend pulled up a stool. "In that case, the drinks are on me."

Chapter Sixteen

The Reverend signaled the barkeep. "Bring a bottle, Leroy. And two glasses."

"What'll it be, John?"

"The best you've got." As soon as the man set down the bottle, the Reverend pulled the cork, topped off Rafe's glass and put a splash in his own. Then he raised it in a toast. "To your future, Mr. LaCroix."

Rafe wanted to hurl his glass across the room. What future? In a few weeks, he'd be sitting in a cantina in Mexico, yearning for Susanna and wondering if Nick had grown to hate him. He'd be damned if he'd drink to that loneliness. He slid the glass toward the Reverend. "Go pester someone else."

John Leaf raised his glass a second time. "Go ahead. Drink up."

"Not with you."

"All right then. We'll invite Betty Ann." The man

crooked his finger toward the girl serving drinks. She approached him with a smile.

"Hi, Reverend. Glad to have you back. How are Abbie and the boys?"

"They're great. You can see for yourself on Sunday. In the meantime, I'd like you to meet my friend Rafe."

The woman beamed a smile, but Rafe had no interest. After acknowledging her with a grunt, he sipped the drink he didn't want. Betty Ann took the hint and made small talk with John Leaf until another customer called her away.

When she was out of earshot, Rafe turned on the Reverend. "What the hell do you think you're doing? You don't know me at all."

A chuckle rumbled in the man's throat. "Oh yes, I do. You left clues all over my house."

"What's that supposed to mean?"

"First off, you're not a thief. You looked at the gun cabinet and browsed the bookshelves, but you didn't touch a thing you didn't need. You ate your own food and did the dishes. You showed some respect."

The man was right. Rafe had done it for Susanna.

"Secondly, judging by where I found the Sears Catalog, you like to read on the crapper."

Rafe couldn't believe his ears. Was there anything

this man wouldn't mention? "I can hardly wait to hear the rest."

"Then here you go. Right now, you're hurting so bad that not even whiskey will help. Betty Ann's wearing a skimpy dress and you didn't even notice. That tells me where your heart is, and it's not in this saloon."

"Sure it is."

"I don't believe you, son." The Reverend nodded at the bottle. "Saloon rats don't turn down free drinks."

Rafe was tempted to reach for the bottle, but why? John Leaf had him pegged for what he was—a man caught between hope and yesterday's mistakes. He tried to sneer, but his anger died when he saw Susanna's dark eyes staring at him. He'd thought her compassion had come solely from her mother. He'd been wrong.

The Reverend hushed his voice. "My wife and I had a long talk this morning. This isn't the kind of courtship we wanted for our daughter, but she's a grown woman. And, as Abbie reminded me, appearances can be deceiving. Susanna knows you better than we do, and we've always trusted her judgment."

Rafe shook his head. "She's a sucker for lost causes."

"So is her ma. We're fortunate men."

In spite of the Reverend's compassion, Rafe felt

like dirt. He pushed the plate away. "Thanks for trying to fix things, but it's best if I leave town."

"Not until you square things with my daughter."

"You don't know what you're asking."

"I think I do," he answered. "She loves you, son. That's the only explanation for what we walked in on. Since you're still here, I'm guessing you feel the same way. If you leave now, this is your life—whiskey, women and regrets like flies on manure. But if you're the man she thinks you are, you'll tell me why you're on the run."

Once with Lem, Rafe had been trapped in a dead-end canyon by a gang of horse thieves. He'd fought his way out and decided to do the same now, but with the truth instead of bullets. He looked Reverend Leaf square in the eye. "I stole money from my old man and left my half brother dead or maimed. It was an accident, but I'm still a wanted man."

As he'd done with Susanna, Rafe recounted the events of his life, starting with the train ride out of New Orleans and ending in the mansion on the Mississippi. An hour later, he was feeling sorrier for himself than ever.

"That's why I'm headed to Mexico," he concluded. "Don't even think about telling me to go back to St. Louis."

The Reverend shook his head. "I wasn't going to.

There's a time to let the dead bury the dead, and this could be one of them. Only you can decide. But what's certain is this. That chip on your shoulder has to go."

Rafe scowled. "What's your point?"

The Reverend's eyes glinted with wisdom. "Son, have you ever made a mistake?"

Rafe thought of Nick's leg but stayed silent.

"I have, more than I can count and they've been costly."

"What's your point?"

"You're bitter."

"So what? My father did me wrong."

A throaty chuckle erupted from the Reverend's lips. "Isn't that just too bad? Poor little Rafe had a hard time of it. You're breaking my heart."

The man was busting his ass, but Rafe didn't know why. "I don't need this shit."

"Yes, you do," the Reverend said. "That self-pity has to go. Do you think you're the only man on earth who's been knocked around? I could tell you stories that would curl your hair." His voice dropped to a hush. "God loves you, son. Susanna does, too. But that bitterness will eat you alive if you don't get rid of it."

Rafe stared at the whiskey. "Some things are more wrong than others."

"That's true, but the cure's the same."

The Reverend dropped a handful of coins on the counter and turned to leave. Rafe pivoted on the stool. "What's the cure?"

"A hard look in the mirror. No one's perfect, Rafe." The Reverend's eyes glittered like dark glass. "You know about needing forgiveness. It's why you came back. But giving it is another matter."

Rafe pushed back the memory of Walter Albright yanking him from Mimi's grave. Instead he focused on what he'd just done to Susanna. "I love your daughter, sir."

"Then stick around."

"I can't."

The Reverend's expression turned wistful and Rafe wondered what he was thinking. He seemed to have stepped back in time, then he blinked and said, "Have you asked her to go with you?"

"We talked about it."

"And?"

Rafe's lips curled into a smile. "Her old man barged in with a shotgun."

The Reverend smiled. "You two need to finish your talk. Let's go see Susanna."

Rafe left money for his supper and followed John Leaf out the door. The Reverend was on foot, so Rafe led his horses as the two men made small talk about

Midas. The sky had turned black with a smattering of stars, but second-floor windows beamed light down on the street. It reminded Rafe of a checkerboard. When they reached Susanna's house, he tied his horses and took the lead on the stairs. He had just reached the landing when she stepped outside. He could see that she'd been crying.

"I'm sorry," he said. "I shouldn't have left like that."

"I'm just glad you're back."

She hooked her arm around his waist and led him inside where he saw Abbie sitting on the divan. When the Reverend walked into the room, Susanna hugged him hard and they made their amends.

Rafe wished all mistakes could be so easily put aside.

The Reverend turned to him next. "Your room's waiting at the parsonage. I'll be up if you two want to talk about things."

After hugging Susanna again, the Leafs left the apartment. Rafe glanced around the front room. "Where's Nick?"

"At the parsonage."

He'd been hoping the boy would give him a reason to stall. After seeing Susanna with her parents, he felt even less sure about asking her to go with him to Mexico. But Susanna seemed more confident than ever. She took his hand and tugged him to the divan.

"Sit down," she said. "I have something to ask you."

Rafe left space on the divan, but she dropped to her knees. Before he realized what she intended to do, she reached for his other hand and curled her fingers around his. The lamp on the end table lit up her face as she looked into his eyes. "Will you marry me, Rafe LaCroix?"

Rafe's stomach twisted. "I have to leave. You'd be giving up everything you love."

"Not everything. And not everyone."

"But your family—"

"I know what I'm doing."

He tried to break his grip. "Then what about your practice?"

Squeezing tighter, she said, "I'm replaceable."

"No, you're not." Rafe thought she was one of a kind. "I don't want to lose you. But—"

"Then marry me." Her eyes burned into his. "I still think we should write to Thomas Smith, but I can live with the uncertainty if I have to. We can have the wedding tonight. You can leave in a few days and find a place for us. As soon as you write, I'll follow with Nick."

The plan had merit, but it wasn't perfect. "I want to be sure of that fresh start before you leave Midas. We can find a church in Mexico."

"No," she said. "I want my father to marry us."

Rafe had his doubts about the Reverend's acceptance. Encouraging them to talk about their mess was one thing. A midnight marriage was an entirely different matter.

"He's not going to like it."

"You don't know him," she said softly. "We'll talk to him together."

Three hours later, the clock in her parents' bedroom chimed twelve times. Susanna was wearing her blue dress with her hair pinned on top of her head. She'd never felt more excited in her life. Her mother had spent an hour talking to her about the decision she and Rafe had made. While Abbie hadn't been as pleased as Susanna had hoped, she had understood.

The problem, it seemed, was her father.

They had spoken to him together and then Rafe had sat with him on the porch for another twenty minutes. Susanna had been looking out the window when she'd seen her father walk alone to the stream. She knew that he'd gone to that spot to think and decide what to do. When someone tapped on the door, she expected it to be him.

"Come in," she answered.

"Hello, Sam." He hadn't called her by the nickname for years.

He was wearing his preacher's coat, which she took as a good sign. After pulling a chair away from his desk, he sat and faced her. "First off, I want you to know that I like Rafe a lot."

"But?"

"There are no 'buts' where he's concerned. The episode in St. Louis was tragic, but I'm convinced it was an accident."

"I believe that, too." But her stomach knotted.

"Even so, he's not done with it, Susanna. Rafe loves you, but he's full of bitterness. That's why I'm asking you to wait awhile before getting married. He needs to sort through that mess."

Susanna quivered with disappointment. She recognized the wisdom in her father's words, but she also believed that her love for Rafe was the surest cure for what ailed him. "I don't want to wait," she said.

"Is there a reason that has something to do with this morning? If there's a baby, it would change things."

Susanna shook her head. "No."

"Then a couple of months won't make a difference. I'll take you to wherever Rafe settles. We'll bring your mother and the boys and have a wedding with tamales and even a piñata."

Waiting made sense, but Susanna was afraid of

what the future held for Rafe. Life on the road held unseen dangers. There were no guarantees that he'd make it to Mexico without encountering the Bentons. If all she could have was a few days, she wanted to grab that chance. Better a wife for a night than a lonely spinster for the rest of her life.

Susanna held her father's gaze. "I love him, Pa. I know this isn't the kind of wedding you wanted for me, but Rafe is part of me. He's the man I've chosen. If you won't marry us, we can go to a justice of the peace."

"Oh no, you won't." Her father had arched his brow, a sign he meant business. "When I marry people, it sticks. I just want you to be sure."

"I am."

When he looked into her eyes, Susanna raised her chin and stared back. She had nothing to hide and no regrets.

Her father blinked first, then smiled. "I never could say no to you. I'll marry you tonight and file the papers tomorrow."

"Thank you, Pa."

"Just remember one thing, honey. You and Rafe can always come home."

It had been a long time since Rafe had set foot in a church. He'd been nine years old and sitting next to his mother. Mimi had been a loyal Catholic and had loved the incense and the awe, the statuary and priests intoning in Latin. He hadn't expected that atmosphere tonight, but that's what he found when he walked into the front room of the parsonage. Everywhere he turned, he saw candles, a hundred of them in all different sizes. A fire was burning in the hearth and the air smelled smoky and warm.

"Are you nervous?"

The question had come from Reverend Leaf. He was standing by the hearth with Nick and Susanna's brothers. The boys were spit and polished, and so was Rafe. In his suit and tie, he didn't look at all like the man the Reverend had found in the saloon.

"I'm more awed than anything," Rafe replied. As he took his place, he wished he had a ring for his bride. Someday he'd give her something special, but that would have to wait.

The Reverend raised his voice. "Ladies? Are you ready?"

The answer came in the whisper of a dress. Abbie entered the room first and took her place at her husband's side. Rafe's eyes stayed on the doorway as Susanna walked into the candlelight with a graceful and confident air.

He'd been a expecting her to wear something modest, but she had chosen her ball gown. The blue silk shimmered as she walked, capturing the flickering candles like stars in the night sky. Instead of a bouquet of roses, an impossible find at midnight in November, she was holding a white leather book. As she stepped closer, Rafe recognized the thick pages of a photograph album she'd be taking to Mexico.

"There's no reason to be formal," the Reverend said. "I'm going to say a few words, then you two will speak your vows."

Susanna handed the album to Abbie and took Rafe's hand. As their gazes locked, he smiled. On a whim he kissed her knuckles, then they both faced the Reverend whose expression had turned serious.

"In the Garden of Eden," he said, "God told Adam to leave his father and mother and cleave to his wife. He intended for Eve to do the same. Cleaving means you hold on tight and don't let go. It's like making a braid, which is what you two are doing tonight. You're each a strand with God's love being the third piece. The tighter you hold on to each other, the stronger that rope becomes. That's what it means to cleave.

"Susanna, your mother and I respect your choice and we'll love Rafe like a son. If you two head south, you'll go with our blessing. Will we miss you?" He swallowed hard. "You bet. But you belong at your husband's side. It's a choice women have made through the ages, one that your mother and I fully understand."

Her eyes misted. "Thank you, Pa."

The Reverend shifted his gaze to Rafe. "Husbands have a duty to their wives. Cleaving to her isn't just about the physical act that brings life into the world, though that's part of the bond. Cleaving means that your wife becomes a part of you. When she hurts, you hurt. When she cries, you cry. That means you put her needs before your own. Will you do that?"

"I will."

Rafe felt the force of the Reverend's regard for a full ten seconds, but he didn't flinch. He'd left this morning because he loved her, and he'd come back for the same reason. No one was going to stare him down.

Slowly the Reverend's expression changed. The corners of his mouth turned up as if he were fighting a smile, and then his eyes started to twinkle. "Don't worry, son. You're marrying Susanna with our full blessing. Welcome to the family."

Rafe choked up. "Thank you, sir."

The Reverend lifted his Bible off the hearth and started to read, "'Dearly Beloved, we are gathered here today...'"

Rafe listened to every word, letting the meaning sink into his bones. He'd never made a promise he'd been so intent on keeping. He said "I do" with complete conviction and listened as Susanna took the same vows.

The Reverend closed the book and smiled. "That's it. You two are married. It's time to kiss the bride."

Rafe pulled Susanna into his arms and looked into her shining eyes. Never mind that the kids and her parents were watching. A peck wouldn't do. With all the passion and sweetness she deserved, he sealed their vows with a kiss that held the promise of the night to come. He didn't want the moment to end, but the boys were starting to snicker.

"Gosh, Pa. Are they *ever* going to stop?" said one of the twins.

"Nope," said the Reverend. "They're just getting started."

Hidden by the night, Garrett stood thirty feet from the parsonage and peered into the window. He'd been watching Dr. Leaf for three days, but tonight was the first time he had spotted Rafe. The night had taken a strange turn when he realized his brother was walking down the street with a minister. Curious, Garrett had opted to lie low. As long as he had Rafe in sight, he could afford to be patient.

The night had taken another twist when he'd followed Rafe and Dr. Leaf to the parsonage. They had been walking fast and seemed excited. Rafe had been carrying a carpetbag, and they had gone into the house through the back door. Lights had popped on in all the bedrooms, and eventually shadowy figures had gathered in the front room.

Garrett couldn't make out the faces in the candlelight, but he could tell that something formal was happening. Flanked by a row of boys and a woman with dark hair, the minister was reading from a book. In front of him stood Rafe and Dr. Leaf. Considering it was just past midnight, the circumstances struck him as odd—until Rafe pulled Dr. Leaf into his arms and kissed her.

"I'll be damned," Garrett muttered. He'd just been to his brother's wedding. With his cane in hand, he headed for Dr. Leaf's apartment. It was time to give the happy couple a wedding gift of his own.

Chapter Seventeen

Susanna grabbed her husband's hand and raced away from the parsonage. "Hurry! I don't want to waste a minute."

"Neither do I." Rafe pulled her into his arms and spun her around. When they were both dizzy and laughing, he kissed her soundly in the moonlight, lingering on her lips and then whispering, "I love you, Dr. LaCroix."

Her eyes misted. "I like the sound of that."

"Me, too."

Arm in arm, they hurried down the boardwalk. They had just reached the end of her block when Susanna saw a shadow moving by her staircase. Rafe saw it too and made her stop.

"Oh no," she moaned. "It's probably a patient."

"I'm not so sure. He's got something in his hand."

Susanna squinted into the alley and saw why Rafe was worried. The man was holding a long object across his body. It looked suspiciously like a rifle. She blinked and recalled Zeke Benton's lifeless eyes. Had the gang come back for revenge? She rarely had calls in the middle of the night, and any of her regular patients would have known that her parents were back and gone to the parsonage. A stranger lingering in the shadows couldn't be taken lightly. She looked at Rafe and knew he was thinking the same thing.

He lifted a split of pine off a woodpile and nudged her beneath a set of stairs. "No matter what you hear, stay put."

"But—"

"Just do it."

With a kiss to her forehead, he went around the back of her clinic. Susanna stayed still, breathing silently, counting the seconds, praying for Rafe until she heard a metallic rasp. It sounded like a sword being unsheathed, but that made no sense. Rafe cried out and then she heard a thump and the sound of a body hitting the boardwalk.

Susanna sped around the corner with her heart in her throat. Her eyes went first to Rafe, standing with the wood still in his hand and bleeding from a cut across his cheek. A man lay sprawled facedown at his feet. She dropped to a crouch and took his pulse.

"Tell me he's alive," Rafe said, wiping the blood from his cheek.

"He's breathing."

Moonlight glistened on her bloody fingers as she did a cursory inspection of the wound and felt the start of a lump. Her best guess was that he'd live. Without better light, she couldn't see his pupils or his face, but her fingers traced a jagged scar. "Oh, God. It's Thomas Smith. The rifle we saw had to be his cane."

"It's a sword cane," Rafe muttered. "I was sneaking up on him when he pulled it. All I saw was the blade. So help me, God, I didn't mean to do this."

Susanna looked up at Rafe and saw his bloody cheek. "How deep is that cut?"

"It's not bad."

Susanna didn't know whether to be horrified by the circumstances or relieved. "Is this man your brother?"

The look in Rafe's eyes tore her to pieces. "Yes, it's Garrett. Susanna, I've got to go."

"No!"

"I hate myself for this—for everything."

"Then stay! Face up to what you did." She pushed to her feet and reached for his hand, but he stepped out of her grasp. Knowing he was poised for flight, she stayed still and tried to make her voice soothing. "You're a better man than this, Rafe. I know you."

But her husband was shaking his head. "This doesn't change a thing. I'll write to you when I get over the border. If you don't want to come, I'll understand."

"We just got married!"

"I'm doing this for you, Doc."

"No, you're not," she said. "You're doing it to save your own skin."

Rafe took three breaths, each one fainter than the last. "I'll write. The rest is up to you."

A cold fury settled in her belly as his footsteps faded into the night. Not only had he run out on her, he'd left her with a mess to clean up. Where was the man who'd risked his life for Nick and sworn to protect her? She had no desire to chase after him. He needed to see for himself that running would do no good. She could only hope that he'd come back on his own.

She also had a patient who needed her attention. Putting aside thoughts of Rafe and a wedding night, she went into the clinic to retrieve smelling salts for Thomas Smith. At least one mystery would be solved.

For the next week, Rafe traveled along remote trails that led south to Mexico. Braving an onslaught of wind and rain, he pushed his horses as hard as he dared, but a blizzard forced him to hole up in an abandoned shack for a few days. He was behind schedule and painfully aware that he'd done the wrong thing by leaving.

Swinging the wood had been a knee-jerk reaction, but he'd had only one thought when he'd seen a stranger lurking in the shadows. Susanna needed protecting. Without a firearm, he had decided to sneak up on the stranger, grab him around the throat and ask a few questions. He hadn't made a sound, but Garrett had sensed the danger and whipped out the cane sword.

Rafe had seen a few of those weapons in his time, but they weren't common. They were usually carried by officers wounded in the War Between The States or men who couldn't handle a gun. When the blade had sliced his cheek, he'd clobbered his attacker with the split of pine. It had made sense until Garrett's head snapped back and Rafe had recognized his brother, scars and all.

He knew it was wrong to run, but he'd been besieged with a loathing that had filled him like a fever. He hated his father and he hated Garrett. And mostly at that moment, he'd hated himself. Running hadn't been a choice—it was his true nature. He'd been too panicked to think about Susanna when he'd left, but he'd spent the past several days composing letters in his head.

I'm sorry...I'm coming home.

I'm in Mexico...the choice is yours.

He had pretty much decided to send the second one. Unless he didn't write to her at all. Either way, he needed to buy supplies. Leaving the shelter of the mountains, he rode into the desert town of Los Manos. Dusty and dry, it was nothing more than a strip of buildings at the crossroads of a cattle trail and a set of train tracks. A lone cottonwood marked the edge of town. Judging by the scars on its lowest branch, more than one man had met his fate at the end of a rope.

Rafe turned his head and saw a splintery building that served as the railroad station. Guilt and anger welled in his belly like a bad stew, and he nudged his horse into a faster walk until he reached the general store. After making his purchases, he walked into a restaurant and ordered a bowl of soup.

He'd just raised the spoon to his lips when he noticed a waitress giving him the evil eye. He'd never seen her before, so he blew on the soup to cool it and swallowed the broth. With his nerves jangling, he listened as she spoke to an adolescent boy. The kid scowled at Rafe and headed out the door. At the same time, a cook came out of the back room and blocked the exit.

Trying to look casual, Rafe ate the soup as he watched the door. When the town sheriff walked into the restaurant, he set down his spoon and waited.

The lawman put his hand on the butt of his gun. "Rafe LaCroix, you're under arrest."

Whatever had happened in Los Manos hadn't involved him, but guilt still burned in Rafe's belly. He tried to hide it, but he felt nauseous. "You're making a mistake. I've never been here before."

"The Bentons rode through here last week. Does that help your memory?"

"No, sir. I'm traveling alone, but I know the men you're talking about."

"I'm sure you do."

"I turned in Frank Benton for the bounty. You can wire the authorities in Colorado."

"I'll do that," the sheriff replied. "But I also have a Wanted poster that says you rode with the Bentons in Colorado, and a witness who'll testify to the rape and murder of Mary Jessup."

The blood drained from Rafe's head. Being accused of such horrible crimes sickened him. He'd left Midas to avoid false accusations and the gallows, and he'd ridden into a situation that was ten times worse. He knew about mistakes. People made them all the time. God only knows what a witness would say at the sight of his bearded face. Even if he shaved, he still bore a mark from Garrett's sword.

With the spoon in his hand and the sheriff glaring at him, Rafe thought about the night in the stable and being tangled in fishing line. This time he felt like a fish in a net being scooped out of a stream. He was breathing just fine, but he couldn't feel the air going into his lungs. His belly was flopping and wouldn't stop.

The sheriff had a heavy mustache that hid his upper lip. As he spoke, his face stayed still, giving him the look of a corpse. Rafe decided he'd be wise to cooperate and gave the man a nod. "I'll be glad to face a witness. I swear, I didn't do it."

"We'll see about that," said the lawman. "Ed Jessup was gone the day it happened, but their daughter saw the whole thing. If she says you're the one, you're going to hang. Now get moving. I'm locking you up."

Rafe stood and raised his hands in surrender. The sheriff took a pair of wrist irons off his belt with one hand and jerked Rafe's wrists behind his back with the other. After turning the key, he spoke to the waitress. "Martha, get word to Ed. He needs to bring Lucy to town."

"They're at the feed store," she answered. "I'll send Ricky."

With the sheriff at his back, Rafe walked out the door and saw Punkin and his packhorse tied to the hitching post.

The sheriff steered him toward the west edge of town. "I'll have a deputy see to your horses."

As they walked, Rafe counted a dozen sagging storefronts, a saloon and a shabby hotel. Dry and dusty, the town looked dead on the outside, but behind the smudged windows he saw angry faces peering at him through faded curtains. The sheriff's office was an adobe set apart from the main street. It had a small window, a thatched roof and a sign that read "Tom Beck, Sheriff."

When the man opened the door, Rafe walked into the office and headed for the cell. The bars were flat metal and welded in a grid, the surest way to keep a man from escaping. After undoing the wrist irons, Beck opened the cell door and waited for him to step inside.

Rafe froze in place. If he walked into the cell, he might never get out. Witnesses made mistakes. He could hang for a crime he didn't commit. He'd also be a sitting duck with Garrett on his trail. Everything he feared was nipping at his heels. He wasn't accustomed to asking God for mercy, but he felt that urge now. He couldn't run and he had nowhere to hide. He needed a break in the worst way.

Please, God.

But instead of peace, he felt a terrible remorse. He'd had this moment coming for years.

Beck interrupted his thoughts. "Do you need a push, LaCroix? I'll be glad to give it to you."

Rafe stared at the wall at the back of the cell, taking in the shape of a man's shadow. It was his own, but he barely recognized it. The angle of the sun made the figure tall and the sweep of the cross-bars gave it outstretched arms. He felt the same awe he'd experienced when Nick's leg had been spared and the same peace that had come from the tangled fishing line.

Staring at that shadow, Rafe knew that his running days were over. More relieved than afraid, he stepped inside the cell.

When the door swung shut, he felt the deepest contentment he'd ever known. He knew exactly what he had to do. As soon as the Jessup girl cleared his name, he'd sell his horses and buy a train ticket to Midas. He'd go to Susanna and beg her to forgive him. Then he'd find Garrett and face his brother like a man.

Rafe wished he didn't look so trail-weary. He hadn't shaved since leaving Midas and dust had caked in the creases of his clothes. He looked like he'd just crawled out of a hole.

As the front door creaked open, he saw a wedge of light followed by the silhouette of a stocky man wearing overalls and heavy boots. He looked directly into the cell, staring at Rafe with bitter eyes and the unkempt appearance of a man without a wife. Gray whiskers mottled his cheeks and his skin looked ashen. Behind him lagged an adolescent girl in blue calico. Unlike her father, she couldn't bring herself to look into the cell. Instead she seemed entranced by the dust motes in the shaft of light.

"Good morning, Ed." Beck stood and shook the man's hand. "We've got one of the Benton gang. I'm sorry, but I need Lucy to identify him."

Rafe saw no point in arguing about his association with the Bentons. Lucy reminded him of a sparrow and he felt like a hawk. It was best to seem friendly, so he made his voice bland. "Hello, miss."

She barely glanced at him and then mumbled at the floor.

"Speak up, girl!" Jessup demanded. "Is that him?"

"I'm not sure."

Rafe's stomach dropped to his boots. The sheriff glared at him. "LaCroix, take off your hat."

Rafe did as he was told and raked his hand through his hair in a vain attempt to look presentable. Dirt coated his palm. His whiskers itched and he smelled his own sweat.

Please God... Daring to hope for a break, he stood square in front of Lucy and her father. Still looking at the dust motes, the girl sniffed. Her father gripped her shoulder. "You have to look at him, Lucy. I know what you saw, but this is important. Your ma's depending on you."

She glanced at Rafe and then looked back at her feet. "That's him. He hurt Ma. I saw him—I saw *them* and she was screaming."

"She's wrong!" Rafe gripped the bars and shook. The metal rattled like dried bones—his bones. He was going to die.

The sheriff gave him a thoughtful look, as if he was considering the possibility of Rafe's innocence, but Jessup charged at the cell. "You son of a bitch! I want to see you hang!"

Rafe stared into the man's eyes and saw a rabid dog. Jessup was past reason. Locked in a jail cell without an alibi and identified by a witness, Rafe knew he was as good as dead.

Sheriff Beck pushed up from his chair. "Settle down, Ed. LaCroix's entitled to a fair trial."

"I don't give a damn what he's *entitled* to," Jessup declared. "He killed Mary. He *violated* my wife. He's going to hang, damn it!"

"He probably will, but not today."

Jessup wiped his eyes with the back of his hand. Tears glistened on the patches of skin above his scraggly beard, but they did nothing to soften his rage. "There's no *probably* about it. LaCroix's going to die."

Rafe was gripping the bars so hard that his hands hurt, but he was also aware of Lucy cowering by the door. He felt no anger toward the girl—only pity. She was making a terrible mistake and she knew it. Rafe had shared that exact misery. After maiming Garrett, he'd felt like a paper boat being carried down a river, racing with the current until it lost all purpose and form. Rafe hurt for the girl, but he couldn't convey that understanding.

"Lucy, let's go," Jessup said.

As the door slammed shut, Rafe dropped down on the cot. Air hissed from the pallet and filled his nose with the stench of urine and sweat.

Beck sat back at his desk. "There's a circuit judge that'll come down from Albuquerque. The trial will start when he gets here."

"When will that be?" Rafe asked.

"Three days. Maybe longer."

Three days of purgatory—of waiting to die and knowing that he'd never see Susanna again. To live with guilt was a daily torture. To die with it was a special kind of suffering. Rafe wanted to be mad at the Almighty for leaving him in this mess, but he couldn't escape the sense that he'd had this moment coming for a long time. In the end, he'd brought this misery on himself.

The sheriff rocked forward in his chair. "There's a new attorney in town. His name's Charles Archer. I'll ask him to come by."

The news did nothing to allay Rafe's fears, but he said, "Thanks."

"As for the trial," Beck continued, "I'll do my best to see that you get one, but I can't guarantee it. Jessup has this town pretty riled."

Rafe had seen a lynching in Gunnison. A horse thief had been dragged out of a saloon and strung up before the law arrived. He and Lem had joined the crowd, watching with macabre fascination as the rope snapped tight. The man had kicked twice, lost control of his bowels and hung there like a piece of meat.

Blinking hard, Rafe recalled the cottonwood at the edge of town. He hated the thought of dying, but one thing bothered him even more. That was knowing Susanna would come to him if she got wind of this mess. He might have risked it if she could have given him a solid alibi, but the Jessup place had been attacked long after he'd left Midas and only shortly before he'd arrived in Los Manos. Besides, women lied for men all the time. Who'd take her seriously? Not the judge or a jury of men intent on revenge. Rafe would still hang, and her good name would be tainted by his. As much he wanted to clear his conscience in person, he couldn't imagine asking her to share this hell. It was far kinder to send her a letter.

"I need to write to someone," he said to Beck.

"I guess that's all right."

The sheriff opened a drawer and removed a stack of newsprint. He brought it to Rafe along with a pencil. "No man should leave this earth with a guilty conscience."

Rafe nodded, but he didn't see how a letter could wash him clean. With the trial in his future, he'd be dead before Susanna read his amends.

As she had done every day for the past two weeks, Susanna closed her clinic at noon and walked to the post office to check for a letter from Rafe. If today was like the others, she'd find letters from friends but nothing from the man who had walked out on her. She'd go to the Midas Hotel and join Garrett for a lunch at the café. She'd report the lack of a letter and ask about his health.

The man had ended up with a lump on his head

but nothing worse. What Rafe had lost had been far more profound.

As she opened the door to the post office, Susanna greeted the clerk with a smile. "Anything today, Will?"

"A couple of things."

Her heart pounded as she took the two envelopes. One was from a classmate in Baltimore. The other was addressed in Rafe's writing but had no return address. She peeled back the flap and started to read.

Dear Susanna,
Please know how much I love you and how deeply I regret leaving like I did. If I could, I'd go back to our wedding night and face Garrett. I'd stand there like a man and take my licks.

I'd trade my soul to have that chance, but the choice isn't mine. I won't go into the details, but I'm convinced you're better off in Midas than you'd be with me right now. If by some miracle I can come home, I will. But if you don't hear from me in a month, I want you to annul our marriage. Trust me that it's for the best.

Nothing can take away the love I feel for you. It's been a comfort in the past few days but a torture, too. I'm more lonely for you than I can say and wish that we'd had that first time. I wish a lot of things.

Tell your father he was right. Life without you isn't worth living. Tell your mother that I wish I'd known her better. As for your brothers, I'm glad to have met them. Last of all, tell Nick I love him. Things aren't working out as I'd hoped, but it gives me comfort to know you have each other.

I love you, Susanna. I pray that someday you can forgive me.

Yours, Rafe

Susanna turned over the envelope and read the postmark. A water stain blurred the ink, but it looked like Los Manos. She'd never heard of the place, but it sounded like a border town. As hard as she tried, she couldn't read between the lines. He was protecting her but from what? Was he still in Los Manos? And worst of all, why did he sound like a man getting ready to die?

Clutching the envelope, she hurried to the Midas Hotel where Garrett was seated at a table. He pushed to his feet and smiled. "Hello, Susanna. Would you care for—"

"I've heard from him." She handed Garrett the

letter and sat in the chair, watching as he skimmed the page.

He refolded it neatly into thirds and passed it back to her. "I'll take the next train to Los Manos."

"I'm going with you."

"That wouldn't be wise," he replied. "It's a rough town."

Susanna respected his warning, but she had no intention of waiting in Midas. Whether Garrett liked it or not, she had something to say her husband. When she'd taken those vows, she'd meant every word, including "for better or for worse." Rafe had shown her his worst when he'd run off, but she still believed in the better man she had married.

"I can be ready in an hour," she said. "When does the next train leave?"

"Not until tomorrow." Garrett smiled at her. "I don't suppose there's anything I can say to stop you?"

"Not a word," she said. "I have something to say to my husband, and he's darn well going to listen."

Chapter Eighteen

Lying on the cot with his arm covering his eyes, Rafe inhaled the freshness of the day. He'd been in jail for seven long days. Sometimes he caught a whiff of diesel from a train or bacon cooking at the restaurant. In the past few days, he'd discovered that facing death sharpened a man's senses. It also made his dreams as vivid as life itself, and they were always about Susanna, even the vinegar scent of her hair.

The one smell missing was the stench of his cell. For that kindness, he owed a debt to Charles Archer. Fresh out of law college, the man was determined to protect his client's rights. He'd insisted that Rafe be allowed to bathe and shave before yesterday's court appearance, and he'd shamed the sheriff into providing fresh bedding.

Archer was also dead set on giving Rafe the best defense possible. He'd asked dozens of questions about where Rafe had been. In the end, he'd said that the odds weren't good, but that he wanted to present evidence about Frank Benton's bounty and call Susanna as a character witness. Rafe had agreed to contact the authorities to verify his role in Benton's capture, but he refused to involve Susanna.

The attorney had tried to persuade him, but Rafe had held the line. He didn't want Susanna anywhere near a gallows.

Lying on his cot, he rehashed the start of the trial. Thanks to Archer, the judge had agreed to delay the proceedings until the authorities reported back on the Benton bounty. Rafe had felt a ray of hope, but threats had exploded from Ed Jessup's mouth.

"You're going to hang, LaCroix. I'll do it myself if I have to."

The judge had gaveled him down, but nothing could stop the hate pulsating in the room. At least thirty pairs of eyes had drilled the back of Rafe's head. When the proceedings ended, the crowd had spilled into the street with men and woman alike calling him vile names. Beck had been forced to fire a shot in the air. The crowd had backed away, but Rafe hadn't felt any safer.

With his feet shackled and his hands tied behind his back, he had been at the mercy of Beck and the crowd. Someone had thrown a rock and he'd ducked.

It had broken a window and sent glass flying. The next night he'd heard drunken threats as a bottle shattered against the adobe.

As soon as Beck left, Rafe expected the taunts to start again. A deputy had been hired to keep an eye on things, but Rafe had no confidence in the man's abilities. Rather than dwelling on being lynched, he closed his eyes and relived dancing in the grass with Susanna.

The creak of the office door jarred Rafe out of his dream. Staying flat, he bent his neck to get a look at the visitor. The first thing he noticed was a fancy cane with a ruby-studded handle. Rafe knew the design. His father considered it an Albright family emblem. He also recognized the bent spine of the man asking the sheriff for a private moment with the prisoner.

"All right," Beck said. "But I'll be right outside."

Garrett waited until the sheriff departed, then he faced Rafe. "Hello, brother."

In all his years on the run, Rafe had never once imagined that Garrett was the man he'd been calling his guardian angel. The name had been sarcastic when Rafe first thought of it, but the compassion in Garrett's eyes made him wonder if his brother had been looking out for him all along.

Rafe knew that he owed this man amends, but

blurting "I'm sorry" seemed cheap. It was fitting to give his brother the first word, so Rafe pushed to his feet. "Hello, Garrett. You finally caught up with me."

His brother motioned toward a chair. "Do you mind if I sit?"

"Go ahead."

Garrett used his weak arm to drag a chair in front of the cell while he leaned on the cane. He sat with an awkward bend of his knees, took two cigars from his inside pocket and handed one to Rafe. He struck a match, lit Rafe's cigar and then managed his own.

Rafe took a puff and then sat on the edge of the cot. The cigar was either a peace offering or a last smoke for a man facing a firing squad. Given Garrett's twisted expression, Rafe would have bet on the firing squad. Either way, his brother deserved this moment. "How did you find me?" Rafe asked.

"Dr. LaCroix received your letter two days ago."

Dr. LaCroix... Blood rushed to Rafe's head. Susanna was using his name. It was an honor he didn't deserve. A second thought rocked him to the core. She had shared the letter with Garrett, a sign that she trusted him. With the cigar dangling between his fingers, Rafe looked at his brother's scars. The ridges had turned pink with time, but that night was bloodred in Rafe's mind. "I thought I'd killed you and the boss wanted me to hang. That's why I ran," he explained. "I'm sorry, Garrett. I should have gone for help."

Garrett's face stayed still. "I didn't wake up for two days. When I discovered I couldn't move my left side, I hated you for what you'd done."

Rafe felt as light as the smoke rising to the ceiling. "You must be looking forward to the hanging."

"No, Rafe. I'm not."

For the first time he could recall, Garrett had called him by his given name—not *bastard* or another epithet. That gesture mattered more than the cigar.

"It took awhile," Garrett continued. "But I learned to walk again. Having one eye isn't so bad except at night. What matters is that I came to see that night for what it was. We were both in the wrong—you for stealing, and me for treating you like dirt when the boss brought you home. I knew all about Mimi. So did my mother. I hated you as much as you hated us."

Rafe managed a dry smile. "That's saying a lot."

"We were a couple of hotheads having a brawl. What happened was as much my fault as yours."

Rafe could almost hear Susanna whispering "I told you so." He could only hope she'd have the chance to say it to his face. But he still didn't know where his father stood in the matter. "I doubt the boss saw it that way."

Garrett tapped the ash. "You can ask him yourself. He's coming for the trial."

Bile churned in Rafe's belly. For years Walter Albright had treated him like mud on his shoe. Rafe tapped the cigar and watched the ash flutter to the floor. "I don't understand why."

"He's got his reasons."

Rafe didn't know what to think. He hated the man for what he'd done, but he couldn't avoid seeing him now. "When do you expect him?"

"Any day."

Rafe blew a halo of smoke and sent a prayer with it. "I hope I live that long."

"I know about Jessup. I'll post a guard. As for the trial, I understand you have an attorney."

"His name's Charles Archer. He's a good man."

"Excellent. If you don't mind, I'd like to have supper with him."

"Sure."

Rafe felt a trickle of hope. If he could get out of this mess, he'd have a chance to patch things up with Susanna. The thought of her reminded him of their wedding and he looked at Garrett. "I owe you another apology. I whacked you pretty hard the other night."

Garrett waved it off. "I don't blame you for that. I thought you'd bolt if you saw me, so I stayed in the shadows. It looked damned suspicious."

Rafe appreciated the understanding. "I was more worried about Susanna than anything else."

Garrett smiled. "She's a fine doctor and eager to see you. I'll bring her in the morning."

Rafe shot to his feet. "She's here? But it's not safe."

If the town got wind of her, she'd be a target for their hate. Rafe could live with a bull's-eye on his back, but he couldn't stand the thought of Susanna enduring the taunts. "Keep her away from me," he said to Garrett.

His brother frowned. "It's too late. She checked into the hotel as Dr. LaCroix. She's determined to testify at the trial."

Knowing Susanna was a block away was the sweetest torture Rafe had ever endured. He had to clench his teeth to keep from asking Garrett to bring her right now, but dusk was settling and the jeering would start. His apologies would have to wait until morning. Surely he'd live that long….

Rafe locked eyes with Garrett. "Tell her I'll see her tomorrow when it's safe."

"I will," Garrett replied. "Now get some rest. I'll post extra guards."

As Garrett left, Rafe gave in to a small smile. His guardian angel was still on the job.

Susanna stood at the hotel window, looking down the street at shadowy buildings and praying that Rafe was safe. She wished she hadn't honored Garrett's request to visit him without her, but it had been the right thing to do. They had needed to settle their differences in private.

Knowing that Rafe had apologized to Garrett meant the world to her. As soon as the trial ended, they'd be headed home to Midas. She refused to think of any other outcome, but she hadn't escaped the hate brewing in the streets. At supper, the waitress had deliberately spilled coffee on Susanna's dress, and the hotel clerk had refused to offer them accommodations until Garrett threatened to withhold all railroad business from the man's establishment.

Susanna had seen too much of the squalid town and couldn't wait to leave with her husband. Peering toward the jailhouse, she was thinking about changing into her nightgown when a flare of orange light caught her eye. Another flame blazed and moved toward the first one. She saw another torch and then more flames than she could count. The dragon's breath was headed straight for the jail. A lynch mob...

Susanna ran to Garrett's room and pounded on his door. He jerked it open. "What is it?"

"There's a mob," she cried. "We have to stop them."

"I thought this might happen. Stay here."

"No! If Rafe's hurt, he'll need me."

Garrett gave her a thoughtful look. "I suppose it'll be safe. I have guards waiting downstairs. Get your coat."

Susanna didn't care if it was safe or not. She wasn't about to wait helplessly at the hotel. As she grabbed her wrap, she wished that she'd brought her medical bag to Los Manos. After hurrying down the hallway, she caught up with Garrett on the stairs and followed him out the hotel door. Six men dressed in brown dusters and armed with shot guns had assembled on the boardwalk.

At the sight of Garrett, a short man stepped forward. "I've positioned six men in front of the jailhouse."

"Good work," Garrett said. "Let's go."

The men formed a phalanx and strode down the street. Protected by the wedge, Susanna glanced at Garrett's face. "Who are these men?"

"The railroad keeps a security force. I sent for them when I had Rafe cornered in Midas."

"Thank God."

As the guards closed in on the jailhouse, Susanna

saw a crowd of men with torches and a deputy standing in front of the door with his arms crossed. Six
more security agents stood at his flanks.

Garrett gripped her elbow to hold her back. "Stay
in the shadows."

Susanna stopped by a post, watching as Garrett
unsheathed the sword hidden in his cane. He positioned himself in front of the sheriff and then raised
the silver blade to command the crowd's attention.
Fire from the torches turned the blade to gold.

"Who the hell are you?" someone shouted.

"I'm a man who wants justice." Garrett's voice
boomed over the whip of the flames. "Now go home,
all of you."

"Not until LaCroix swings."

Susanna squinted through the glare of the torches,
but she couldn't see who had spoken.

"It won't happen tonight," Garrett insisted.

Susanna could barely breathe as the mob stood
its ground. She could feel heat from the torches and
worried that someone would set the roof on fire.
Garrett was still holding the sword high, a sign that
he had no intention of leaving. Finally, a tall man in
the back drifted into the night. One by one, the other
rioters followed until everyone was gone, except for
one man. Susanna saw his rabid eyes and knew she
was looking at Ed Jessup.

The torch turned his skin orange and his eyes into empty sockets. "I'll be back, Albright. I swear it on my wife's grave." He hurled the torch to the ground and walked away, fading to nothing as the flame suffocated in the dirt.

Susanna shivered with dread, but Garrett was composed as he addressed the deputy. "Go home, young man. My men will stand guard."

"Don't mind if I do."

As soon as he turned the corner, Garrett motioned for her to come out of the shadows. "The door's unlocked. Go see your husband."

The deputy had stepped outside at the first sign of trouble, but Rafe didn't expect to see the dawn. The night air was thick with smoke from the torches, and he could hear the mob jeering at the lawman. At the most he had five minutes before the mob stormed through the door and dragged him to the hanging tree. Only one thought filled his mind. He couldn't die without saying goodbye to his wife.

He had no paper, but he'd kept the pencil he'd used to write the letter. After retrieving it from under the cot, he dropped to his knees in front of the wall and wrote "Susanna" in his finest script. Racing against the chaos in the street, he drew the roses she should have carried at their wedding and wrote "I love you."

He finished the message with his initials and stood, ready to face the mob.

Trapped or not, he wouldn't go without a fight. He had Susanna to love and Nick to raise. With his heart pounding and his fists in knots, Rafe looked out the window for signs of violence. But instead of more shouting, he heard a sudden hush and a man bellowing at the crowd. He watched as the orange hue in the window faded to gray and finally black. He didn't know what to think when the doorknob turned and someone slipped inside, keeping the back of a coat to the cell. The visitor spoke to someone on the outside, shut the door and then faced him.

Susanna's brown eyes nearly dropped Rafe to his knees. The danger might have faded to the shadows, but it was lurking like a monster. "You shouldn't be here," he said, trying to mean it.

"Then where should I be?"

His throat went dry. "At the hotel where it's safe."

"The mob's gone. Garrett's posted a guard."

Rafe was foolishly grateful to see her and appalled at the risk. If the crowd doubled in size and the men tried again, she'd be in grave danger. As much as he wanted to hold Susanna in his arms, Rafe knew that he had to talk fast and send her to the hotel.

"I'm sorry I left," he said, rushing the words. "We took vows and I broke them ten minutes later."

"You panicked."

"But that doesn't explain why I didn't turn around. Can you forgive me?" His voice had cracked with need, but her eyes stayed steady.

"I already have."

"I love you," he said.

Smiling, she said, "I love you, too."

Rafe knew it was time to send her away, but he needed to touch her. With the bars between them, he stuck his hand through the grate and reached for her. But she didn't see the gesture. Her eyes were focused on the ring of keys hanging behind the sheriff's desk. If she let herself into the cell, he'd never find the strength to send her away. But neither could he let her go without a touch, a kiss even.

With his heart pounding, he watched as Susanna took the keys, lifted the desk lamp and approached the cell. With a twist of her wrist, she opened the door and stepped inside. Rafe took the lamp and set it on the floor. Facing her at last, he brushed her cheek with his fingertips.

Her soft skin soothed his worries and inflamed his need. Just a kiss, he told himself. Bending his neck, he brought his mouth to hers and sweetly brushed her lips.

"You have to go now," he said quietly.

"I don't see the need."

"The mob—"

"Twelve men are standing guard."

A thousand wouldn't have been enough for Rafe's peace of mind. He kissed her again, more deeply this time, pressing the silk of her lips into his memory. She had to leave before he lost his will. If he touched her again they'd be making love on the cot and he wanted to give her so much more. Knowing it was best for Susanna, he stepped back. "Go on now," he said in a ragged voice.

With a glimmer in her eyes, she walked to the cot and picked up one of the blankets. Turning, she held it up to the bars, tied one end and then fastened the other to make a wall of sorts. The lamp cast their shadows against the wool—a man and a woman three feet apart but aching to be joined.

When she held out both hands, Rafe took them but kept her at arm's length. "This isn't what I want for us," he said hoarsely. "It's a goddamned jail."

Susanna tugged his hands downward, drawing their bodies together like beads on a string. "What exactly do you want?"

"A bed big enough for both of us. Soft sheets and a mountain of pillows. Put it anywhere but here and I'd make love to you all night long."

"Close your eyes," she whispered. "Tell me what you see."

Rafe gave in and stepped into a dream. He didn't have the strength to do anything else. "I see you," he said. "And me...in a bed big enough for two. It has a red velvet spread and I smell roses."

"Then that's where we are."

Their lovemaking started in that dream, but it didn't stay in the land of make-believe. As soon as Rafe kissed her, his senses came alive with the taste of his wife, the way she moved her lips, her soft breasts pressed against him. He wanted to feel her writhing under him, grasping for him, but as much as he craved her body, a deeper truth had struck home. Susanna wasn't the only virgin in the jail cell. Her body was pure while his was experienced, but no woman had ever owned his heart. As far as first times went, Rafe was newer at love than she was.

He eased back on the kiss and looked into her eyes. "Come lie with me."

"I thought you'd never ask."

Together they moved to the cot. It was too small, so they stood facing each other. Rafe loosened her hair and undid her buttons, watching her face as a glow spread from her throat to her eyes. When he pushed the suit off her shoulders, she gave him a seductive smile. And when he sent her skirt to the floor in a puddle, her underthings went with it. Was there anything more glorious than a naked woman with love in her eyes? Rafe didn't think so, unless it was a man who felt the same way.

Susanna smiled at him. "My turn."

A minute later he was buck naked and warming his wife with his bare skin. Tiny or not, the cot would have to do. He brought her down with him, being careful not to crush her with his weight. Then he gave her all the love he could find. They were lost in each other—kissing, touching, suckling—when the lamp died and plunged them into a world without sheets or walls. Rafe rolled her to her back and stroked and kissed until she was moaning. Then he whispered, "You're mine," and joined their bodies with a tender glide.

"Oh!"

"Did that hurt?"

"Just a little," she said, her eyes wide. "Whatever you do, don't stop."

Rafe held still until she began to rock on her own. She moved slowly, as if she were testing the water, then she pulled back her knees, bringing him as deep as a man could be. He slid out and then back in, gauging her reactions for pain, but Susanna was already arching to meet him. Her first time…their first time. He picked up the tempo, aware of her every move until she cried out in surrender.

Never before had Rafe felt such utter possession of

a woman. And never had a woman so fully owned him. Driving forward, he followed her into the oblivion of being loved, spilling his seed without fear. Sweaty and spent, he collapsed on top of his wife and pressed his temple against hers. When he kissed her, he tasted tears. "Do you hurt?"

"Not anymore. I want ten thousand nights just like this one."

"Me, too."

But danger was lurking outside the jail. If Jessup had his way, their first time would be their last. Rafe had no regrets about making love to his wife, but he was just as sure he wanted Susanna safe at the hotel. After easing out of her, he snuggled close and stroked her hair. He had to tell her to go…but she was kissing his neck and exploring his chest. When she traced the line of hair that ran past his navel, Rafe decided talking could wait.

Chapter Nineteen

Susanna woke up at dawn and realized she was alone on the cot. Blinking away the fog, she saw Rafe fully dressed, standing by the wall and holding the blanket open a crack so he could see out the window.

"Good morning," she said in a husky voice.

"Hi."

He'd answered without turning his head. A kiss would have been nice, but Susanna understood his nerves. They had made love twice, but she hadn't slept in her husband's arms. He'd been on guard all night, watching for the first sign of trouble.

"You'd better get dressed," he said gently. "Beck'll be here soon."

"I guess so."

But Susanna was in no mood to hurry. Yawning, she stretched against the straw tick and sighed. They'd had a glorious wedding night, but the future was far from secure. Glancing at Rafe, she saw that she'd caught his attention. "Any regrets?" he asked.

"Not a one," she said.

With Rafe's eyes on her, she put on her underthings and traveling suit. Barefoot, she padded across the cell and leaned against his arm. He dropped the blanket in place and pulled her close with an urgency that matched last night's coupling. Only instead of sexual release, he needed reassurance.

"It's going to be fine," she said.

"I wish I could believe that."

"Charles Archer seemed optimistic at supper last night. He said my testimony would help."

Rafe held her even closer. "I want you to promise me something."

"What is it?"

"If things go badly, I don't want you to stay for the hanging."

Susanna put her hands on his chest and looked up. "Don't talk like that. You're going to be acquitted."

She felt the rise and fall of his chest and knew that he didn't share her confidence. When he loosened his arms and stepped back, she saw a coolness in his eyes. "Promise me you'll leave."

"Absolutely not."

"But Susanna—"

"If you're found guilty, we'll file an appeal. Your father has connections, Rafe. We'll use them."

His lips curled with disdain. "I've thought a lot about the boss. I don't have anything to say to him."

Susanna was appalled. Garrett hadn't explained Mr. Albright's reasons for seeking out Rafe, but how could his motives be anything but good? "You *have* to talk to him."

"I'm sorry I stole from him and I'll pay him back. But that's it."

"Maybe he wants to apologize to you."

Susanna watched as bitterness creased Rafe's eyes and hardened his mouth. This was the man who had hunted down Frank Benton and mocked Timothy Duke. As surely as Ed Jessup wanted to see Rafe hang for his wife's murder, Rafe had punished these men—deserved or not—for the sins of his father.

He looked at her with disgust, then jerked the blanket to the floor. A ray of sun made an arrow into the cell and landed at his feet, not quite touching his boots. "You're naive, Dr. Leaf. Get out of here before you get hurt."

"Darn you, Rafe."

"You just proved my point. As mad as you are, you won't even cuss."

Susanna got right in his face. "What you call naive,

I call trust. I married you knowing full well what it would cost. Don't you dare treat me like a child."

"But you are," he insisted. "How can you tell me to talk to Walter Albright after what happened to Mimi? The man made her life hell—and mine too."

"He also gave you a roof over your head and an education. That counts for something. And he sent Garrett to help you. I can't believe you're so bitter that you won't even speak to him." She hadn't meant to sound superior, but that's how the words came out.

When Rafe glared at her, she knew that his anger went bone deep. She didn't want to fight with him, but she couldn't back down without losing more than the argument. If he couldn't set down his bitterness, it would destroy him from the inside out. She raised her chin in defiance. "I won't apologize for speaking my mind."

"Neither will I," he said with a chill. "This marriage was a mistake. Get an annulment."

Susanna felt as if she'd been kicked. "Last night meant something to me."

"Like I said, you're naive." His eyes glinted with the hardness she'd seen the night he had kidnapped her. "You had an itch and I scratched it. That's all it was. No one has to know. Now go back to Midas like a good little girl."

Susanna had never struck a person in her life, but she was close to it now. Boiling inside, she flashed on her talk with her mother.

You don't have to rush, sweetie. If he's the right man, you'll have your tomorrows.

She had seen the wisdom but hadn't wanted to accept it. Now she wondered if she'd be spending her life steeped in his bitterness. Susanna steadied her voice. "We rushed into this, didn't we?"

"That's for damn sure."

Susanna grabbed for her shoes. She had no desire to annul their marriage, but neither could she stand the man slouching against the wall. "I'm going to the hotel. We both need time to think."

"That's fine with me."

They were shooting bullets with their eyes when the front door swung wide. Sheriff Beck, shadowed by four men, walked in with his hands over his head. The tallest man had a pistol pressed to the lawman's back and two others were armed with shotguns. The fourth was holding a length of rope in one hand and a black hood in the other. Terror ripped through her as she guessed what had happened. To get past the guards, Jessup had used Beck as a shield. Judging by the shouts in the street, a crowd was gathering. Last night a dozen guards seemed like a small army.

Now she wondered if fifty would have been enough to control the mob.

Beck looked at Susanna. "What the hell are you doing here?"

"She's leaving right now," Rafe answered.

Jessup aimed the pistol at Susanna's head and cocked the hammer. "I don't think so, LaCroix. Maybe I'll shoot her first. Then you'll know how it feels."

Susanna would have dodged for cover, but the cell offered no protection, nothing but Rafe's shadow and then his body as he stepped in front of her. "I'm the one you want, Jessup. Let her go and I'll make this easy for you."

The man holding the shotgun spoke up. "Take him up on it, Ed. I won't hurt a woman."

Susanna couldn't see Jessup, but she could feel the hate spilling out of him. After a huff, he shifted the gun sight from her head to Rafe's. "All right, LaCroix. Your life for hers."

"No!" Susanna cried. "He's innocent!"

But Rafe had already stepped from the cell. She wanted to kick and scratch at his captors, but the man with the second shotgun was aiming in her direction. Rendered helpless, Susanna watched as the man with the rope tied her husband's hands behind his back and then raised the black hood over his head. Rafe turned his head and looked straight at her. His eyes shimmered with remorse. "Susanna, I—"

But the black hood fell into place, muffling his final words.

Jessup spun him toward the door. The man with the shotgun jerked his chin toward the cell. "What about these two?"

"Lock 'em up," Jessup replied. Then he shoved Rafe into the street.

Susanna charged for the cell door, but the man with the shotgun was already shoving Beck behind the bars. He slammed the door and then aimed at the sheriff. "Give me the keys."

Beck motioned toward the wall behind his desk. "They should have been on that nail."

The man glanced at the empty spot, turned back to Susanna and took aim. Panic spread through her smallest veins. As long as she had the keys, she could escape. "I don't know where they are."

"Don't lie to me, lady. I'll shoot Beck first and then you." He pumped the shotgun to make his point.

If she argued, Beck would end up full of holes. Trapped, Susanna reached into her coat pocket and shoved the keys through the bars.

The man snatched them from her fingers. "That

was smart." With a twist of his wrist, he locked the cell, tossed the keys on the desk and left.

"Help!" Susanna shouted at the top of her lungs, but she doubted anyone would come. The security agents would be trying to save Rafe, but maybe a passerby would take pity on her.

Beck put his hands on hips. "Save your breath, miss. Everyone's headed for the hanging tree."

"Where is it?"

"East of here. Just past the tracks."

Susanna peered out the window where she saw puffs of smoke from a locomotive. Yesterday she'd arrived on a similar train and had seen a cottonwood on the edge of town. Even barren of leaves, it had struck her as pretty and she'd commented to Garrett about its cross-arm branches. He'd looked away and now she knew why.

Terror stole her breath and made her heart pound. When the room started to spin, she dropped down on the cot. The ropes squeaked like they had last night and the straw tick crunched—but just once instead of over and over with the joining of their bodies. So much had been left unsaid. To grieve was part of life. But for a husband and wife to be torn asunder with anger in their hearts, that was a special kind of wretchedness.

Susanna couldn't stop the tears. How long would it

be? Would she know when it was over? She wished she wasn't a doctor. She knew the science of death by hanging, but there was nothing clinical about the agony in her heart.

Raising her head, she looked out the window and wondered if she'd know when Rafe took his last breath. She wanted to believe she'd feel it as her own. Even more, she wanted to believe that Garrett and his army would come to Rafe's rescue. Grabbing on to that hope, she faced the corner of the cell and dropped to her knees. She was about to beg God for mercy when she saw a bouquet of roses penciled on the wall. In the middle of it, Rafe had written her name in a fine script. Below it, he'd left his initials and the words, "For my wife."

He'd bid her goodbye, and this time he wouldn't be back.

As soon as Jessup shoved him into the street, Rafe felt the mob surging like floodwater. He couldn't see a thing because of the hood, but he could hear the hateful jokes and a chant calling for his death. Every town had a hanging tree and that's where they were headed. With Susanna out of harm's way, he intended to fight every inch of the way.

He knew he didn't have much time, but each second gave Garrett and the security agents a chance to get to the tree first. Blind and stumbling, Rafe zigzagged like a drunk. When one of his captors slammed the butt of the shotgun into his shoulder, Rafe crumpled to his knees and fell on his face.

"Damn you, LaCroix!" Jessup jerked him up by the collar and shoved him forward. Rafe deliberately fell again, but the ploy ended in two men gripping his biceps and dragging him down the street. The chants turned to a roar as they neared the edge of town until he was surrounded by calls of "killer" and "murderer."

Suffocating under the hood, Rafe heard the pant of his own breath. It muffled the catcalls but couldn't block the whinny of a horse. When the crowd suddenly hushed, he shuddered. They'd reached the hanging tree.

He struggled against the ropes binding his wrists, welcoming the sting of air on torn flesh, because it meant he was alive. He'd be dead if Jessup and his cohorts got him on that horse. With only his instincts to guide him, Rafe made a show of being exhausted. Just as he'd hoped, one of the men let go of his arm. Rafe kicked wildly and landed a boot in the man's crotch.

A curse filled the air, followed by the thump of a man landing on his butt.

Rafe pulled free from the second man and headbutted his fat belly. To his utter relief, the hood rode up past his nose. Even in the midst of the fight, he knew that he'd never breathe fresh air again without remembering this moment. Before he could shake the hood loose, Jessup pushed him to the ground, yanked off the hood and pointed the pistol at Rafe's temple.

"You're *not* going to die easy," he said. "Get up."

Rafe went limp, but Jessup had the strength of a madman and dragged him to the swaybacked horse standing under the cottonwood. In spite of the crowd, the horse stood still, as if it were part of the plot. Rafe didn't have a friend in sight. As Jessup pushed him on to the horse's back, another man pulled his legs into place. When a third man climbed a stepladder and dropped the noose around his neck, Rafe surrendered to the inevitable. Even if Garrett mustered his small army, it was too late to save his life.

In a final act of mercy or retribution—he didn't know which—Jessup stepped back and bowed his head in prayer. Then he looked at Rafe. "If you've got anything to say, LaCroix, now's the time."

Susanna was on her knees when two men wearing tan dusters walked into the jail. She pushed to her feet and waited for the bad news about Rafe.

The older man tipped his hat. "Dr. LaCroix, I'm Detective Russell Montgomery. I have orders from Mr. Albright to see you safely on the train."

"Does this mean it's over?" she said in a near whisper.

"No, ma'am. It means I'm supposed to put you on the train."

"But Rafe—"

The man ignored her and turned to Beck. "If there's a key handy, I'll use it. Otherwise I'll shoot out the lock."

"It's on the desk," Beck replied.

The younger guard found it and opened the door. "You better hurry, ma'am. The crowd's breaking up."

Susanna struggled into her shoes and then allowed the detective to escort her out the door. Some of the onlookers had reached the jail and were walking with their necks bent in shame. One woman was crying, and another was muttering about men who deserved to die.

Susanna looked east, beyond the buildings to the top branches of the cottonwood, barren and lifeless against a sky so blue that it hurt her eyes. She heard the clop of hooves coming around the corner and turned. The undertaker's wagon, drawn by two black horses and driven by a shriveled man in a black top hat, rolled down the street. She had to face the facts. Her husband was dead.

The security agent touched her elbow. "Don't think, ma'am. It's possible Mr. Albright's men arrived in time."

As much as Susanna wanted to believe him, she couldn't muster that much faith. "This may be difficult, but I'd like to take my husband's body to Midas."

"I'll check with Mr. Albright, ma'am."

Her body felt leaden, except for the trembling in her belly, as she walked with the guards to the waiting train. She thought briefly of her carpetbag in the hotel but didn't care enough to fetch it. When they reached the station, she saw a locomotive with brass trim and only five cars behind it. She guessed that Garrett had used his family connections, but whatever help he'd summoned had arrived too late for Rafe.

Detective Montgomery helped her up the steps and motioned for her to sit on a divan in a private passenger car. A porter appeared and asked if she needed something to drink. Susanna shook her head and he exited the car, leaving her to weep alone.

Chapter Twenty

Rafe surveyed the men and women who had come to see him die. He looked hard at each face, expecting his usual bitterness to rise like bile. But instead of anger, he felt only a terrible pity. The mob had lost its soul and Ed Jessup had lost his mind. But Rafe felt a peace that settled around him like a mother's embrace.

He knew Susanna would find the drawing on the wall. It wouldn't take away the sting of their parting, but she was a wise woman. She'd see the love in the pencil strokes and know his heart. Last night they had become one body, cleaving together just like the Reverend said. Not even death could erase that love.

As he looked at the angry mob, Rafe thought of Garrett with gratitude. They had made their amends and he could count on his brother to look out for his wife. The only regret he had concerned the boss.

This morning Rafe would have spit on him. Now he understood the man's need to make amends.

His death would deny the boss that peace, but Rafe knew of another soul that needed pardon. He searched the crowd for Lucy Jessup and found her standing alone and slightly apart. Knowing about mistakes, he called out to her. "I forgive you, Lucy."

The girl gasped and stared at him wide-eyed. Then she looked back down at her feet.

Rafe felt her shame, but he had no sympathy for the bloodthirsty crowd. Sitting tall, he shouted, "You're hanging an innocent man today. I want you to remember that."

"Who says?" shouted a rabble rouser.

"Murderer!"

"Death's too good for you!"

"Slap the damn horse!"

Rafe took in the sneers and the disgust, the gruesome taunts and even a few women with tearstained cheeks. He wasn't fooled. Their grief was for the Jessup family—not him. The mob wanted to send him straight to hell, but Rafe knew that wasn't his fate. Because of Susanna, he'd finally learned that love was stronger than hate. He felt her presence in the sun at his back, and he saw her outstretched arms in the shadow of the branches. Looking straight ahead, he waited for Jessup to send him to heaven.

Only the man didn't move. Rafe's gaze dropped from the blue sky to the crowd where he saw streams of dust as people stepped aside for a dozen men in brown dusters. Tall and arrogant, they strode through the crowd, each one armed with the truth and a bladeless ax handle.

Rafe knew what the weapons meant. The railroad's toughest agents carried them on trains for times when a gun was a danger to innocent passengers. As the men strode toward the tree, the crowd stood in stunned silence. Rafe heard a rifle being cocked and glanced to his right. Two men were positioned on the roof of the railroad station, each one aiming at one of his captors. Two more rifles clicked and he looked to his left where another set of guards had set up a perfect crossfire.

"Hold on, Jessup," said the man on Rafe's left. "I don't want to die today."

"I don't give a damn what you want."

"Don't shoot!" called the man who'd chickened out. "We'll let him go."

All Rafe had to do was stay on the horse and he'd live. But he could see Ed Jessup weighing his options. He could send Rafe to eternity, but they'd be making the trip together.

"Don't leave your daughter," Rafe said. "I'm not worth it."

Before Jessup could decide if he agreed, the twelve guards emerged from the mob and formed a wall in front of the horse. The agent in the middle looked hard at Jessup. "If that nag moves, you'll be dead before the rope gets tight."

Jessup didn't budge, but his cohorts raised their hands high and stepped back. The guard strode forward and gripped the horse's halter, then he raised the ax handle over his head and held it high to give a signal. Rafe looked toward the railroad office where a group of men in suits were filing out of the door. In the lead was the man Rafe had hated most of his life.

Walter Albright had aged in the past five years. His brown hair had turned to iron, but his eyes hadn't lost their intensity. Rafe felt that gaze hard on his face. Behind his father he saw Garrett with his cane, a man who looked like the governor of the New Mexico territory and two men wearing copper stars that marked them as federal marshals.

As the men gathered by the tree, Garrett unsheathed his sword and severed the rope from the branch. It slithered past Rafe's shoulder and landed on the ground like a dead snake. When he bent his neck to shake off the noose, Garrett slid it over his head and then untied his hands. Free at last, Rafe slid off the horse and faced Walter Albright.

"I have something to give you," the man said. "I'd be grateful if we could talk in private."

"Of course." Rafe had something to say as well.

His father nodded and turned to the crowd. "Ladies and gentlemen, my friends and I have no wish to circumvent justice. If the evidence is worthy, Mr. LaCroix will stand trial. But if today's actions are an indication, you are *all* far more guilty than he is. *This was a goddamned lynching!*"

Albright's voice boomed like thunder. "What happened to the principles that this blessed country is founded upon? What happened to a man's right to be heard before he's condemned?"

The boss hadn't directed the question to him, but Rafe felt guilty as charged. Susanna had been right about listening to his father's side of the story. At the thought of her, he turned to Garrett and whispered, "My wife—"

"I sent men. You'll see her soon."

Relieved beyond measure, Rafe directed his attention to his father, who was lecturing the stunned crowd. In that stillness, Rafe became aware of Lucy Jessup staring at him. He knew she was searching for her courage, just as he should have done when he'd left Garrett to die.

Come on, Lucy... Come on...

After taking a breath, she waved her arm and

shouted, "Listen to me, everyone. I was wrong. I have to tell the truth."

Walter Albright nodded at two security agents who cleared a path for the girl. Looking small and afraid, she walked toward the hanging tree and positioned herself in front of the crowd. "I didn't lie when I said this was the man, but I wasn't sure, either. Now I'm sure it's *not* him."

Lucy turned to her father. "I'm sorry, Pa. I know you wanted me to say it was true, but it's not."

The man slapped the girl hard across the face. "You're lying now!"

Before Rafe could blink, a guard grabbed Jessup's wrist, spun him to the ground and hogtied him with the lynching rope.

The man whom Rafe guessed to be the territorial governor stepped forward. "Ladies and gentlemen, I'd say that settles the issue."

Rafe couldn't tell if the crowd was disappointed or relieved, but no one uttered a word as they drifted away. The governor turned to Rafe. "Do you want to press charges against Mr. Jessup and his friends?"

No," Rafe answered. "But I'd like him to spend a night in jail for smacking Lucy. I'd also like to see this tree turned into firewood."

The governor nodded. "Consider it done."

After some discussion with his father, the governor

and the marshals left for town, leaving Rafe alone with Garrett and his father. Lucy cleared her throat. "Mr. LaCroix?"

"Yes?"

"I'm sorry for what happened. I don't see how you can forgive me."

"It's all right," Rafe answered. "I've made a few mistakes myself, including one as bad this one."

The girl mumbled again that she was sorry and walked away. The guilt would linger for a while, but it wouldn't haunt her like it had Rafe.

Walter Albright took command of the situation and faced Garrett first. "Son, if you don't mind, I'd like a moment with your brother."

"Of course," he replied.

When Garrett was out of hearing distance, Rafe's father reached into his pocket and withdrew a gold band studded with rubies. As the sun reflected off the ring, Rafe recalled the hundreds of times he'd seen it on Mimi's finger. He'd thought it was a meaningless token and had figured it had been buried with her. Seeing it now brought his mother back to life.

His father tilted the band so that the rubies caught the light. "She loved red, but you knew that."

Rafe knew something else. "She loved you, too."

"Yes, she did." He sounded wistful. "But she loved

you more. This isn't how I planned on telling you about the last time I saw your mother, but we don't always get to choose where and how we make our confessions."

Susanna had been right. Walter Albright needed to make peace for things Rafe had never considered. "That's true," he answered.

"As a young man, I made a terrible mistake. I married for money instead of love and then lacked the discipline to keep those vows. My wife and I paid the price every day until she died, but you and your mother, and even Garrett, bore the consequences as well. For that I'm sorry."

Rafe thought about what the Reverend had said about letting the dead bury dead. It was time to move on. "It's in the past."

"Is it?" The older man's jaw hardened. "I can't help but think about how Mimi died."

Rafe understood the question and all it implied. Had she bled to death from a miscarriage or had she visited a back-alley abortionist who'd killed her? They were at the root of Rafe's hatred for this man, but what did they really know? Only that Mimi had loved them both.

"I've wondered, too," Rafe answered honestly. "In fact, I hated you for it. But deep down I know that Mimi would have loved that child like she cared for you and me. You made sure we had food and a roof over our heads, so money wasn't a factor. As for what people thought, shame had no place in her life."

Walter Albright looked doubtful. "The last time I saw her, she had to know about the baby, but she didn't tell me. We had a bit of a spat—more like a real row—about your schooling. We both knew that someday I'd invite you to work for the railroad. I wanted to hire a private tutor so you could stay in New Orleans, but Mimi wanted you to have the credentials of an East Coast education."

Rafe felt the truth in his bones. "She was always pushing me to do well in school."

"When she died, I tried to honor her wishes. I know it was hard for you, but I thought it was for the best."

"I can see that now."

"What troubles me is the baby. I never knew, and now I wonder if she thought I was ashamed."

"Were you?"

"Only of myself." Walter Albright looked straight into Rafe's eyes. "It wasn't until I lost you and almost Garrett that I saw the railroad for what it is—a business and not a child. I vowed that night to make things right with both of you."

Rafe felt the noose coming off his neck all over

again. "You have, sir. I owe you my life. After the way I left, you would have been right to forget I'd ever been born."

"A man can't forget his children. It won't fix past mistakes, but I'd like to make up for lost time. I understand you have a wife."

Rafe felt a surge of pride. "That's right. She's a doctor."

"That's what I heard from Garrett. I'd like to fund a full clinic for her." The man's eyes misted. "The gift will be made in Mimi's memory."

Rafe choked up. "Thank you, sir."

The boss nodded and then clasped his hands behind his back. "I've also heard that you're a hell of a bounty hunter."

The pride in his father's voice touched Rafe to the core. "I did all right."

"You did better than that," Albright said. "Thanks to the Benton capture, you have a reputation equal to my best agents. I'd like to offer you a position with the railroad."

Respect shone in his father's eyes. The older man wasn't telling Rafe to take the job. He was asking if he wanted it. "What do you have in mind?"

"You'd be overseeing security for the Southwest. If you're interested, there's an office on the third floor of the Midas depot."

Rafe thought of the men in tan dusters and all they stood for—bravery, justice and protecting innocent lives. He'd ride the rails when he had to, but he'd be even happier to spend his nights with Susanna.

He smiled. "I'd like that, sir."

"Then it's settled. That leaves us with one last item of business. I hope it's not too late to give you and your wife a wedding present?"

Rafe felt chagrined. "We had words, but I plan to grovel as soon as I see her."

"Perhaps I can help you out." His father's eyes twinkled. "Garrett tells me there's a parcel of land outside of town that would be suitable for a house. I figure you'll need six bedrooms and a stable."

A bribe wouldn't win Susanna's heart, but making peace with his father would prove that his bitterness was gone for good. Rafe smiled at the older man. "Sir, we'd be honored to accept. It's kind of you and I don't deserve it."

"It's a gift, son."

"Even so, you're not the only one here with amends to make. I was wrong to steal from you and even more wrong to leave Garrett bleeding like that. I know all about mistakes. I am truly sorry for running, and even more sorry for all the ugly things I've been thinking."

"Consider it forgotten."

When Rafe held out his hand to shake, Walter Albright put Mimi's ring in his palm. Then he curled Rafe's fingers around the band of gold and cupped his hand in both of his. Looking down, Rafe saw the thickness of the old man's arthritic knuckles. Time had changed them all.

"I've kept Mimi's ring in my pocket for thirteen years," his father said. "I think she'd like you to have it."

Rafe lifted the ring to the sun and thought about love, mistakes and forgiveness. He couldn't think of a more fitting wedding band for his wife. "This means a lot to me."

"Then it's yours to give to Dr. LaCroix." His father's eyes turned a deep blue, then he gave Rafe a smile that bordered on rascally. "I thought you and your wife might need some time alone. I told my steward to give you my private car for the trip to Midas."

"Thank you, sir."

In spite of Rafe's warm tone, the older man looked disappointed. That's when Rafe realized that he'd once called this man "Papa" but had taken to calling him the boss like everyone else. Rafe held out his hand. "I'm years past calling you Papa. How does Father sound?"

"I'd be honored."

Backslapping hugs weren't Walter Albright's style, but his voice had choked up and he was gripping Rafe's hand with all his might. "Welcome home, son. Now go make up with your wife."

"Dr. LaCroix?"

Susanna looked up from her damp handkerchief and saw the guard who had brought her to the train. Perhaps he had word about retrieving Rafe's body. "Yes?"

"You can see your husband now. He's in the boss's private car, so if you'll follow me…"

The man motioned toward the door at the end of the car. As much as she dreaded seeing Rafe's corpse, she welcomed the chance for a private good-bye. She stood and followed her escort, vaguely aware that the train was starting to roll. After passing through a second car, the guard stopped on a connecting platform and knocked on a mahogany door carved with an ornate W.A.

When no one answered, he opened the door, motioned for her to enter and then closed it, leaving her in an alcove that entered into a sitting room. She could see light through the windows and a partition that blocked off what she guessed to be a sleeping compartment. Rafe's body was most likely in that private space.

Susanna took three steps and halted. On the wall by the bedchamber she saw the shadow of a man shaving with a straight razor. It didn't seem likely that she'd walked in on Walter Albright. The guard wouldn't have made that kind of mistake. Nor would the elderly man have had broad shoulders and muscular arms that matched the ones that had held her last night. She had heard of grieving widows seeing visions, and that was the only explanation that made sense. Except the shadow was humming a waltz. Mystified, she watched as the man came around the corner, bare-chested and golden in the morning light. The sun glistened in his hair and made it shine. Best of all, he had Rafe's blue eyes.

"You're alive," she blurted.

A smile curled his lips. "Is that a medical assessment?"

"No, it's a shock." She could barely breathe. "I saw the hearse—I thought—"

In three strides, he crossed the room and pulled her tight against his chest. All she could do was press her cheek against those hard muscles and listen to the beat of his heart. His body molded to hers, leaving no doubt that he was flesh and blood. "It was close, Susanna."

She put her hands on his chest and looked up. "Tell me what happened."

Rafe led her to a divan where he wrapped her in his arms and shared the struggle with Jessup, his father's intervention and Lucy admitting that she'd been wrong. "You were right. My father had worries I'd never considered."

"I'm glad it's settled."

"I owe you amends, too," he said. "I said hateful things in the jail."

"So did I."

Rafe smiled at her. "I guess we had our first fight."

"Just so it's not our last," she quietly. "I don't mind a bit of arguing, just so we always sleep in the same bed."

His eyes twinkled. "That won't be a problem. My father offered me a job in Midas. How would you like to be married to the man in charge of security for the Southwest region of the Santa Fe Railroad?"

Her eyes shone with happiness. "I'd like it a lot."

"There's more," he said. "You know that piece of land west of town? Father wants to build us a house for a wedding present."

"That's wonderful! I can see patients there."

"You won't need to. He's also building a clinic in Mimi's memory. If you'd like, you can have a wing of rooms for kids like Nick and Melissa."

Tears welled in her eyes. "That's been my dream as long as I can remember."

Susanna's heart was brimming when Rafe reached into his pocket and withdrew a ruby-studded ring. As the band shimmered in the light, she thought of Midas and the king who had given the town its name. Everything he touched had turned to gold, the worthless kind that could buy things but not joy. A different king had touched Rafe and he'd discovered his father's love, a gift worth more than all the gold in the world.

Rafe slipped the ring on her finger. "This belonged to my mother. I'm hoping you'll wear it as our wedding band."

With the ring in place, Susanna touched his cheek. "I'd be honored."

Pictures of their courtship flooded through her mind. They'd had a first kiss and a first argument. They had made vows and she was wearing his ring. They had made love and she felt complete—except for one thing. Susanna smiled into Rafe's shining eyes. "Do you remember my deepest secret?"

"You bet I do."

As her husband stood and pulled her up with him, the train sped into a curve, throwing them together as he braced to absorb the speed. When the train steadied, he scooped her into his arms and carried her into the bed chamber where she saw red velvet covering a wide bed and mirrors lining the walls.

A bottle of champagne was angled in an ice bucket, and a bouquet of red roses had filled the room with a sweet perfume.

Susanna's mouth gaped. "Does your father always travel like this?"

"The flowers are for you." He set her on the bed and smiled. "Look at the card."

She read it out loud. "To Mr. and Dr. LaCroix. We'll arrive in Midas this evening. Until then, enjoy the champagne and roses. I've taken the liberty of contacting the Reverend and Mrs. Leaf with the good news. With respect and love, W.A." Then he'd added a P.S. "Dear Susanna, I'd be honored if you'd call me Father."

Tears of joy welled in Susanna's eyes. "We're going home, Rafe. I can hardly believe it."

She grabbed his neck and pulled him down on the bed. Then she kissed him full on the mouth, rolled him to his back and straddled his hips.

Her husband gave her a wicked smile. "I thought you wanted to sleep like spoons."

"I do, but not just yet."

With the train rocking, they made love until they'd each had their fill. Satisfied at last, they slept all the way home, nestled together like spoons in a drawer.

* * * * *